From behind, in the shadows, movement. Smaller ones, some very small, others closer to his size, all emerge. All click with a few grunts mixed in, all come to the edge where Darrian is clinging to the flattened boulder with her free hand.

And I watch this oh-so-delicate woman, a woman I have torn open the night with, touched and been touched by, now too far from me to save, in absolute surrender to a half-circle of North American Great Apes!

The smallest ones begin to get squirmy, move away to play by the water's edge. The old one, all melancholia and grace, simply reaches out a nonchalant log of an arm and with a gentle brush, touches the offered wrist of Darrian Stone. In a great movement back, she pulls off towards me, almost royally, clearly not in retreat, more like joyful acknowledgment of the message. The apes break their ranks, click and coo and cough, going about various odd jobs now after the morning matin.

Darrian returns to me, nuzzling my neck, wrapping an arm around my waist, all wide grin and raw joy.

"Darrian." I can barely whisper, devastated by awe, an almost unbelieving witness.

calling
RAIN

KAREN MARIE CHRISTA MINNS

calling RAIN

KAREN MARIE CHRISTA MINNS

The Naiad Press, Inc.
1991

Printed in the United States of America on acid-free paper
First Edition

Edited by Katherine V. Forrest
Cover design by Pat Tong and Bonnie Liss
    (Phoenix Graphics)
Typeset by Sandi Stancil

Library of Congress Cataloging-in-Publication Data

Minns, Karen Marie Christa, 1956–
Calling Rain / by Karen Marie Christa Minns.
        p.   cm.
    ISBN 0-941483-87-8 : $9.95
    I. Title.
PS3563.I4735O98   1991
813'.54--dc20   90-21910
                                                         CIP

For Nell Mohn,
who came looking.

To
Dian Fossey and Dr. Kate Livingston . . .

with
special thanks to

Teresa DeCrescenzo
and
Katherine V. Forrest
(editor, author and guardian angel
of wordsmiths).

About the Author

KAREN MARIE CHRISTA MINNS, a Gemini writer (1956), believes in the absolute necessity of heroes. She also answers all of her mail.

Works with Naiad Press include: *Virago* (1990), a lesbian vampire allegory, nominated for two Lambda Awards — Debut Writer and Best Science Fiction/Fantasy; *Calling Rain* (1991), an eco-feminist adventure, *Romaunt* (1993), a video-news love story. Minns is currently writing her fourth novel, *Ephemeron,* which takes place in various parts of the Universe.

W here the hell do you think you're going?"

The rough voice pulled me back onto the road. I hadn't even heard the Ranger, his footsteps drowned out by the old pickup that had just dropped me off.

"Uh, nowhere, just hiking." It sounded pretty lame.

"This is a closed area, Miss. You have to have special permits to hike back-country or off the regular trails. Can I see some identification?" He took a step closer.

I backed up, knowing I couldn't outrun him with these spanking new, blister-causing, twenty pound, unflexed boots or my overloaded cherry-red L.L. Bean pack. Shit. It was starting to rain anyway.

"Okay, okay, it's in the pack, let me dig for it. I need my rainsuit, too." I was trying to move slowly, the guy was big, had a rifle to back up the khaki uniform and I didn't like the way he kept licking his bottom lip. I hoped it was only nerves.

I found my wallet, dropped two credit cards on the mossy side of the road as my ring caught in one of the hidden zippers — supposedly a great new feature of this year's pack. Didn't matter — they were both up to their limit. Poor fool who found and tried to use them. My driver's license was next out on the gravel. I scooped up all three, holding them out for inspection. The ranger didn't so much as twitch. Great. Power games. Just what I needed after the last fifty-mile hitch up from the Greyhound station. What an asshole. I wanted his badge number. I straightened up, moved forward to give him the now soaking I.D. He finally smiled, that bureaucratic, shit-eating grin that some of them have. He knew exactly where he had me. Suddenly the cool emerald of the forest seemed very menacing. I was like Dorothy on the way to Oz without benefit of even Toto . . . terrific. Even if this guy was for real, who knew if he might try something? Lately I'd been reading about a lot of missing people and unsolved murders and this soggy state. I stepped back quickly.

"You got a problem, lady?" His eyes never dropped from mine.

No. I shook my head. No problem, just want to get the hell away from you, Bub. No problem at all. I went back to my shucked pack and rummaged around for the day-glo rainsuit. I knew it would just make this dude's day when he saw it, but it was

2

really beginning to pour now and I could take the snide remarks better than the numbing wet.

"Sorry, lady, we have to verify these down at the Station. Follow me."

Guess I wasn't quite the menace he originally suspected because he turned his back to me and started for his Rangermobile. I followed, of course, furious, knowing he wasn't even going to give me enough time to pull my pack together or put on the rain gear.

Running, half-dragging the overburdened bulk across the soaking macadam, I tried hoisting it to my hip. I felt like one of those semi-demented mothers with three kids clinging to her body as she rushes to make a plane.

Coming to the curve I saw he'd left the Rangermobile running, its exhaust like a small ghost flying from the tailpipe. Cute. Real cute. He jumped behind the wheel, gunning the engine impatiently. Okay, okay. I got it. Jesus!

He kicked the passenger's side open and I scrambled in, desperate to at least get the pack on the seat, sure he would only wait long enough for my body and then drive off with the pack open to the rain on the road. I slung the hulking thing over my hip and onto the seat, then tried to climb in on top of it . . . grace. He made no move to help.

"Buckle up," he growled through the hair on his face.

It was the last thing he said till we got down to the Station.

* * * * *

3

The Station was a small cabin, all tight, smokey and reeking with that particular scent of outdoor-male sweat. It had been kept that way for years, judging by its potency. I attempted to smile. How long had it been since I had to think about the way some men believe all women act? This was the weirdest scene I'd ever encountered.

A desk was jammed against one wall, more to catch paper than to sit at. No chairs to sit on there anyway, they were gathered in a loose semi-circle in front of the stone fireplace that was huge, easily big enough for one of these guys to step into. I wondered what they burned in there ... then decided against dwelling on it.

The room was steamy. A rocking chair and a cracked "almost leather" overstuffed chair completed the semi-circle. The rocker was occupied by a sleeping Ranger, his feet rustically propped against a pile of split logs. I kept expecting the strains of a beer commercial. To the right of this room was a tiny kitchen emitting cooking smells — beans, taco-fry, making my stomach growl. I hadn't eaten anything besides a Mars Bar on the bus.

A gun rack made from antlers held an odd assortment of rifles, their stocks gleaming like oily baby bottoms, their metal barrels giving off that blue light and unmistakable gun scent. My father was a New England deer and rabbit hunter. So were my brothers. I knew guns. I hated guns. I recognized the smell.

"Well, come in, try not to get mud all over the floor. You damned college kids think this is some kind of hostel or something. Leave your boots off at the door." The Ranger was a tad less growly now, the prospect of the fire and hot food probably mellowing him out.

I slid the slippery pack from my shoulder, set it balancing against the wall. The sleeping Ranger snorked himself awake, grunting and grimacing as he stretched. As I bent to untie my sodden laces I felt the men watching my ass. Shit. This was beginning to feel like a scene from *Deliverance.* I turned around, shucking the wet boots, realizing this was less an issue of tracking in mud than of keeping me from getting out of there very fast. Shit, shit, shit. Had to be careful now . . . go slow.

"What now, Charlie?" The other Ranger was fully awake and moving up from his chair.

"Found her off trail around Bear Bend. Figured she was a damned college kid, what with the storm coming in and all, might be better to pick her up now as well as after dark. You just know her parents are going to call up here when they get the weather report on the news. Just trying to save us some work."

"Take her back to town?" The awakened Ranger scratched his cheek, yawning again. He seemed about the same age as Charlie, late thirties or so, just starting to get a little bald in the front, no fat on the edges yet, though. I had to give him that. It was clear they both had hiked up and down the mountain more than once.

"Well, for Christ's sake, she can't stay up here — got a better suggestion?"

"She wants to go camping, hell, let her camp — put her out back. I'm sick of these know-it-all kids with their high-tech gear and their no-tech experience driving up here and us having to save

5

their sorry asses every time the weather changes. Let her tough it out if she wants. Won't be risking much ... ten to one she's going to be begging for a ride back down by morning." The guy patted his gut. "Not bad for an old man, eh?"

I moved back to my boots, pulling them on hurriedly. "So, I don't get any say in this?"

"Hey, honey, one look at you and your credit cards and that's all the say I need. Your pack's about thirty pounds overweight, your gear still has the price tags on it, and I bet you've got hamburger for toes in those new boots. I don't want to ruin my night slogging through the woods in a downpour looking for you, you know? My partner's idea is fine. Your choice, either load it all back into the jeep and we take you down or you can camp out back. Now, what's it going to be?"

"Look, I'm not just a college kid, okay? I'm up here on real business. Do you know Professor Darrian Stone?" I was pissed and cold and trying to look six feet tall — big, real big. They'd simply have to take me seriously.

"Ahhh no, tell me it ain't so ... please!" The Ranger, now fully awake, banged an empty coffee pot on one of the desks.

"What ... why?" I looked from one to the other.

"Lady, the woman is nuts, you don't want to be bushwhacking up the mountain looking for Dr. Fruitcake. Believe me, she'd just as soon shoot you as invite you in." Charlie turned and took a coffee mug off another set of antlers on the wall.

The front door suddenly swung open. The sound of the heavy rain caught us, compelled us to turn. A rush of pure, fresh-washed air poured into the room.

I'd taken only a few steps inside but still never felt the person pass behind me, never saw movement, only heard the door and felt the rainy air and just beyond, a retreating shadow pass into the woods.

"Sitting Mule — one of the half-breeds. We let him do some of the heavy chores around here, comes inside when it gets too howly out. He was sitting in the corner there, drying off when you came in. I get so used to him I don't even notice. Probably has to piss. Now, you listen and you listen good. Nobody gets to Dr. Stone unless Dr. Stone invites them. That's the rules. We get the invitation from her first, see, so we know who to expect. She hasn't had anyone up there but her Indians, not since *Geographic* left, got that? Indians say she's gone deeper — 'under the trees' they say — just means so deep we can't reach her. She isn't expecting any little college chickie to show up, trust me." Charlie poured some instant coffee from a jar into his mug.

"All right, okay, maybe she isn't waiting, but she knows who I am. I sent a couple of letters to her. I'm sure once I get up there and meet her face to —"

"She'll raise holy hell and send you packing so fast you won't have time to tie those fancy new boots! I've seen it a hundred times, lady. Look, spend your vacation down in one of the regular campsites. This is nice land, lots of fine hiking, climbing, lots of kids your age around. Get your gear dirty, relax, go home and show everyone the nice pictures you took. Use your freeze-dried stew and buy some postcards. No loss of face, we won't tell a soul we found you. You'll feel like a million bucks when you leave, a real wilderness woman! Hey, it took the pros from the press three years before she'd let them close enough to film her ... We aren't even allowed beyond a mile from this Station. She had some big clout to get the muckey-mucks to give her that kind of jurisdiction. You have to get a pile of forms, have them signed, notarized, then leave all your gear here, she's paranoid about guns, contamination, you name it. Fucking precious apes, all these years we had to deal with the bears, now it's apes. Anyway, after you do all that and wait around a few months till it's approved, then we have to escort you to the first fire tower on Remmel. She sends her bloody Indians to take you up to camp — even that's only a small camp — nobody knows where the real research goes on or if there's more than one base. We've only spoken to her face to face a couple of times in seven years. Go on home, kid, it ain't worth the trouble." The awakened Ranger gulped his now-made coffee, then offered the hot water to his buddy.

"She doesn't like men much, either. Who knows what might happen to you up there, huh?" Charlie winked lewdly as he stirred the instant coffee.

"Well, least not white boys. She's got enough Indian meat to take care of *emergencies*, I'm sure." Awakened Ranger burped, wiping off the bottom of his moustache with two fingers.

"You guys are sick!" I backed up, suddenly aware that no one really knew where I was. I told my parents I was going to spend Thanksgiving vacation with a professor — not exactly a lie — they still thought I was at Smith. Shit.

"The kid's right, Charlie, we shouldn't speak so unprofessionally about the good Doctor. Tell you

8

what, kid, you go up there and meet her and then you come back and give us *your* opinion, all right? Fair? Now, you just call us if you need any help with that little old tent, okay?"

"Thanks boys, guess I can manage." I shouldered my pack and started for the door, struggling not to scream. My back was almost knotted with fury and tension. Hold it in. Hold on. Get out.

"Just remember, girlie, this is *our* country up here. We're the law. We can boot you out in a minute. Show us respect and we can make it easy, any wise-ass lip and you're history — clear?" Charlie was back to growling threats.

Why did I get the feeling that this Station was not the pride of the U.S. Forestry Service?

"Yeah, clear." I slammed the door behind me.

The rain was beyond rain, transforming itself even as it hurtled earthward, thousands of hot needles aimed at my face and hands. Even the huge ponderosa pines offered little protection. I was a stranger in the forest and the forest knew it — as if the Douglas fir and spruce parted themselves and directed the stinging rain right at me.

At least I'd made it out of Rangerland. Fuck them both. When I got someplace dry I'd write a scathing letter to the Park Service and tell them exactly how this particular section of back country was being managed. No wonder Darrian Stone steered clear of here.

I'd dragged my sodden pack at least a mile through the brush, switching back and forth, trying to carefully edge my way up the mountain. Finally, I had to stop.

Night was coming in blacker than the storm. I looked around for the driest mud I could find . . . at least it wasn't running downward in little streams. Everything including me was covered with dirt, pine needles and pieces of plants. Even my sleeping bag was soaking. A sopping mass of three-hundred-dollar useless down. I tossed it outside the tent. I wrapped whatever clothes were merely damp around me, mummy style, then, curling into fetal position, I tried to concentrate on warm.

The tent dome was all green and light brown, almost invisible in the brush. This was a plus — no Rangers could spot me in the downpouring dark. Now, somehow, I realized I'd forgotten to attach the rainfly — had forgotten, in fact, because it wasn't packed in the sack with the rest of the tent. Fuck. The tent was leaking in four separate places. The rock directly under my left hip was the only thing keeping me from being marooned in a big puddle in the middle.

Miserable. Still, I wasn't dead. Supposedly, in all the mountain manuals I'd been reading lately, that was a plus. Had to focus on the challenge, I was finding my best self here, no prep-school Barbie Doll with glasses, no wimp from the city, I was proving . . . something, right? Yeah, yeah, like Joe Campbell's "bliss following," or something close. Screw the "how-to-survive-hints," I was in the middle of a hurricane, freezing my ass off for one reason. Be real, it was because of Darrian Stone. Dr. Darrian Stone. When else had I ever wanted anything this much?

It wasn't even the drama of the North American Great Apes Project — though that was a pull in itself — I mean, how many of us had grown up with Bigfoot stories at summer camp or on TV? But even with that mystery blown wide open by her it was the hard, cutting, almost razor-sharp image of her that did it for me. The last year at Smith had nearly been a washout. What did I really want to do when I got out? My blue-collar family lived in silent terror of the College as if it were the Catholic Church itself guiding their daughter's destiny — okay, they worked hard to get me there but so had I! For years, kissing ass in that goddamned factory town, being "nice," dating the right people, licking up to the city fathers, getting the scholarships and grades and honors that were a straight ticket out of purgatory. I loved my folks. I worried about my family. They would never get out. For them the highest honor was to live and die where the family had first landed a couple hundred years before. To make furniture in one of the handful of factories still running. To make good marriages and babies enough to insure the next generation could take over your job when you're tired. And here I came along, the weird kid, the one hanging out in the woods around town, not to hunt — which could have been tolerated in a tomboyish way — not to make out with the neighborhood boys — which would have been less tolerated but still understandable — not even to do drugs and drink. No, there goes Nikola, into the woods, just to ... what? To draw. To dream. To get away from them all. How to say you

11

wake up most nights from a sound sleep, your eyes scanning the dark room, looking, just looking — for what? For whom? How to tell a family that loves you but can't make you quite "fit" that you wonder how you can love them back and not die a bit each time, because to love them means to pledge a loyalty that won't allow differences? And you, Nikki, you've always known you're different.

The art scholarship to Smith was the escape hatch. Smith bowled over the parents, bowled me over with the beauty of the campus and the fact that ideas were allowed, encouraged, expected. Shit, for three years I was drunk with it. It was a matter of course that Nikki, the artist, Nikki, the outrageous, Nikki-the-newly-discovered-sapphist-now-womanizer would have extreme reactions to all issues . . . ha! I had found my niche at Smith and the idea of having to leave at the end of this year was . . . what? Like waking in the dark of my hometown all over again . . . lost. Alone. Grad school? Where? And more importantly, why? As much as I loved doing my art, as much as I counted on the "life of the artist" and the tolerance and good cheer it reaped for me, I was not prepared to "do" beyond school — it seemed as much of a waste as the factory would be. Commercial art went against everything that I did believe it, and it meant the City. I needed the woods like water, like air. Some throwback in our family line, perhaps, who knew? But the same call that impelled my father and brothers to hunt each fall courted and cried for me. Not to kill and conquer, no, but to just "be." What could I do with that? Not a lot of call for someone to hang out with the bears and draw these days.

You needed contacts for contracts to illustrate nature magazines or even textbooks. You needed technical skills that took years to acquire before you could compete with the artists already in the field.

Let's face it. Once, finally at Smith, so much had come easily (even learning how deeply my love for women ran) that to contemplate another huge battle for grad school was beyond that which I could handle. For the first time in my life I'd actually felt comfortable and I couldn't bring myself to think about what commencement could mean.

There was no more family support. They'd expected some amazing return for their investment — at least a son-in-law and better yet, some great prize-in-the-sky that would allow me into graduate school for fine arts or a job in New York. What they saw was this Nikki talking and dressing and acting so different, who did she think she was? Where was she going now with her high-and-mighty ways — who would take care of her when she got too old to be considered cute anymore? I was wasting my college education, so hard fought for and won, wasting it on drawing pictures of trees that would be better used cut up and sanded down, re-rooted into someone's living room. This last year at Smith I was supposed to figure out who I was, what I wanted — where I was going. Instead I'd concentrated on partying, bed-hopping, painting all night in the studio and trying to charm my way through the requisite other courses that would allow me to graduate. Not exactly lost, no, but I'd fit the category drifting.

I didn't like to drift. It scared the bejesus out of me, though damned if I would admit it. Something was going to happen, and as long as I could draw and as long as I could get outside often I'd be okay, just fine. Don't think far ahead — one day at a time — revel in the joy of brilliant, fascinating, coddled women eager to share my bed, never let them know that even after those delicious, split-open-ripe nights, sometimes I'd still wake up in a dead-sweat, eyes wide, peering and trying to pierce the dark.

Then, one month into anthropology 205, sitting with a hangover and the vague, musk-oil scent of Jennifer Knowles still clinging to my skin, the lights go down in the class and a video punches on ... and for the first time in my life I learn that Remmel Mountain is about eight thousand, six hundred feet straight up into the misted sky of Washington State — clearly not the tallest peak, but one that marks the edge of where people feel safe camping — one that marks the edge between forest and wilderness.

Close to the Canadian border, on the northern end of the Pasayten Wilderness, Remmel Mountain is where primatologist Darrian Stone has a base camp. Where scientist Darrian Stone has established, documented and continues to study one of the greatest discoveries in the fields of primatology, anthropology and biology of the twentieth century: the North American Great Ape!

Tadah! Heavy music. The *Geographic* theme song, initial credits, and what the hell, I'm sitting up, headache forgotten, actually paying attention to this documentary.

Maybe it was all that green; killer forests there. So much wild. Maybe it was the day or simply that the filmmaker was truly a gifted person. Didn't matter, doesn't still, whatever made me sit up and take notice was secondary because there in front of me, in the middle of a mountain camp on the northwest coast, was the most magnificent woman I'd ever seen. I think now, flashing back, the cameraman knew it too. He came in slowly and then, as the story unwinds, as she is introduced and begins a three-minute monologue about her work on Remmel, he just zooms in closer and closer until the viewer is almost swallowed up by her eyes — the forest rides in them. Greens and golds, burnt siennas and tawny oaks — like a hit of epinephrine to an asthmatic, this picture still gives me a rush. Darrian Stone — okay, just a tape, but the first image I had. Jesus H. Christ.

Darrian had turned forty, just, or so my faulty math powers figured, so this tape was taken when she was younger. She had just recently gone public about the apes when *Geographic* was first allowed into her camp. Shit, for me, well, it was like a vision of the Holy Grail or something. Still no way to explain it, I can't even paint it — truly a first. I mean, I nearly fell off my chair in class, right into those eyes. Like I wanted to go up to the screen and just ... just touch her face ... Didn't matter that about twenty other people would witness the mad act ... I was that lost. Shit! And here is the kid who has never so much as blinked over any rock star or movie idol, this was a whole new feeling, a whole new world, and I fell hard.

Darrian Stone shone. I mean, here was this lone woman, on the top of some rain-soaked mountain, living with Indians and looking like a designer's idea of Dian Fossey. Even back then Darrian wore the silver and denim and leather like a movie version of herself. There was a kind of self-conscious vanity that made her endearing to me — I could feel it, see it the way she spoke to the cameraman, the way she moved them through the forest. And yet her humility when she was talking about the apes and the Indians — almost reverential. It broke something in me, something that had been high and hard — dammed up — something that not even seven different lovers in three years had been able to touch. She was cracking the single most interesting American folkloric mystery, proving its truth, bringing in the forensic material that would blow everyone out of the water ... and yet she was totally unaffected. She had solved the mystery of Sasquatch, of Bigfoot, and yet she was this really tall, beautiful, vulnerable woman whose voice made me go liquid. Something about her brilliance, the intelligence shining in those eyes — but more — there was power, too, as if she had become part of that steaming forest, not just someone studying or visiting there, but an actual part of it. They called the video *Out of the Mist* — of course playing on the Fossey parallel — but in an odd way, with this woman, it worked. I wanted to know her. Bang. Smack between the eyes, it hit me. I had to know everything about Darrian Stone.

I bought a copy of the video. I played it almost non-stop for two weeks. My housemates were ready to strangle me with it. Finally, when even the dog would slink out of the room when I had it on, I realized it was time to act on the obsession.

That first, long-winded, star-struck letter ...

where was it tonight? God, it had taken an eternity to write. Spent more time on it than any paper I'd ever tried to write my entire student career. I just didn't want her thinking I was this sorority rich bitch out for a field trip and an easy 'A'. For the first time in a long time I wanted to prove, had to prove, that I was deadly serious. Had to comb through three years of "play" to find a few hard kernels of what I'd accomplished, something to show her — what? What did I want? What would I say if she wrote back? "Hey, like, Dr. Stone, I love the woods too — can I come up and play with you and your apes?" Right. But I did love the forest — and maybe there was something — maybe she could use an illustrator, or even someone just to — to — what? What?

My friends thought I was nuts. I was pathetic, at this age, to have the hots for a middle-aged scientist lost in the bush. There were enough professors around open to "possibilities," why did I have to entertain this fantasy? Why, indeed? Just something, something in the colors in her eyes, and this sounds so stupid, but, if you looked at the tape long enough, listened hard enough, there was a sadness there. Something about Darrian Stone resonated in me as purely as a bell — I *felt* her.

Okay, a strange way to explain it — but for the first time in my life I wanted something, someone — not in that fleeting, crazy craving way, not like pepperoni pizza or a new Porsche or good sex — something deeper — something I had no words for — still don't. And worse of all, this "something" hurts. Deep.

So, I mailed the damned letter off to the

producers of the tape and got a form letter back. Darrian Stone received her mail c/o the Ranger Station on Remmel Mountain — no agent — not even a foundation yet to do the paperwork. Any contact had to go that uncertain route. Best of luck.

Yeah. Okay, so another to the Ranger Station based at Okanogan National Forest. No reply on that one, either. Like burning bits of paper without prayers on them, in Catholic school, being told that the rising smoke carried our words to God — those letters almost as transparent. And like the prayers, I got no direct answers. No immediate results.

Enough playing. I had to have a plan. Going out of my skin sitting in classes, the studio, hanging out with my friends, all I could think about was Darrian Stone . . . and being deepwoods with her. Everything I had lived for seemed so trivial, so easy, so soft around the edges. This new burning was sharp, it hurt, didn't cease. I had to find a way to get directly to the woman. If I could see her, meet her, talk with her — somehow she would know I wasn't a bullshitter — she would feel this same ringing note, recognize it — she had to.

And I had no choice but to split. All the money I'd saved, worked for in the summer as a docent in the local museum, all the bucks the parents had scraped together for my final year at Smith — I pulled it out of the bank. A one-way ticket over Thanksgiving break, one hundred pounds of camping equipment from the L.L. Bean catalogue — and a map of Okanogan . . . it seemed like a lot. It seemed like nothing.

I told everyone at school I was visiting relatives. I told all the relatives I was staying with a prof at

school. And I wrote a final letter to Darrian Stone
telling her every reason I could think of why she
should just meet with me once. I enclosed a rough
resume, all the letters of reference I'd ever used for
jobs, school, special favors in my department. I even
sent a copy of my birth certificate and proof of all of
my shots — what the hell do you mail to someone
when you are in thrall? Just as long as she didn't
think it was a prank or I was an ax murderer ...
just so long as she didn't think I was some pervert
pretending to be sane. When I got there I'd show
her my drawings — hell, I'd floor her with my
technique. I'd repair roofs, clean toilets, write press
releases — whatever she said. It honestly didn't
matter. And when it was done, I'd come off the
mountain. I would know what else I was supposed
to do, then ... That, too, rang pure as a Tibetan
prayer bowl in my heart. I'd meet Darrian Stone and
I'd know. Yeah.

The sound of the storm bawling, screaming in
high rises and then moaning back ... Recite the
names of Indians around me ... I'd been practicing
the entire bus trip out ... Ozettes and
Quillayute ... Sleep coming with the rain ... Hoh,
Skokomish, Snoqualmie ... sounding like the storm .
.. Tulalip, Quinault, Makhah and Yakima ...
Winomish and somewhere, somewhere below me ...
Chief Joseph's grave.

It is the absence of rain that wakes me. The
unrelenting drilling has stopped. Not even the
melting chorus of trees breaks the silence. Night

surrounds me. I've slept through the soaking day. Have to pee ... bad ... so much water and cold, no surprise.

I stretch cramped legs, wondering if I could light a fire or should — whacko. Rangers might follow the smoke directly to my camp.

The tent zipper sticks, probably rusting. I nearly take down the dome as I fight to get out of its nylon belly. Jesus — the air is like the inside of a refrigerator!

Carefully I stand as straight as last night will allow — walk to a bush — watch my hot pee stream in the dark ... Damp ... gray night, not the pitchy black I expected ... Must be a moon rising somewhere behind the clouds.

Before my eyes can adjust something cracks a branch behind me. I swing around, my head light, hot, reeling — am grabbed by "It!" All fear crams down my throat — the air only coming as if through a narrow straw, my lungs on fire, I am pinned, the muscles binding my own like iron ... A long, dark tunnel, no chance to call, to scream, to struggle ... a melting, going down ... useless ...

"You've got a bad cough. It's going to hurt to breathe deeply for a while. Don't try to talk. Drink this."

"It" had a very human voice.

I opened my sticky eyes. A golden glow ... the soft hissing of lanterns, smell of fire, some food, not a hospital, not even a "Bigfoot" cave.

I hurt. I really, really hurt. Breathing was like

20

sucking razors into my lungs. My back and chest were heavy with white pain. My throat felt meat-raw, burned. Even the light made my eyes ache. Couldn't raise my head more than a couple of inches. It was as heavy as a crystal punchbowl and about as empty.

"Don't try to get up! Julian brought you in, you're lucky. We've lost a lot of people on this mountain from hypothermia. Here, drink."

"It's" voice was all velvet, no rough edges and soothingly familiar, but just on the other side of recognition. Couldn't focus, couldn't see, not enough to peel back the skin of light and look inside.

"We'll talk later ... I promise. Now, drink this and then try to sleep." The voice moved off, down the dark tunnel, pushing me back, back toward the narrow end ...

Better. Awake and better enough to know it. Pity. If I'd been sick longer maybe somebody could have gotten word up to Darrian Stone and she'd really know that a serious person was dead set on reaching her. First thoughts ... I sit, all the way up, for the first time in ... days? Hours?

"Long enough!" The liquid, golden voice of "It" is beside me.

"What?" I turned, surprised, a little unnerved.

"You've been here long enough. I think, tomorrow, we can take you up the mountain ... Nikki."

"It" is a woman. Her long, silky hair brushing past strong shoulders. Tall, or seems so as she

21

stands by my cot. Dark face, tanned, eyes like twin chestnuts. Oh, I could fall into the warmth of that color . . . Must be feeling better. I grin, embarrassed, taken by this soft angel.

"I'm Farquhar, Dr. Stone's assistant. She's left word that it's all right to bring you up, that is, if you still want to go?" The woman tries to hide her own smile.

Farquhar! Of course, I recognize her now, know why the voice seemed so safe, so much like "home." But on the video she looked so much younger, no older than me. Now, this woman is stunning, but with the web of worry etching her face, outlining the eyes, around her smile . . . what had happened? What was going on up here? Where was Darrian Stone?

"We looked through your backpack. Julian thought it was necessary. I hope you don't mind. We're usually very private up here, as you may have already surmised. However, we have to know who strangers are. Julian was in the Ranger's cabin when they brought you in. He thought you had to be the same woman when he came upon your tent two days later — after the storm. Still, he couldn't be certain — and you were very sick. It doesn't take long up here. The mountains make harsh judgments." Farquhar reaches out a slim hand and gently, gently touches my reddened cheek.

I feel . . . dirty. That residual film of illness that remains until you scrub down, hard. This woman is the kind of person I've only read about. Like a New Age joke, almost — almost too peaceful. Yet no fake. Sudden tears, they splash down, baptize her fingers. Christ — is it the fever? I stutter, try to apologize,

don't know why. Shyly she pulls back, moves like a
shadow, so quiet, so lithe. The dark eyes don't look
into mine but discreetly over my shoulder. If this is,
indeed, Farquhar from Darrian Stone's facility then I
am right — no way can Dr. Stone be a psycho!
"Did Dr. Stone ever receive my letters? Where is
she? Why did you let me up here? Why didn't . . .
Julian . . . why didn't Julian just tell the Rangers
where I was? He couldn't be that old Indian inside
the Station — that guy was so little — how could
he . . . ?"
"Don't waste your energy, Nikki. You've got a
long hike tomorrow. We think you can make it but
you'll have to conserve strength, take it very, very
slowly. It would be optimum for you to remain here
for a few more days but a major storm is moving in.
After first snow we can't get up to Darrian till
spring. If you have even a single doubt about joining
us there for that length of time you should
reconsider — now." Farquhar kneels down beside the
makeshift cot. Her eyes grow wide, this time looking
straight into me, this time seeming to dance with
the lantern light.
She knows my answer.
For a brief moment I think of my parents, grad
school applications, deadlines, even the stupid
Rangers . . . Forget it! A final look into Farquhar's
face and I know I'll send them all cover letters,
explaining everything — later. My parents knew of
Darrian Stone — hell, everybody in America knew —
my roomies would tell them if my letter didn't arrive
first — not hard to figure, given the maps of
Washington, the camping gear catalogs and copy of
the videotape left in my dorm room. Hell, I'd already

23

blown the year's money getting to Remmel, so, so, so.

"You'll have to come up the mountain in silence, Nikki. People track us, plant radios, bugs ... we are under constant surveillance. It won't be safe till we reach the sub-alpine zone. Somehow, most intruders give up around there. At base camp you won't be allowed to communicate down the mountain ... not for many weeks. It sounds harsh, but there are good reasons. A break as small as news that some college kid has been "kidnapped" by Dr. Stone's people — and the press would tag it that — would be enough to crack us wide for any governmental scrutiny. More people on the mountain, more danger to our work. They'll use any excuse to move deeper into the sanctuary." Farquhar's eyes, though solemn, still crackle with light.

The words are reactionary, almost crazy — wouldn't people be more apt to come looking if they already knew I was headed for Remmel?

Again, as if she can read my mind, Farquhar answers, "They only search for a few weeks in the winter season after the first snow. We have radio contact but we won't confirm that you're with us — not for a while. The Rangers can attest to the fact that you showed up and were a tenderfoot — simply implausible that you could have made it up the mountain, in the storm, on your own. Because you're a college student it will be assumed you're on a joy-ride back to the city, on a lark. No one can do anything till first thaw. I know how bizarre this must sound, but you have to trust — to believe — Darrian's work, our work. It all hinges on the

24

balance of silence. Can you make this promise, Nikki?"

Farquhar takes my two hands, pressing her cool palms against my tight, hot skin. It is so easy to allow her these minute connections — not like me — not like me at all. I am a New England child, much as I fight it, all bristle and cold bone until I'm absolutely certain of someone's intent, sure of their affection. But here, this strange, beautiful, achingly familiar woman is holding my hands, crouched over my bed, asking me to come away with her into the uncertain winter and tell no one.

I allow it . . . all of it. For an entire life so much had come to me through my own manipulation, my own striving — almost too easy. There had never been a burning focus, only a vague desire, an unrest, like sand in a shoe — but never a fierce need, a drive. Suddenly, in this curious place, a hunger that allows no other thought, no question, no remorse. It scorches my past like so much wrapping paper — and under the gauzy envelope, at the center: Darrian Stone. And this Farquhar too — her herald — they are who I'd come so far to find. Not just miles, but my life. My pulse pounds as if in answer — yes, yes, again, yes!

Farquhar nods, her eyes full of flame. "Sleep deeply tonight, Nikki. Tomorrow you are going farther than you have ever imagined. Goodnight." She leans over my cot, and, almost too soft to be real, her lips brush my forehead. I close my eyes, my breathing filled with ache.

* * * * *

25

Awake in the still lap of darkness. The air, expectant, expecting snow, I suppose. Rubbing sleep from my dreamless eyes, my muscles still screaming for rest, then, the sudden Cyclops of the lamp, steaming tea held out by the glorious Farquhar! No vision, no Castanada hallucination, a real, flesh and blood scientist this morning — hair swept up into a neat, black bun, eyes full of flight but dead-on serious. Her parka is already zipped, her heavy boots laced, only the hand holding the tin cup of tea is ungloved. She is still calm, no distance, thank God, she is still who I opened to last night, but today there is an aura of time, a feeling of speed barely kept in check.

"We let you sleep in a bit because you've been so ill, but now it's time to move. Your pack is by the door. Hurry!" She picks up two towels, nudges me out of bed like a mother cat with her kitten — gentle but serious. I realize I'm wearing only a bemused grin as I stand, grab for the towels, head in the direction she pushes — a shower. I move as fast as my bent and bruised bones will allow.

Outside it is full-on morning but the light is gray. Huge, scattered flakes, lacy as doilies, travel — but their drop is less downward than sideways . . . a bad sign.

Farquhar, a huge pack strapped to her slim body, waits beside a small, dark, wrinkled man. I pull on my own scarlet bag, struggle awkwardly with the buckles, the weight. My head is already beginning to ache.

Farquhar smiles, winking obviously at the old man. She adjusts my straps, eases the pull against my sore shoulders.

"Julian will be taking you up ... slowly. I'll go on ahead. I've got important mail and supplies that Darrian is waiting for; I don't want to keep her any longer. You just stick to the pace Julian sets, all right, Nikki? It might seem he's going too slowly but trust him, he knows the terrain ... and the weather. Don't worry. You'll be at base camp before nightfall. I'll be waiting for you both — with Dr. Stone. Have a good hike!" Farquhar touches my face with the tips of her glove.

The earthy smell of doeskin fills me. Such a simple act, but it breaks me wide, again the stupid tears rise. How silly to flash on words like "tender" on this rugged hillside in the snow. Yet, with her, it fits. Okay, I'll trust this Julian, but only because she trusts him! I watch her strong strides as she bushwhacks out of sight, the huge pack almost dwarfing her already tall frame.

"How far?" I turn to ask Julian.

His eyes sparkle, light as a match behind them, alive. "Far enough," he grins.

We are off. Right. Far enough.

Clearly the air was colder. Our breaths left train-plumes in the space around us. I was sure my heart was loud as a locomotive. Even if I hadn't been ill it would have knocked me out ... the altitude, the pace. We must have risen over a thousand feet in a few hours — all of it straight up. Julian handed me some bread and cheese and an orange as we took a breather. I was surprised at the small pack he carried especially in comparison to

Farquhar's burden. Even my pack outweighed the rucksack he was hauling.

"Julian, I don't mean to be rude, by why does Farquhar have to carry most of the mail and supplies? Seems a little unfair to me."

"I'm for you." The quiet man didn't look me in the eyes.

"What?" I stood up suddenly, orange peels mixing in electric panic with the clean snow. A horrible image of me wrestling this old guy off my bones in the woods — who would believe me, the stranger? They all trusted him, right, even the Rangers! Oh shit.

Julian read the shock in my face. His expression was stone but his color deepened. He poked a booted toe around the base of a rock and muttered, "I'm for you ... if you can't climb ... just in case." His voice betrayed no hurt, yet was very, very cool.

Man, I am the world's biggest ass! In case I can't make it ... just like the first time he carried me to their cabin. Now my face was scalding. Idiot!

"Julian, I'm such a jerk. I ... apologize, God, I'm sorry. Please, forgive me?" I took a snowy step towards him, then stopped, unsure, embarrassed, ready to be left to freeze on the nearest log.

He still didn't meet my gaze but extended a gloved hand. "I accept."

I took it, unable, this time to look at *him*. We finished our cold lunch in silence, listening to the tiny pitpitpit of the changing snow around us, smaller now, icy, cruel against exposed skin and branches, all signs of a major pile-up.

I rescued every bit of trash, vowing to do penance, to make camp under my own steam, even if it meant death. And someday, I swore, I'd give Julian a ride down the mountain.

The storm came in on us in one long howl. I'd never heard such inhuman sounds before — nor seen such monolithic trees. I kept expecting them to thin out as we climbed, but they continued on, an army still and dense. Maybe we'd taken a turn off Remmel and were on another slope. It would be so easy to get lost even without the added curtain of ice and wind. I wasn't sure what hour it was, let alone the direction we were moving. Funny ... all my adult life time seemed so important, the exact measure and record crucial, calendars, punch clocks, schedules, datebooks, watches, organizers. How nothing mattered in terms of minutes or even days, all that mattered was finding someplace warm, out of this storm, and, ultimately — Darrian!

Julian never looked back. A matter of pride, or more likely he could hear my wheezing cough and was able to measure my progress, or lack, by the sound. He didn't slacken his pace though, or offer to carry so much as my pack. I took it as a good sign. A thumbs up.

Farquhar had had the forethought to remove my sleeping bag, tent, and extra clothes. Now my second pair of shoes, few personal items, even the minimum gear I still carried rubbed in places I didn't know I had — blistering my armpits, the small of my back, hips and collarbone. Any place a strap bit in, took hold and kept time to the softshoe rhythm I marked through the thickening snow. I wondered how much farther, the sweat trickling down my back then freezing right over my tailbone. Couldn't even carry on a conversation ... just as well. I doubted Julian would much appreciate a white-girl motor-mouth on the trail he was cutting for us through the big trees. I wanted to stop every other step but my pride, and Julian, wouldn't allow the luxury, I was sure. Slogging through the now thigh-deep white, I guessed this was the way a prizefighter must feel in a losing, final round.

Julian stopped. Stopped so suddenly that I walked right smack into his back, my glasses scrunching against my nose painfully. They were completely ice-coated and now reduced to nothing but greasy smears.

"What, what?" I gasped, swiping at the murky lenses with my mitten.

Julian turned around, touching my shoulder, smiling, pointing. Clearly, off to our right, a marked trail, the snow not exactly shoveled, but definitely pushed aside.

From the miles of shucking underbrush this now seemed like a freeway. Julian broke out a canteen of very sweet tea. I drank two long, wonderful mouthfuls. The metallic bite made my tongue pucker but it was oddly refreshing. Julian finished the tea off, burping happily. We couldn't be far away, now.

Warmth began to leak back into my extremities. Darrian Stone. Would she even be there when we arrived? God, I could be set up in some faraway visitor's cabin, or worse, a tent! She'd be holed up in this storm in her own quarters ... I might not meet her for days ...

Couldn't hold this unbearable thought. Too much

illness ... the brutal hike ... I would lose it, finally, in front of them, just simply break down. No, no, it would be all right ... too much of an investment to think otherwise. Just put one boot in front of the other, bide my time, mellow out. Okay, okay.

Julian picked up his pace. While the smell of woodsmoke began to mingle with snowscent, the wind hid any signs of a settlement nearby. The howling had deepened, becoming almost enraged. I understood that we really had been in serious danger as we climbed. Julian had hidden it from me. Had we even so much as tarried at lunch we would have been caught dead in the gale. A second time I owed my life to this Indian man.

I reached out tentatively, squeezed his sinewy shoulder. Any mouthed thanks would only have been torn from my lips by the wind. He didn't even flinch, only tapped my fingers with his gloved palm.

A final stand of lodgepole pine, now totally frosted, bellowing in response to the rip of the wind. Even my eyelashes were icy. Before Julian stepped over the last branches, I knew we'd made it. He held them aside, waiting patiently as I struggled, pulling snow down on both of us as my packframe hit a low bough.

Then, no more than five feet from us, a deep, slow laugh barely audible between the pauses of wind. A strange, musical laugh. But it was replaced by the familiar parka and long unmistakable legs of Farquhar!

Pulling into sight behind her, the person who laughed into the storm's face ... Taller, even, than Farquhar, the wind whipping a dark ponytail back behind her handsome head, as if she were galloping towards us, dressed in denim and dark green, exactly as I knew she'd dress.

She moved toward us, hugging Julian madly, and he thumping her merrily on the back in quick return. Then he laughed, too, for the first time, relief and exhaustion finally betrayed in his voice. Here the wind died down just long enough for us to listen to each other. I felt very, very insignificant ... the lone boarder at a family reunion.

Even so much as one step towards them seemed impossibly arrogant. So I waited, bent under my pack, fighting the rising lump in my throat, the tremble in my knees.

Darrian Stone came to me. Taking off her glove, extending her hand in that bitter cold, she stood open, unguarded, ready to meet me, the stranger.

Christ, I would have recognized those long, strong fingers and sculpted veins anywhere ... I shucked my ice-crusted mittens and touched my freezing fingertips to hers. Fire and frost ... my stomach fell into my socks. A little gasp that I prayed the wind masked, escaping from my lips, a sound I'd only made a few times before ... all raw hunger, all astonished joy.

"Nikki? I'm Darrian, Darrian Stone."

Farquhar broke the electricity, yelling above the blizzard, giving up, resorting to a rough shove, trying to push me ahead up the rapidly drifting path.

It was so dark and "furry" that I could barely make out Darrian's tall form at the head of our small line. Julian held my elbow needing my guidance this time.

My lungs felt flat, as if a huge boulder were slowly squeezing my chest to pancake width. Each cough forced me to stop, gasping, dying with the indignity of making them wait even that much longer in the screaming blizzard.

The main cabin was farther along than I'd guessed. Safety? Privacy? Protection? We had easily another eighth of a mile through the hard snow. My head was really pounding now, God, I wondered about altitude sickness. For some people, it hit them at about nine thousand feet. Still, this could be close enough. My stomach gurgled with remembered tea. So hard to even gasp . . . but no way would I give in . . . not now, at the feet of Darrian Stone . . . Finally, the miracle of a blurred porch.

Darrian stood there, in the circling flakes, waiting, impervious to the gritty snow as it lashed at her bare face and head. She held the door open as we made the final few yards. Inside, the light like stepping underwater, as if we'd moved under the frozen face of a pond. Clean, blue, not warm. The fire in the fireplace little more than hissing coals. Obviously Darrian had been waiting for us for some time outside. This went right to my heart. The prestigious scientist freezing her ass waiting for a college student . . . and of course Julian.

"Get the woman warm, Farquhar! Julian, just sit, will you? My God, I can carry wood, I'm no cripple, not yet, anyway!" Darrian clomped out, back into the swirling white, re-entering minutes later with an armload of firewood.

"Nights like this I'm thankful we spend half our time cutting wood. Nikki, get out of those wet clothes. Put your pack into the room down the hall — the one with the door open. For now it's yours. Farquhar says you've been ill. Please, no relapses, we don't have any safe way to get you down and I make a lousy nurse at best. Go, go!"

No arguments. Things happening too fast to think about them. It was as if I'd been expected for months, like a long lost cousin that you welcome but are unsure of . . . okay, I could understand. I'd make myself useful, she'd see, indispensable even, pay back for the risk they were taking, the burden. No way I'd be sick again.

"Seems you enjoy these bedside scenes." Darrian was standing over me. Dark. The wind had stopped. I could hear the fire in the front room as it munched a meal of logs.

"What?" I sat up too quickly. The darkness was suddenly sprinkled with tiny, exploding points of light. Falling back against the pillows I realize I've got nothing but my thermals on.

"The hike up took a lot; you'll get used to it. A number of people start to feel the altitude up here . . . some never fully acclimate."

"Sorry. Guess I'm more tired than I thought." I wanted to curl up and die, then thought about what a problem that would cause.

"Don't be embarrassed, Nikki. If it hadn't been for Julian my first winter, I'd have been nothing but a popsicle. He helped me build this cabin after the snows. The original tipi I spent the winter in has long since been recycled. I still remember *my* first hike up here — no lost honor, little preppie." Darrian smiled.

"I'm no prep! Dr. Stone, seriously, let me explain, please! I know how this must look, but honestly —" A coughing attack interrupted my tirade.

Darrian, thumping me on the back, waited till my hacking was under control. Then, she let me know where I stood: "I apologize for the preppie crack. Anyone under the age of twenty feels like . . . a school kid. Nikki, look, I didn't ask you to come.

You don't owe me any explanations of why you aren't physically up to our standards. However, we do not owe you anything either. From what I hear from your college, this little jaunt may be more of a getaway than anything else . . . correct?" Darrian sat at the foot of my cot.

I attempted to sit up, at least to something approximating eye level. My chest felt seared.

How to get it clear with her? All of those months dreaming in the dark at Smith, and now here I was, away from the rest of the stupid world, where no one could haul me down, and here was Darrian Stone, sitting on my bed! Even through the sickness she made me blush, heat creeping across the expanse of wool between us, creeping up and filling me. What had Smith said to her, and when?

"Of course I checked out your credentials — we don't simply ignore letters when they arrive, especially when there is such a high-pitched plea inherent in them. If you hadn't checked out I would never have allowed you up this far, regardless of your wishes. If you stay through till spring, as I'm afraid you must, you'll have to pull more than your weight, Nikki. I don't want to get into this now. We'll talk later. Best you get some sleep. The toilet is down the hall — indoor plumbing, our one convenience. If you need me, my room is on the other side of the cabin. There's food and water in the kitchen. We'll discuss things in a few hours. Sleep now." She stood, stretching her long arms, and moved to the door. She moved like a tall shadow, meaning she hardly seemed to move at all.

"Dr. Stone, how am I supposed to just sleep? You

don't believe me, believe why I've come up here, believe I can contribute ... can work hard for you ... I'm not some ..." The tears cut me down, again, dammit! Throat scalded, can't say any of what I'd rehearsed for months. Anger, frustration, and something more like — like a kind of homesickness. Shocking; missing people who knew me for what I was, solid, no flake. I needed someone to stand up and say that — so that Darrian would stop, just stop! I couldn't take the harshness in her voice, the disappointment so obvious as she stood in the dark by the door. This the worst nightmare of this entire nightmare journey: Darrian Stone doesn't much like me.

"Nikki, slow down. Maybe you should know this. I don't expect anything, anymore, from anyone. Now, goodnight."

She walked out, shutting the door firmly behind her, shutting me off from the rest of them, like a child sent to bed before all of the grownups. I was reduced to that! How cold and black in this dinky room! I pulled the comforter up and over my aching chest, trying to breathe, to remember who I believed I was ... maybe, even, to sleep.

The light: sacred as in a sanctuary and just as impersonal, the light woke me. From the black maw of blizzard came this miracle of brilliance. Pure, dazzling its way through the chinks in the log wall (no wonder it's so damned cold!) breaking into diamond points all over the room. Whatever it touches it illuminates ... a kind of benediction. I feel wholly well, for the first time in how long? Cold, but cleaned out, new, almost filled with the light.

I peel back the covers carefully, not wanting to break the illusion of wellness, knowing, too, the shock of the floor against sleep-warmed feet. No disappointment there. It pulls the breath straight out of me, makes me have to fight back a coughing attack. Like some lowly root vegetable shucked from the warm garden and rudely tossed into a refrigerator. Still, there is the light. It is worth the nip of the floor, and the immediate tug of bladder.

I rush to my pack, grab jeans, flannel shirt, shove them on directly over my longjohns. God bless every cotton manufacturer working for L.L. Bean. Within seconds, the layers thaw blood and bone back to working temperature.

The door squeaks crisply. I ease it open as gently as Darrian closed it the night before. No one awake. No sounds or smells of coffee. No smoky fire scent. The door to the bathroom also creaks. Jesus, not easy, straddling a freezing toilet seat with your jeans and long underwear around your ankles. The two things Smith taught us: hold your liquor and pee straight. I had a fifty-fifty chance with this handicap.

Hitting the handle there is a strange sound, some kind of special solid waste unit or something — figures. Wash with water almost as cold as the air. This is the most awake I can ever remember being in my life.

Outside, the hall is a bit lighter now, coming closer into full morning. Almost back to my room when a soft voice calls from the front room.

"Good, you're up. I wondered if you were a morning person. That's a point in your favor."

Her back is to me in the living area. She sits, cradled it seemed, in an oversized rocking chair, an Indian trade blanket tucked around her. Watching (for what?) out the diamond-iced window, her body seems surrounded by a halo.

I can't focus through that blazing light! It's almost as if she sits dead-center, in the middle of a star, untouched, merely absorbing the energy and then throwing it off effortlessly around her. I couldn't answer.

"You *are* better, aren't you?" Darrian turns the chair around to face me, her face now black as her back had been moments before.

"Definitely, oh, yeah!" I stammer, little sunbursts going off in front of my eyes.

"You know, Nikki, you can tell everything about a houseguest after the first evening." Darrian moves away from the window glare, coming towards me. "You can tell if they're morning risers or late night folks — especially valued, but decidedly different. You can tell how adaptable they are going to be, or if they're cranky and requiring lots of care — not so valued up here. You can also tell who keeps their promises, by the morning light." Darrian grins.

I'm still blinking at the black spots, trying to listen, read her voice, read between the lines. "What promises?"

"Oh, like pulling one's own weight, wanting to be helpful — those kinds of promises. Come on, Nikki, you can learn the intricacies of a cast-iron stove, you can make our tea. I'm in charge of the oatmeal and toast. There's enough wood left over from last night so we won't have to gather any till later. Come, come, I'm sure someone with your grim determination can make a pot of tea!"

Suddenly I want my toothbrush, mouthwash, comb. No time to dash away. Darrian is already steering me toward the tiny kitchen, one huge hand planted firmly on my shoulder.

The kitchen faces west and so the light there is more subdued than the eastern window dazzle. It, too, shows winter through chinks in the logs. The cabin is so much bigger than I expected ... but it was also a lot rougher. Hard to believe she's been living up here like this for so many years. Tough.

Darrian hands me a box of kitchen matches and tells me to light the fire (already set up) inside the pot-bellied dwarf that passes for a stove in the corner. I fiddle, hemming and hahing, trying to figure out where the hell I'm supposed to put the lit match. Before I can burn my fingers, Darrian wheels around, half-shaking her head in frustration and half-laughing. She takes the box from me. Then, she reaches around and hits an unseen handle on the side of the stove. Lo and behold, the dwarf's belly sprouts a hole big enough for a two year old to climb into.

"This is where you stoke it ... no huge blaze to start, okay? Big fires don't impress me. A year or so ago another preppie — sorry, another student, nearly burned us down. Remember, small fire, intense heat — a little like you, no? All right." Darrian has her back to me on that one.

The flush scalds across my face. Glad she's leaning over, lighting the stove. In seconds there is the smell of shavings catching alight. Only a single feather of smoke and then it disappears ... the flue pulls well.

"Hope you like oatmeal. It's our staple till spring. Lost my whole henhouse two seasons ago, bear or cat, still don't know for sure. Just a few bits of fluff left. Well, we can get by on powdered eggs another winter."

"Uh, do you bake up here?" I feel like Mary Ellen Walton on the TV show as I place the kettle carefully on the top of the rapidly heating stove.

"Would that destroy your image of me, Nikki? the old hard-nosed she-devil-scientist baking?" Darrian is facing me, her smile unlined in the gentle light, her hair falling in loose tendrils, curly as the single plume of smoke from the stove. Her eyes, darker this morning, still holding the forest in their depths.

I feel my knees twitch. Shit, I have it bad! Fight her finding out ... I know what she'd think if she only knew how I feel about her, was continuing to feel, even with the disapproval or maybe, more, because of it.

"It's just, well, maybe I thought somebody else up here did that sort of thing. You know, what with all your research and stuff I didn't think ..."

I feel her move rather than see it. Almost as if her body heat passes in a gentle wave and washes over me, flooding through the layers I've pulled on. God, this is almost too much ... almost scary. I then realize it's the stove! I pull away, from her, from it, bumping my hip awkwardly against the sinktop.

41

"You've been reading too many articles about the primatologists in Africa, my dear. No, up here, I do the cooking most of the time. I find it difficult to turn over power in the kitchen. It's just too small to have things out of order. We have to take special care because of the wildlife, too. Someone absent-mindedly leaves the pantry open and there goes a half-season's dry goods with the first raccoon. Anyway, dammit, I'm a terrific cook. Just ask Julian, or Farquhar. That old Indian lives for my brown bread and baked beans. How do you think he's survived this long around me?" Darrian smiles wide now, allowing my retreat.

Christ, I could fall into that look! I want, want . . . what? The blush burns redder. The scream of the tea kettle saves me.

"Morning!" Farquhar at the door, her own blue longjohns peeking out the top of her flannel shirt. At least I was dressed right.

Farquhar's hair is neatly piled up, again, a dark bun capping her fine head. This morning she looks more like the woman of the video, the lines washed away by sleep, or maybe by just being back up here — with Darrian.

"I was educating young Nikki on the finer points of our 'Mrs. B.' They may yet end up friends." Darrian reaches cleanly over my head, opening a cupboard for the tea canister.

I am grateful to the gods and goddesses that she's left the blanket on the rocking chair. Her soft white jersey pulls as she takes the canister down — cupping her full breasts — her nipples clearly outlined against the worn fabric, the morning waking them. I feel the familiar warm ache, low.

Farquhar has also noticed. At least she stops for a moment, and I see her watch Darrian. Jesus, no, they couldn't be! It flashes that maybe they are lovers. Of course. It would explain a lot, including how physical and easy Farquhar was with me, another woman's woman. Of course she could tell — my vibes, whatever, why I was so drawn to her. I try to avert my hungry look for Darrian, watch for more clues from Farquhar ... then I catch her catching me. Shit.

Her eyes flash brown sparks ... her lush mouth unreadable. She makes the connection, I know it, feel it, sure as her hand against my face the day before. Ashamed ... it's not for lust that I've come to meet Darrian. Okay, so my whole self is, is just, well, open to her, but that isn't why I'm here. How to let Farquhar know that? One more item confusing our agenda. At this rate they'd send me down the mountain in an empty tea tin. I try to change the subject, change Farquhar's look.

"Uh, 'Mrs. B.'?" I stammer.

"Yes," Darrian says, "as in Butterworth — those maple syrup commercials — or don't they still sell that stuff? See the resemblance?"

Farquhar's face betrays nothing but amusement, but I can still see the questions in her eyes.

"Uh, where is the teapot, the cups?" I'm struggling to sound even.

"Big ceramic pot over there. Cups in the other cupboard. Honey in a jug inside the pantry. Farquhar, can you scrape some out, please?" Darrian rescues me, oblivious to the war-of-glances being fought over her.

Then, she bumps against me again. I turn, clutch

43

the teapot to my belly, not even looking as I claw for the cupboard handle.

"I can probably reach it more easily." Darrian is in a full press against my back. I feel like I'm really going to pass out this time, the sweat beading up on my forehead, running down my back. My entire body feels scorched with the contact. Have to get out of there, fast.

Darrian senses something. She turns, watches me back away, back directly into Farquhar this time, jump as if I'd sat on the stove. She raises her eyebrows questioningly, then breaks into another mind-melting smile.

"Nikki, excuse me, sometimes I forget, strangers don't realize in these tight quarters we're all just family — crashing around in here is part and parcel of that — I'm sorry if it feels too familiar."

Right. Family. Sure. Especially after all the preppie crap ... the woman was driving me nuts! Just move out to the table and set it up for our "family breakfast." Shit.

Julian helped clean up when we'd all finished. As silently as he joined us he left. Farquhar with a brief "bye" had also split. What was I supposed to do? Darrian was off in her own room, typing, from the sound of things behind her closed door. Okay, I'd unpack. Back to my little cell. That should take all of five minutes.

On the tiny table that served, I suppose, as a desk, I plunked out the diary and the drawing book still at the bottom of my pack. Both were soggy but salvageable. The diary was virgin — I knew it would be filled halfway before the bloody week was through. So much to decipher around these strange people — they talked in code or not at all. A few pens tumbled out onto my cot, a broken pencil. The rest was basic toiletries and a couple sets of jeans and sweaters — I stored the now-empty pack under my bed.

A small closet caught the clothing. It was clear what went in — the design of the room demanded that. Like a barracks. This "guest-room" was not made to entice anyone to stay for very long. I wondered about Farquhar's quarters — and Julian's. My extra sneakers were at the foot of the cot, ready to go. All my fancy stuff was somewhere below us, at the little home of Farquhar — kiss a few hundred bucks goodbye — what an ass! For the use I got out of it I could have simply taken my old Girl Scout rucksack and an army blanket. Now what?

Didn't feel like writing, not yet. Wait until it was safe. All I need is for Darrian to sneak in and find a diary complaining or questioning *anything*. Even I'm not that stupid. Hell, I'd spent my teenage years paying for the time my mother found my supposedly locked-up journal, in tenth grade — never again. Maybe Darrian was finished typing — I could ask for work. Seems reasonable, seems right.

Back in the living area, no sound except the wind outside and a little whine from the chimney. Darrian's bedroom door still closed tight. I knock, expecting her to scream for me to get lost, or worse, to open it wide, a look of absolute rage on her face at the intrusion. Neither happens. Don't dare, not in a million years, to peek inside. Maybe now, everyone out, a great chance to check on my surroundings, get my bearings. Might even pick up a few Stone clues.

One third of the cabin is taken up by the front room, our main living area. Huge windows face out east, surprising because of the care taken to haul those little panes of glass that make up the bigger windows themselves — they let in lots of cold air, too. On the other hand, this is the direction any visitors would come from, so it made sense.

The fireplace on the northern wall was as huge as the one in the Ranger Station. It helped throw warmth and light from the coldest end of the house. All stone, tall enough to step into, the mantle was easily five feet across. Wood was piled next to it, between it and the front door. An old, Indian rug, small dark spots showing the effects of shooting sparks from the fire, lay about three feet in front of the hearth. Behind it was the worn leather couch, it, too, covered with an Indian blanket. I wondered who the hell had brought the couch to Remmel. Behind the couch, open space — only Darrian's rocking chair occupied it.

So far, no one else had come even close to sitting in that "throne." Darrian ruled here, clearly, totally. Even Julian was relegated to assistant status inside this space. This *was* Darrian Stone — from the books on primates, feminist novelists, texts of psychology, art and Native Americans, lining the bookcases (that ran floor to ceiling next to her bedroom door), to the well-ordered kitchen and the venerable Mrs. B.

I gently touched the rocking chair, watched it move, thought again, of Darrian, this morning, a burning star, shattering the light.

A narrow hallway leads past her bedroom's western wall, and across from it is another closet. Tentatively I open it, finding only extra outdoor gear: boots, backpacks, tools, parkas, a few lanterns. And then, way in the back, two rifles and a shotgun. This feels strange — the first thing I've come across that doesn't carry the feeling of Darrian. There are also boxes of bullets and shotgun shells on the floor. I back out quickly, making sure not so much as a stuff-sack is out of place. Maybe the guns are for the bears that murdered her chickens . . . maybe.

Back in the living area, the round dining table dominates the space closest to the kitchen. It can seat eight easily. The mail sack Farquhar carried is now perched, like a small, sitting child, in the middle of the table. I have to fight the urge to open it, see if there are any letters about me inside. Damn college, what did they tell Darrian anyway?

The hallway that leads to our bedrooms also has bookcases opposite our doors. These seem less Darrianesque — maybe Farquhar's influence? Farquhar the reader — what kinds of things would she most likely keep there? I thumb through a few fat volumes — technical mountain guides, books of trails, more than a few modern art books. Again, did she carry them all the way here? Gifts from visitors? Lots of psychology and anthro volumes — more Native American lore, less spirituality and more history here — that made sense. Farquhar's family tree somewhere? Here too, cookbooks! And I thought Darrian was the house chef. Either an exaggeration (to further intimidate me) or maybe these were also Darrian's? Still, if the scientist and the beautiful Indian were lovers, wouldn't their books be as mingled as their lives? Darrian and Farquhar together — it made my stomach twist — why hadn't I even allowed for that possibility? If I had known it would I have come this far? Of course, it didn't change a thing. Getting laid or even tangled up with someone hadn't been a problem since my first year at Smith. Hey, I was a Don Juanita — no lack of self-confidence there — no need to come trekking for a lonely scientist. No, Darrian was a pull for other reasons, reasons I still couldn't label, or didn't want to label. Darrian and Farquhar, I could handle that. Yeah, okay. It made getting accepted perhaps harder — maybe the school had even told Darrian a little about my "social life." Wouldn't put it past them, depending on who she talked to. If she knew, she didn't act as if she knew. And if she didn't — fine, that explained the preppie punchlines.

Farquhar was too obvious for there to be a doubt, now that I'd looked closely. Her woman's energy was in high gear, and this morning, coming on me staring at Darrian like that, I saw it in her eyes, saw something that hadn't been there when she looked at me before. Shit — I wonder what Julian thinks about all of this? could he possibly know? If he was the one up here with Darrian that first winter it must have been before Farquhar, so he would have witnessed it happening between them — but he seems so conservative, old-line, somehow. This was confusing, intriguing, and I had to figure it all out just to save my sanity. Winter lasts a long time in these mountains.

At the end of the hall, past all of the bedrooms and the bath, completely running the length of the back of the house, was a screened-in porch. Plastic sheeting lined the inside of the screens for the winter. Surprisingly, it worked like a greenhouse — adding heat and light to the cabin. Maybe I should beg a few strips for my own room.

A few hand-made chairs and a large pine table overflowing with green plants completed the furniture out there. I guessed that if people lived anyplace long enough they were bound to collect stuff. Funny, thinking of any of the three of them with a green thumb. Off the large porch a door led to the back, the forest immediately there, ready to swallow this cabin at first sign of vacancy. A woodshed was just down two steps, a razor sharp ax propped against the woodpile. A line of blood beaded up on one thumb as I tested it. Clean shavings breaded the snow — clearly someone has already been chopping this morning.

I go back inside. Two more tin and wood shacks are beyond the cabin. I suppose they are the research buildings, small as they are. Darrian and the others are probably holed up out there, barring the door to my entrance.

Okay. I got the picture. I'd wait until I was invited. Meanwhile I'd sit inside, pull down one of the history books, get educated, stun them all with my vast knowledge of . . .

Voices coming out of the woods! I hightail it to the front room, immediately guilty, the ghosts of a Catholic childhood haunting me still.

* * * * *

"Well, it isn't a complete loss. If we get the roof repaired by tonight it will be fine. Good thing the place wasn't heated. All those records would be mush now." Darrian's boots clomp onto the back porch. I imagine her pulling them off, setting them close to the door.

"Yeah, maybe, but if the shed *had* been heated, the snow on the roof would have melted and . . ." Julian's voice trails off.

They come down the hall, Darrian at the lead, as usual, her face ruddy from the cold and . . . what? She doesn't say a word when she sees me. Julian, following, winks as he passes.

"Julian, we wouldn't have to patch it in this cold if you'd simply listened to me earlier." Darrian sits heavily at the dining table, wrestles the mail sack open, pulls out a handful of envelopes. She seems to need to always be doing something — one task hardly complete before the next catches her. I can't even think that fast.

"It's not the records, Darrian, it's that the maps and growth charts can't be replicated . . . besides, it's bad for you to be working out there without any heat!" It is the most I've heard Julian say the entire time I've known him. My stereotype of "the silent Chief" goes the way of "dirty old man in the woods." What an ass I am, still.

"Julian, you know the only way to heat that place is to rig up a kerosene stove — too risky. Besides, we'd have to have the junk brought in and I don't want to give those yuk-yuks below any more excuses to come into camp. I'm fine. Just have to remember to wear my down and gloves. Anyway, only part of the roof caved in. That happens in heated buildings, too. You know how much snow weighs. Stop worrying. You'll get wrinkles." Darrian propped her stocking feet on a chair.

"Yeah." Julian wandered out into the kitchen, the sounds of tea-making ringing back.

"Want some tea, Nikki?" Darrian didn't even glance up from the letter she was reading.

"I didn't think you even knew I was here." I sounded like a little kid coming up to her father when he got home from work, unsure of his mood. I knew it all too well.

"Don't be ridiculous. Sit down. Julian! Make an entire pot, will you, please?" Darrian kept on with her reading.

A muffled grunt came from the kitchen. I sat. Across the table from her. Her lips were almost ruby ... her hair deep chestnut against the whiteness of her skin ... so white for someone who spent her entire life outdoors. Maybe it was only the cold.

"This afternoon, if you're feeling up to it, I'd like you to help with the roof on the records shed. You do know how to hammer and saw, don't you?" She kept on reading.

"Well, maybe not as well as you, but I've built a few bookshelves at school and —"

Darrian put her letter down, laughing.

"Hey, what's the joke? Look Dr. Stone, you seem to find a lot to laugh about around me. Maybe, maybe it isn't so cut and dried as you think, huh? Maybe I am serious about working and maybe if you give me half a chance you could find that out for yourself! Dammit! I gave up school, friends, even my family to come here this winter, just to, to meet you!"

My anger shocked me. It was the crack about the bookshelves, her laughing. I could handle the sarcasm, even the judging, but not her laughing outright at me.

Darrian threw the letter across the table. It hit me squarely in the chest. "Nikki, what is it that you want?"

Shock. Absolute. I can hardly respond, "I, I . . ."

"To be filled up? To find direction — isn't that how maudlin psychiatrists label it? Or is it a broken heart? Who did you really leave back at Smith, Nikki? Maybe I sell you short — maybe it's fame and fortune, a germ of an idea for a novel or a play? Or do you want some inside scoop for your doctoral dissertation? What, exactly, do you want from me? How dare you get indignant! You are the one who came here, uninvited, I might add, getting the law involved in the worst possible way, costing my people time, supplies and very nearly their lives in rescuing you. Then you come barging into my camp, fainting dead away, babbling about wanting to help when you finally come around — and yet you can't even light a bloody kitchen stove. This is a private, sophisticated research facility. Millions of dollars have gone into this program for the past seven years. Internationally recognized individuals have begged, literally begged, to come up here to study, yet you have the gall to force yourself on us just because a couple of your student letters weren't answered fast enough to satisfy you. What the hell do you really *want*, Nikki — tell me now, because there are a few things I need to tell *you*." Darrian's eyes were laser beams, crackling green-gray, focused right at my heart.

Where was the wondrous woman who had been on the snow path less than twenty-four hours ago? Where was the being-of-light who'd greeted me this morning? Who was this banshee?

"Nothing to say? I thought as much. I want you to know what your being here is going to cost this facility. First, there is no way to get you down till spring thaw, approximately six months from now. There is no mail up or down until that time. I have to radio your presence here to those fools you met below, tell the, no, *convince* them, that you are fine, in no danger, not being kept here against your will. Then they have to convince whatever family you have. How many parents are willing to accept the third-hand words of strangers when it comes to their children? Barring the very real possibility that they will try to get the police up here. You arrive, in camp, sick, without benefit of medical records or history —"

"I've had my shots! I'm not allergic to anything!" I was pathetically grasping anything, anything to stop her tirade. Had to calm her down, just cool her out.

"That doesn't make you any less of a threat to the Indians. Nor to my animals, nor to me. You're bringing every East-Coast-God-knows-what with you — who knows where you've been or who you've been with? You were sick the moment you arrived. The first thing you did was pass out when you entered this cabin. Do you realize that you could wipe out every animal you profess to want to help? You could kill every last person you say you want to aid.

These are the hard facts, Nikki, the issues that mark the researcher and separate the true scientist from the student on a field trip. Now, I have to make our carefully planned provisions feed an additional adult for six months. I have to gauge fuel levels and emergency medical supplies — even clothing, if we run into trouble. I've been crucified by the press, lately — how do I know you aren't simply a plant? This is what *I'm* dealing with, Nicole, what *I* have to consider. From the first second of receiving your letters I've had to mull these things over. I've continued to consider the issues, even as I hauled your sorry butt into bed last night and made your oatmeal this morning. To top it off, before I can even sit down and do a full interview with you, the damned records roof blows in. Can you begin to fathom why I might be a wee bit bent out of shape when *you* dare to get upset?"

Darrian's face was the furious face of a stranger. People had been right about the mood swings, the viciousness just under her professional surface. I was afraid of her — truly afraid.

Finally, Julian entered with the tea. Funny, it had only taken the time for the kettle to boil, but it had seemed like hours. Julian's face was now another mask. In silence he sat between us. In silence Darrian poured three cups. She handed two to him. He passed one to me. I waited for the scalding liquid to cool, thankful only that the trembling in my hands had stopped.

Finally, the silence was broken.

"Needs honey." Julian pushed himself away, tramping off to the pantry.

"We all do." I stared into the bottom of my cup.

Darrian glared back, I could feel it. Then, shockingly, I heard her snicker.

I looked up in disbelief. Somewhere, past the maniac, the great woman had returned ... maybe this middle ground was the real Dr. Stone?

My voice was barely a whisper, "Will you just answer one thing, please?"

"What?" She was back in control, the anger drained from her body.

"Why did you even let me in this close?"

Julian was in the doorway, his teacup in one hand, the honey pot in the other. He was staring at Darrian, too.

"Because ... you were the only one." Darrian pushed away from the table in one quick move.

The porch door slammed.

Julian sat in Darrian's chair. He didn't look at me.

"Julian, what in hell did she mean, the only one?"

Julian sipped his tea delicately, maddeningly adding honey in slow, golden dollops. Finally, he put the spoon down.

"In all the time since the press first began to hurt us, to hurt her, you are the only one who has tried to come here and meet her — face to face — to find your own answers. The only one." Julian finished the tea in one last gulp. He stood, brought his empty cup back to the kitchen.

Oh. Jesus. Oh

Word got down the mountain — I don't know exactly how — but no one came looking. When Darrian cooled off she relegated me to the lab. Just a shed, one of the tin jobs out in back, by the records building with the new roof. I suppose she wanted to keep an eye on me.

Darrian had devised a way of identifying the North American Great Apes without having to dart them or to noseprint them — so many of the innovations she'd worked out just knocked my socks off. Humble as it was, that lab was this Ali-Baba treasure cave of research. I doubted even the Leakey Foundation itself knew more about forensics in anthropology. I was split on being out there — part of me felt punished or as if I was being watched. Another, deeper part was blown away that she trusted me alone with all of her primary work. Like everything else at Remmel, including Darrian herself, it was a conundrum. Just go slow, breathe, remember why I'd come. Remember.

The lab had a small generator for power, mainly for use with the microscopes and slide projector. It also housed all the cameras, film and video equipment, medical equipment and assorted apparatus an outfit like ours needed on a daily basis. My part in all of this? Simple. It was shit. Absolute shit.

Long before I was even allowed to see footprint casts of the North American Great Ape I was put to work cataloguing shit. Ape shit, to be exact.

Each morning, after oatmeal and fruit and about four cups of heavily honeyed tea, I'd bundle up and be shooshed out to the lab. Once there I'd don a mask, goggles, dissection gloves, and apron, and spend the entire morning going over, under and between stool samples — very glamorous. I kept imagining my parents, when someday they'd find out the truth about why their eldest child had left a perfectly good Ivy League college career.

Parasites, disease, content of digestive tracts — all needed to be recorded and then the records filed. I was also filling in notebooks with my drawings of whatever turned up on the slides. Darrian said not a word the few times I started to get cabin fever and insert such memorable characters as "Mr. Big One" or "Stoolie" between the sketches of the more conservative slides.

Three or four weeks into it I went loco. Darrian was still barely speaking with me, still sore about the way I arrived, I guess. I felt like a cholera victim — quarantined till death.

Then one morning, just before she and Farquhar were heading out, Darrian turned to me: "Nikki, tonight, if you're interested, there are some slides I'd like you to see."

I lost it, completely. "Isn't it enough that I'm already dreaming about shit smears — do I have to have them as after-dinner-entertainment too?"

"Perhaps you've got a point." Darrian's voice was strange. She slipped out the back.

Farquhar grabbed me by my shoulders, the strength in her grip, the anger on her face knocking the wind right out of my tantrum. "Nikki! She meant photos ... the apes!" Farquhar gave me an exasperated sigh, let go, followed Darrian.

Dammit! Who would have believed the old bat was going to finally break down, give in, right there, that morning? Why now, all of a sudden? Was I so absolutely out of line — *so* out of it — just for expecting more work? The usual ... shit?

"Looks like you blew it, kiddo." Julian was finishing his breakfast at the table, scanning topos as he drank his never-ending tea.

"Julian, I cannot read that woman! Do you think I should run out there after them?"

"Too late, they're gone. She moves fast on these mountains. Sometimes I can't even track her." Julian smiled slowly, his old face a mass of worn lines, tired tolerance.

In the lab, the more slides I completed the worse I felt. Of course I was dying to see the ape photos — had been tiptoeing since I got there, hinting gently, broadly, at how much I'd give to be able to visually identify the animals whose "returns" I was cataloguing each day. Damn! For a research post specifically set up to study these animals, there was precious little talk about them. I wanted to help — with all of it, the conservation even more than the rest — it was why I'd tracked her this far. Why I'd come in the first place. Her articles, her videos, all of the work she'd published pointed to *the* area of need being in protecting, in conserving the habitat of these primates — she didn't need another file-clerk for stool samples. She didn't need another student to wash dishes or haul firewood. Had I misread those looks on the film?

I knew that every scrap of solid evidence we compiled, each statistic, bought her more credibility, more academic strength with the foundations giving her money. I knew that every primatologist on the planet wanted a piece of the action. But she was asking for more than "additional studies." Her voice, the eyes (those damned forest-eyes) — all my life I'd looked for that light. Maybe other people found their hunger through movie stars or rock-and-roll or teachers, parents, the local mayor — regular-walking-around-types who filled them with that sense of life, of something bigger than themselves, a connection, a cause, a belief to fuel them. But I'd never found it. Not in the nuns and priests of my Catholic school days nor in the people and professors at Smith. Like a flashlight running under its own power, my batteries were low, I was dying, really dying. Then, the tape of Darrian Stone. Her hunger infused me, overtook me, became my hunger. Her hunger went beyond the scientific community, the fat-cat foundations, the pure-research ideologies. She wanted to save something bigger, beyond herself. Maybe I'd missed that in other causes, maybe something in me had made me able to gloss over exactly this point in the past. Whatever the reason, Darrian had hooked me, and I wanted to do this thing *with* her, not in a lab with a microscope and notebook but out there — my ass, too, on this mountain. I had to find her, to tell her these words — the first that had come as a kind of explanation — the most articulate I'd been, to myself, to Farquhar, to Darrian.

The day was warmer than it had been in weeks, the sky thick with yellow-gray clouds that held in what little heat there was. It would make following their trail a bit easier — footprints in slush — even I could handle it. Packing lunches for them, I rehearsed my apology. Even if she was riled when she first saw me she just had to listen. I knew she'd get it. I wanted to be one of them, part of her "tribe . . . no more shit limbo.

Julian was back in the records shed. No need for him to see me. I'd be back before dinner. The fewer questions, the better.

Muddy mustard sky. Never saw anything like it before. Pale winter sun trying to bite through the deep-set clouds. As long as this warmth keeps up it feels safe. In my pack are sandwiches, apples, and at the last minute I grabbed one of the cameras. Who knew what I might see? Maybe a few good shots could be a kind of amends, too.

Time, as usual, loses me. Leave my watch in my bedroom like the rest of them. No conscious boycott, no *Easy Rider* gesture, just take it off one night and forget to put it back on. Begin to wake with the light — then the sounds of the morning in the cabin; coffee and tea-rites, oatmeal and running water sounds, the scrape of Darrian's rocking chair as she moves from the rising sun ... these are my new alarm clocks. The rest of the day is marked by shared meals, work. We just stop when it gets dark again. Moonrise puts some animals to bed, stirs the others from their diurnal sleep. Could hear them outside the cabin, roaming over and around, would fall asleep wondering if the apes were watching. I never found any signs, though. No more need for my watch. No more need for lots of things. Julian has an old Timex. Pulls it out occasionally, just to see if it's still ticking. Can't even imagine Farquhar with something so mechanical on that slender wrist.

Farquhar ... mystical dancer with the Indian profile; scientist and scholar and healer and lover of Darrian Stone — what were they doing out in these woods now? Was this how they got to be alone? Maybe this was why Darrian had kept such a low profile with the press ... a good dose of homophobia could make the project disintegrate.

Damn, sometimes, most times, lately, I felt like a deaf novitiate in a convent full of hearing people. All of them so involved and comfortable in their routines, in their beliefs, almost impossible for them to realize I didn't "get" half the rules. Darrian would go on for hours about Remmel, the camp, hardly ever about the apes and never about her life before the apes — the two times I'd asked it was met with silence. The Farquhar-as-lover theory held even there

. . . most of the time they'd be on their own tracks, quiet. Some classical music for the tape recorders, that was about it.

Only meals were rowdy — rowdy by our standards. The communal thing, complete with our own ritual of Darrian leaving a little bowl of whatever we were eating out on the steps. Later, when Julian would bring it back, it would, of course, be empty. Nothing mysterious about that. The human animals were in a definite minority up on Remmel. I didn't ask about the custom. Figured when they were ready they'd tell me — or not — let me watch, live with it, figure it out. Like the watches, like learning this new way to tell time, to be quiet so often.

No wonder Darrian was such an easy target for the press. Even in her own home she was more than just a woman, more the Abbess, the chief. Never direct orders, not really, not since I first arrived. More, we just "knew," and Farquhar was always by her side. Whatever further explanation was necessary, Farquhar gave it. She was the softer facet of Darrian — translator, almost a kind of bodyguard (as if Darrian needed it), administrative assistant, constant companion. Darrian tall and wild and white, raw-boned, her beauty the handsome sculpture that some great seacliffs possess; rounded out, pounded into perfection by the elements, always changing but so solid, so centered. Farquhar, on the other hand, lithe, the Indian dancer; her body flowed around obstacles rather than withstanding or attempting to go through them. Her hair as long as Darrian's but darker, like her eyes. She was the night without moon, the stars sparkling inside her, laughing even as they burned through the dark. Darrian was the frosted light of full-moon; a glow so brilliant it could cause momentary blindness; lead you off the path as it dazzled, striking back even the stars.

Older, wiser, larger than Farquhar, Darrian was still vulnerable to the younger scientist, would only settle back, be calmed, by the quiet dancer. Like the moon waxing and waning, giving the stars their own dark nights, Darrian would *only* move for Farquhar ... and Julian watched, bemused, the elder of all, uncomplaining, unjudging, strong as the Douglas fir.

Christ, I could taste the envy. Where was the room for me? Would there ever be a space? Compared to these three I was less real than a passing plane, transient as the weather and probably as unpredictable. No wonder I got shit patrol. Damn, damn, damn!

Must be past ten, had to have been walking for over an hour. Still, nice to notice my body was changing (even as my mind), no more leg cramps scrambling over the talus and snow, lungs less congested, only coughing fits first thing when I woke. I expected that to clear up as it got warmer. I gulped the mountain scent and breathed easily.

I am becoming part of this place. Say it over, believe it. There is room for me.

A wide gap in the trail is mud. Boulders litter the place. The sun's already baked them dry. If Darrian and Farquhar came this way they'd have jumped over the muddy spots and travelled along the stones. Great, no more tracks. It made me nervous. Beyond, an alpine meadow, then more crushed rock, finally, a sharp plunge back into old-growth forest. Shouldn't have been daydreaming so much. Julian always tells me to be a better scout out here. Fuck it, I'd lost their trail for sure.

Okay, no panic. Worse comes to worst I can signal for help, but dammit, it's the last thing I want on this particular excursion. Better to cool out, remember to follow the water line. I had to find them soon, no matter how fast they'd travelled I'd only missed them by minutes, less than half-an-hour max. Unless they could fly they'd only left the trail a short while before.

The dense growth didn't help, visibility was cut to a few yards as I go down the slope. Listen. Birds gone quiet ... a snap of twig ... bootprints along the snowline ... nothing. Nothing except the scream of ravens breaking cover directly in front of me.

Of course, every animals in a five-mile radius knows where I am, recognizes me for the stranger I am. Light seems odd. Sickly yellow graying out, then, the first fat drop. A large "splotch" on my hat, hard enough to come through the felt crown, and cold. A sudden chorus of smaller "plops," more than tree melt. Shit, it is rain! No choice. Have to get back fast, before the noon sun retreats. The rain will turn to ice in a matter of hours. Julian's told me enough cautionary tales about hunters and miners found frozen, their tools still stuck to their hands. I take him, always, at his word. Swallow a long drink of the tea in my canteen, try to stay calm. Brings back a flash of the tea in the blizzard from Julian that first hike up here ... at least this won't be anything close to that storm. At least I hope it won't.

Then I hear it. Such a minute noise, almost like

it comes between the droplets. A second sooner and I would have missed it altogether. Then, again. This time I feel it more than hear it . . . an intentional sound . . . quick snap of wood . . . a low cough.

Turning to my right, slowly, realizing that I am downwind and whatever it might be must have had my scent for some time, I try to be very, very still. Maybe it's only a mule deer.

The smell hits me, carried up on the rainy breeze. At first almost nauseating, oily, overpowering. Human, almost sweaty and with that tinge of fear smell that I can sense on my own skin, too. Behind three boulders, about fifty feet away, maybe closer, the hair reddish, long, the animal or man, seems to be sheltering either from the storm or from me. Shit, this ain't no deer! Grizzly? Not in the lower forty-eight, even in Yellowstone they're getting rare, and anyway they'd be in hibernation now. Still, if this isn't a bear then it's a big man in a grizly jacket. A bear of a man, stinking to the high heavens. Darrian warned me about some of the crazies up in the deeper woods. Still, I was past the area where survivalists dared but not beyond the scattered remnants of old-time-mountain-men territory — she'd had more than one run-in with them over the years. This was my first. Damn, didn't even have my Swiss Army knife with me.

Crouch low, low as I can. Whoever is out there knows I'm here, but if I act non-threatening, nonchalant, maybe, if the rain slows and the sun comes out we can each pretend to ignore the other and get out of here . . . please God. Oh, to be propped safe and dry among the stool samples. No squinched legs or freezing toes. Want to cough, to clear my throat of its accumulated terror. Seems like eons since the guy moved . . . maybe he's dead.

Sometimes old Indians went off to die alone. Was I waiting for a corpse to make the next move? On the other hand, if it was a poacher or a mountain man in a bearskin coat then maybe I should try to get a picture for Darrian — she used them for identification with the Rangers, sending off snaps to the Rangers on a regular basis. Also to eco-groups and even the Mounties. We were so close to the border it made sense. Lots of good hiding out spots in these mountains. She warned me to stay cool if I got close with my camera, a lot of these dudes now knew exactly what it meant to have their picture taken . . .

I pulled out the 35 mm, trying to keep my hands steady, holding my breath, hoping the sound of the rain would be enough to mask the autofocus. Now, if the guy would only turn his scraggly head a few more degrees I could get a decent profile.

Then he reached out for a branch. In that one move I saw enough to make me drop the camera completely and wet my pants. His arm was twice as long as any human arm I'd ever seen. The nails were black and big as Karloff's in *Frankenstein*. I couldn't muffle the cry that bubbled from my throat. At the choking sound he turned his head so fast I swore it was on a swivel. The bulging forehead, the reddish tinge to the skin, the dark, humanoid eyes, the matted hair and open mouth all contributing to my vast horror.

The animal, if you could call it that, never stood. It simply let out a high, inhuman scream, then charged over those boulders directly for me. Prayers not thought since childhood formed in my brain, no words from my lips, nothing even to scream, only the sounds of the pelting rain and the crash and road of this seven-foot animal.

Deadmeat, deadmeat, the mantra beat to my heart's pulse. I want to close my eyes and become either devil or angel but just be out of my body, free of this butcher-sack, hey God, look out, I'm coming up! Then, from behind me, another scream, a sudden silence.

Three soggy ravens burst from undercover, my heart sends a missile bolt to my head, the sky opens and drops a deluge on us all. Only then can I turn my gaze from the dead-stopped animal and see what has halted its flight — the green of Darrian's parka. Below her, not ten feet away, Farquhar. My teeth chatter, my body shivers, I can say nothing. No thing. The animal, unmoving makes another coughing sound. I snap around, unable to stop myself, sure it's the wrong maneuver but I can't break mid-flight. Still, the animal remains controlled.

Darrian makes a noise in her throat, follows it with a sharp clap. At the cracking sound of her hands there's a red blur and the animal bolts for the trees. I do not breathe.

Years, months, centuries or only minutes? The ravens resettle in a branch right over my head. Obviously put out by these stupid humans who sent them needlessly into the rain, they preen and cluck, puff and cackle.

Finally, Darrian looks full into my face. One quiet motion, I'm to follow. I try to explain, why I'm there, about the poacher, the picture. For my efforts I get a rude poke between the shoulder blades. I swear, to all the monsters of the forest, I will never argue with Dr. Stone about anything as long as I live, amen.

Julian and Farquhar are sitting already, when we get in. Darrian shoves me toward my room, ordering "Get dry!"

I listen to the heavy clomp of her boots as she slams from my room and heads for the kitchen. Peeling off my clothes I sneak to the bathroom to wash my reeking jeans and try to clean off the feeling of the wasted day.

Hell, what's going to go down next? What would it be like to try to rejoin the living? Through the wall I can only hear Darrian's voice when it approaches yelling:

". . . well, why the hell didn't you notice she was gone? The storm . . . two of them, a male and a female . . . turned to identify . . . Farquhar realized . . . yes, yes, a single bluff charge but . . . they don't know *her!* Too low . . . maybe someone up there . . . spooking them down . . . do we have a choice?"

Silence again. My own breathing sounding like a dump truck with a broken muffler — then the back door slams twice. I wait long moments before daring to peek out. Maybe it was safe?

Farquhar has the fire roaring. Night reflects its black eyes against our windows, the fire throws back patches of gold and rust. No one has bothered to light the pressure lamps.

Tucking in my flannel shirt I fight the constriction in my throat. It just plain aches because I can't tell . . . can't tell why I did what I did or how terrible I feel about doing it.

Farquhar looks up from the hearth where she's

68

finished stoking the flames. Her smile cuts me, it's the only kindness I've known all day.

"Come over here, you. Sit down." Farquhar pats the old couch. She sat at the farthest end from the fire.

"Nikki, Darrian's too upset to talk to you so I guess it's up to me. Come here, I'm not going to bite your head off!" Her eyes are so dark that like the windows they reflect the light of the fire.

I hesitate only a minute, then come and sit beside her. Christ, one big lumpen, ugly mess — why is it that women feel ugly when they feel bad? Somehow it seems to settle in our bodies. No man I knew, not brother or friend, ever dealt with embarrassment by shifting his physical view of himself. Oh sure, maybe hands-in-pockets or a little stammering, but never this consuming belief of being monstrous in face and shape. It is exacerbated by Farquhar's long, cat-graceful body and handsome face — even the dancing fire of her eyes seems to laugh. Tears bead up clouding the lenses of my glasses. The salt bit, bitter.

I wipe the lenses on the front of my soft shirt, my hands gone all trembly. Wonder if I'm going to end up bending the wire frames all to hell by the time I'm done. I use the time of nothing but shadows and fractured light, a blurry image of Farquhar's face to try to choke out another apology — useless.

Farquhar takes my hands in her own, holding them carefully. The fire spins flickers like miniature searchlights through my round lenses, across our laps. What are we looking for, really?

"I know, Nikki. Darrian knows, too. This

afternoon was our mistake, not yours. We should have been clear about the camp boundaries. It's just never occurred to us that anyone would try to follow us up the mountain. We keep forgetting you aren't anyone." Farquhar gently drops my palms, but her smile is still warm.

Glasses back in place I notice the lines that have now restrung themselves across the planes of her face. I watch her close her eyes, lean back, sigh softly. So much I don't understand, so much almost within touch, a kind of presence with us, often, here in the cabin, but invisible — at least to me. My tears are back. I hate this weak body and its constant betrayal. Dammit.

Without opening her eyes, Farquhar senses my discomfort, the salty welling. "Oh Nikki. It was only a matter of time before she took you to them, do you realize that? The slides, the lab work — just tests of your science, your technique — she wanted you to know as much as you could about their physical makeup before you actually got close. The first time can be ... well ... you know, now — overwhelming. A knowledge of their more pedestrian traits is a definite benefit before encountering them in the woods. So strange, isn't it? She'd planned to give you a kind of formal introduction tonight, like passing the family photo album around after dinner ... but this morning ..."

"I know! So stupid! My big mouth! Farquhar, I just wanted to find you, to tell you, apologize to her; she doesn't have any idea what it means to me, to be allowed to work with you all up here, to be allowed to stay." I lean forward, punctuating the words, wanting to make them solid as rock, somehow, prove their seriousness.

Farquhar opens her eyes as if she's been dreaming and now is back. The fire's reflecting light keeps me from reading what is pooled there. I know she's looking directly at me, so quiet, this woodswoman, almost unnerving, but not quite, just at the edge of it. Like the time at Brownie Camp — what was I, seven, scrawny, short, the older girls not really older at all but resenting me in their tent.

They took me out, one night, almost dusk, to pick high-bush blueberries for our breakfast. We all knew it was beyond bounds but it felt so wicked it was wonderful! Too proud to wear my glasses at camp, I'd bluffed my way through the first two weeks, relying on remembered landmarks, careful listening and studied calm at all blurred objects making sudden moves. But this night there was no moon and darkness came quickly. The older girls thought they'd hide just out of direct sight and then run off without me.

I didn't panic — fear wasn't even close. For me, the woods were cool, friendly, known, their night sounds and smells like a bit of home, the only reassurance I'd had in days. No, the overriding feeling was hurt, then, almost as searing, humiliation. Not only had I been fooled, it was clear that I wasn't wanted. Didn't fit. Now even the counselors would know it when everyone got back to camp and I was missing. Couldn't see so much as the stars without my glasses. So, as I'd done so often at home, I crawled into the rooty lap of a huge oak. Someone would find me or morning would find me — simple.

It was the head counselor of the whole camp, flashlight splitting the dark like a long sword — the beam cutting the dark, falling on me at the base of the ancient tree. Only a few hours lost, enough to scare her, to scare all of them — make penitents out of the other seven-year-olds.

The counselor didn't say a word, no scolding, no lecture. Instead, she sank down against the bark, against me, sighing as softly as Farquhar had just sighed. Maybe she'd read my file and realized my glasses-less rebellion or maybe the other kids had come clean. Whatever it was, for the rest of the session, she'd let me take off by myself when no one would notice, in the daylight, alone, out under the big trees. As long as there was no commotion, as long as I promised to come back. We never spoke about the night but her smile, and the memory of her sigh as she sat next to me in the black arms of that summer night, finding me in that lost evening, those feelings came back often. Now, on top of Remmel, in the middle of winter, Farquhar called them up. Again, I couldn't speak. Again, I felt only seven.

"Nikki, the apes shouldn't have been within five miles of that area. It's far too low for them to be safe. Darrian is upset about that, less about your trying to track us down. She and Julian are up there now." Farquhar is gazing at the fire again, her voice as low as the flames.

"But the rain. She's going to be out in the ice, in the dark . . . and those animals. Jesus!" Fear makes me cold, Darrian in the forest with only Julian for protection, no!

"Ssh, easy. The apes only look fierce. You can see where the stories of Bigfoot originated. Our apes are more like orangutans or gorillas, Nikki — shy, gentle, terrified of humans they don't know. It's more their size and the shock of coming on them blindly that makes them seem . . . like monsters. What worries us is how scattered they are — probably poachers driving them down . . . or, if we're lucky, it was because that young pair sensed Darrian and came out to her. They know her. It isn't on the tapes or in her articles, but it's true. The apes sense and recognize her the same way they do the Deepwoods Tribe that's protected them for centuries. Tonight she and Julian are trying to herd the animals up higher, to safe ground. Don't worry, they won't be alone. The Indians will help. For her, up there, it's actually more secure — at least she doesn't have to keep watching her back. Up there she's with family."

Farquhar reaches over and gingerly touches my knee. Her fingers hold their usual potent magic — like an electrical charge, almost sparking, I can feel the touch run through me.

"Guess I'm the only white guy, huh?"

"Honestly, Nikki — if you don't stop feeling sorry for yourself I swear I'm going up the mountain too. You are pathetic! The best thing you can do is go out and get more firewood so when they do get back the cabin will be warm. Tomorrow, go to the lab and work like hell. You know, it hasn't been so much as swept out in years. And Nikki . . ." Farquhar takes my chin in her hands, drills her gaze into my eyes.

"What?"

"Get it, just get it. Only one week, that's all it took. You've passed ... can you understand it if I put it into those terms? We've lasted this long because we've learned to read outsiders very, very quickly. Hey, don't you know what those New Agers say? Aren't all Indians supposed to be shamans? Julian had you figured out the first time he saw you at the Rangers Station. It took me a little longer, but he's had more practice. Now Darrian, well, she's still too much the scientist to trust the other parts of herself very easily, but she's learning. You're with us now ... really with us ... just slow down, little sister. All right?"

Stupid tears again, boiling up and over — have to pull back, can't let her see the mushpot I've become. No wonder why Darrian loves this woman, no wonder at all. I hear her laugh softly as I head for the bathroom to blow my nose and wash my face. I've passed ... can I believe her?

Coming back, she's still on the couch, the fire very low but still bright, hot. I walk behind her, reaching around those wiry shoulders, feeling the fine bones and taut muscles of her arms. I hug hard, letting her know I've heard her, that what she's told me has connected dots in this puzzle of Remmel.

Farquhar leans her head back, her hair a dark cloud against my cheek. The scent that has come to mean Farquhar rises — clean, green as the rainwashed ferns in the woods — this soothing perfume not something she puts on, but her, just her.

I let go, moving close to the fire, sitting below her, on the floor, my back bolstered by the mass of the couch. Maybe it's easier like this, maybe I can finally ask some of the tough questions. She so rarely talks about herself — or about Darrian in any personal way. Maybe it will be easier for her to answer.

"Farquhar, how did you come here, how did you find Darrian?" I almost hold my breath as I ask, ready to accept silence, ready to be told it's not my business, to go to bed.

But she stretches, another sigh between us. "Are you sure you really want that old story?" I don't look but can see the wrinkled nose and half-frown in her words. She's trying to keep it light . . . it's not light. The stone-heavy seriousness can't be disguised. So glad I'm facing the fire. Still so much Massachusetts in my blood, can't ask outright about their romance, but of course I want the story, want the details.

"Nikki, you're like a little kid needing to be tucked into bed — okay, you asked for it, all right." She pulls her legs up and tucks them under her, arranging herself like all really good storytellers do. I know it won't be a short, two sentence summary — no, her body, her voice, all natural to telling long tales. I settle down, settle back, listening to the rain, briefly worry about Julian and Darrian, push it away, hungry for more than concern, needing to fight the unease with how this all began. There is also more than a twinge of . . . what? Anxiety . . . maybe even a little heart pain? My speculations these past weeks will be confirmed . . . shit, so what? I'll handle it — maybe after tonight I can drop some of the baggage I've collected around these women, get beyond the daydreams I've carried up the mountain.

Maybe.

"When I was at Issaquhah College, Darrian came as a lecturer. She had just started her study of the Pacific Indians in the northwest. I was a senior. I wanted to be a radical Indian anthropologist — turn the tables, I guess, on the white boys — you know, work with my own people, write their real-life accounts instead of interpretations.

"My husband of one year was also a student but he only had one quarter left. Oh, we were crazy in love, Nikki — you know the kind, where the only air you can breathe is what is between you — nothing exists outside of the other — and because he was the only love I had I was that much more taken. A good Indian girl, everyone so proud of this marriage to another full-blood, and both of us in college. He was a business major, really going places. Handsome. Articulate. Dedicated to our people. He caught the eyes of some important men in Olympia. An Indian who could give a speech and who had majored in business — lots of money to be made between the logging and mining operations and the Indians. So they approached him. Increasingly his time was spent off campus, shuttling between the offices of these corporations and the headquarters of the different tribes. The college finally asked him to take a leave of absence until he could devote full-time to finishing up his final projects. By then it didn't matter because, for all intents and purposes, people on the outside already saw him as having his business degree.

"Suddenly, our honeymoon was over. I was alone most of the time. We weren't even going to bed or getting up together.

"He took it better than I did, in fact took it too easily. All I knew was that if this was going to be our life for this period of time then I'd have to swallow my disappointment and just go on with my own studies. I wanted to be the best wife."

Farquhar sighed, her voice almost too full. I was glad I couldn't see her, didn't have to watch this cross her face. "Then came Darrian," I whispered, half to myself.

"Then came Darrian. Oh Nikki, you should have seen her then, like some caricature of the white anthropologist — complete with tape recorders and cameras dangling off her and the piled-up hair-do. She even wore pumps to class when she gave a lecture. We'd wait for those shoes. No pop quizzes or long tests on the days Darrian Stone clicked her way into the classroom. I think back to then and I really have to laugh. She's destroyed every photograph, I'm sure. I can't even kid her about it. A long time ago, the now-star-quality-scientist-and-film-figure-of-the-primatology-set was quite the nerd.

"Still, there was always something, even under the sprayed hair and the tweed suits, something absolutely magnetic about her. Her classes were always filled, people standing in the back, hanging out, without so much as a whisper of a credit, just to hear her speak.

"I always sat in the back, afraid to talk, afraid even to volunteer answers about my own people, keeping silent when no one else would reply. Darrian began to notice me, little by little. She says, today, it was because my papers were the only passable undergraduate writing she'd come upon at the college but I really think it was because of her scientist's mind. It just didn't make sense that a student who worked so hard on her papers and projects and got consistently high test scores would blow off so many lectures by falling asleep in class. Also, like so many white anthropologists, she kept coming upon closed doors in our community. Obviously I was an Indian — she needed some contacts, and she knew I knew that, too, as an aspiring anthropologist in my own right. Who better to try to connect with? I was the smallest fish in that very tiny pond. So one day she got up the courage to ask me after class. I thought I was going to catch it for another nap. Instead, we went for coffee.

"Nikki, like you, I *felt* her — inside myself — all sparks and flame, all liquid warmth. I had never had these feelings about anyone before — not even my husband. Here was this woman — a white woman, an anthropologist to boot, an Indian's worst nightmare. But my feelings, these visceral feelings were very, very deep. As I got to know her I realized she had them, too.

"Of course Darrian has always been Darrian. She ignored the fire. Always my 'good teacher' — still, to this day. Sometimes our eyes would lock in a stare, even in the middle of the most mundane debate there would be a pause, a microsecond of suspended breath, our hearts, our blood, they knew.

"I became more than her passport, more, even, than the student she'd taken under her wing. In this bewildering, wild wonderful space I felt her equal. I knew then that I was walking beside her. It was my power that she helped me recognize, helped me know.

"We never spoke of any of these things. I had no one to speak to about them. I doubted she had any support on campus either. Besides, the only person I'd ever slept with was my husband. To think of Darrian in that way was almost unbearable. My mind refused the images — oh, but my heart had no trouble with its imaginings!

"We began to spend a lot of time together. It was natural for her to begin to be invited to family gatherings, then tribal outings. Soon Darrian became a part of all of our lives. She helped with legal questions, even demonstrated for Native fishing rights and worked on drawing up the papers for land disputes in the area around school. Gone were the tape recorders and the cameras. The changes were subtle and slow, but they came. Darrian grew into the woman you know, Nikki. Funny, I think subconsciously she wanted to look like us. I've never thought of it in this way but it's true. Someday I'll have to tell her. Anyway, my husband's business deals began to peter out. Some of his hasty negotiations fell through. He was not as influential within the tribal councils as the logging companies had hoped. He was too young — business degree or not. They held out cocaine, gave it to him at first. We had no money. I knew he was getting more by dealing. Not his fault — they took a poor kid and flashed around a lot of money, fast cars, clothes, gave him false respect — promised him power in the white world. He was hooked on the drugs and they used them to control him. Like a salmon in a net, they held onto him. He couldn't get away. He was dying, Nikki. There was nothing he could do.

"Darrian tried to get help. But every time he came home from another rehab program he'd end up going right back to the people who hurt him. She loaned him money, and when he used it on the junk then she'd loan me more — groceries, rent, whatever. He resented her. He also saw me looking up to her in a way I'd once looked at him.

"When she got me the position as her assistant researcher he fell apart. Pride, and more, my heart was closed to him. He knew it. He beat me because of it, broke my wrist and dislocated my shoulder. When Darrian found out she went crazy.

"Now, all these years later, it's kind of sad and funny at the same time. Can you see Dr. Stone, armed with her briefcase, crashing down my apartment door, about to beat the shit out of my two-hundred-pound, six-foot husband? She tried, but the cops got there first. They found his drugs, he even had a gun. I moved in with Darrian after that. I filed for a divorce . . .

"Nikki, when I met you, you reminded me of myself — and a tiny bit of Darrian, too. You have her stubborn side, her tenacity, her courage. But you also have a vision that is more like mine. Darrian can't see herself — not even the reflection of herself. She doesn't know how vulnerable she is in the same way she doesn't understand her power. You've come here because you know Darrian's heart.

"Out of all the people who hear about the project, who read her work or see it on TV or who have even met her, only a few recognize her, only a few attempt to climb the walls she's erected to protect herself. Julian, the Deepwoods Tribe — they know. I see. Now you. I watch you, Nikki, I watch you watching Darrian and I recognize your expression. I can almost feel your heart's direction because my heart moves there too. Nikki, I know ... you are in love with her."

God, not true! All the arguments I've given myself rush forward — heavy, hard-hitting, logical. No, I'm only on Remmel because she needs ... what? Help, yes, workers, I'm up here because I love the woods, because it's time for me to leave Smith but I don't know where to go, because somebody has to save the planet, right?

"It's all right, Nikki. Take it easy. Darrian hasn't realized it, not yet, not in this way. She's confused by you, maddened by you and her own feelings about you, but she won't allow herself the luxury of examining them. It isn't her way. She's so private. As close as we are, all I know about her past is what everyone else knows, what's in the press packages: East Coast education, family deceased, her work here. Since I've known her there hasn't been anyone ... but before that? She's terrified of her own hunger, Nikki. I think she's afraid her passion will hurt anyone risking it. I know that's true. Even if we ask for the risk ...."

My face was stone-solid, my lips unable to form

the obvious next question. Farquhar knows, as if she's inside my head, she knows.

"Yes, I did ask. Soon, after I moved in, when the divorce was finalized. I couldn't pretend that she was just my friend, just my mentor anymore. So many nights I thought I'd scream if I didn't say something to her, anything, a hint, a note, some shred of suggestion — but she was always so courtly toward me, she left no openings.

"Finally, when she came home later and later every night, it was as if the nightmare of my marriage had come back. I couldn't handle the retreat, the silence. I came to her bed, Nikki, I came to her."

I moved up onto the couch, across from her. I was stunned. I believed, in my wild dreams, that surely Darrian was the orchestrator of the seduction. Darrian, always the most powerful, the moving force at our center, the strongest, most decisive. Farquhar laughed again, but when she looked at me I saw the tears, her lower lashes jewelled, sparkling with the ruby glow from the fireplace.

Without stopping to think I brushed them away. Maybe she was right, maybe I was in love with Darrian — but this woman across from me, she was inside, too — deep, touching down, taking root in my heart. So bloody brave! I could hardly admit my own feelings let alone take action ... and with Darrian! Jesus!

Farquhar smiled, swiped at her own eyes, swallowed hard. I waited for her, waited for the rest. I owed her this much.

"It's not what you think, Nikki. Oh, it would have been so easy ... I was so ready. She could have had anything she asked for that night. I knew she felt the same heat, held the same power between us, it wasn't a question of our attraction, of our love, but she knew something I could never understand. She held me for a while, Nikki, and I could feel her trembling. Then, toward dawn, she bundled me up and put me back in my own bed.

"We have never talked about it. I know we never will. I love her. I accept her terms. And I am very glad you're here."

The fire is only coals. The rain has stopped. My head and heart are as heavy as the time I woke in Farquhar's cabin.

Overload.

For us both.

I need new air, she needs more space.

I get up slowly, move off for wood. There's no need to explain — anything.

Outside the forest is dipped in melted diamonds, every branch and twig a precious jewel. The moon rises in its own icy sheath, so slowly, as if it, too, is aching.

Darrian, Darrian, where are you tonight?

Do you know how much you are loved?

I gather an armload of wood, go back in.

We pack the fire high, make it ready for their return. Farquhar hugs me goodnight. Another bond between us, solid, fierce, it hasn't vanished with the ending of the story. I was worried it might — it has happened before, other people, other long, strange nights telling secrets only to have them taken back in the light. Not tonight, not with this woman.

"Nikki, when they come in, I'm not sure what will happen. Darrian will most likely be on the rampage, but you have to remember, it won't be about you. Whoever or whatever is driving the apes out of safe ground, we'll pull together and deal with it. We always have, we've got no other choice. You're a part of the project now, it's been years since anyone was allowed in. Those who tried to find her ended up burning her. God, Darrian would kill me if she knew what I've told you. But you need to know. Most of all, you need to know how much she cares. What you decide to do with that is something else, little sister. Goodnight."

Tired, blood-tired, all I can do to strip down, fall under the comforter, listen as the night surrounds us, protecting us, leading us into our dreams.

I woke suddenly. Strange noises outside the cabin. I tore into the hall, yelling for Farquhar — no need, she was already at the front door.

Three men and a woman, dressed in the latest Patagonia-wear (their pants alone could fund us for a month), pointing up at our front door. Farquhar blocked the entrance with her own body.

For a second the memory of the guns in the hall closet burned in my mind, then I decided to wait, to see how Farquhar called it. I wouldn't even let the strangers see me, even know another person was there.

One of the men held a video camera, pointing it past Farquhar, actually trying to shoot inside. I was furious. Where do people like this come from?

Running to my room, pulling on jeans and a sweater over my long undies, I tried to be ready as

I could if Farquhar needed me to go for help. I sat on the bed, my face sweaty, my heart pumping hard, listening for the sound of the front door being closed, listening for Farquhar's quiet footsteps in the hall.

Then she was in my room: "Nikki, it's the damned film crew from station KVWA. Some locals reported seeing big animals on the mountain, low. The Rangers got word, leaked it to the press — the bastards! Someone, somewhere, is getting paid off — guess that explains yesterday. Now they want a statement from Darrian. They'd just love it if she blows up at them on camera. Nikki, you have to stall them. Go outside, introduce yourself. Lock the door when you leave. Tell them I've gone to get Dr. Stone. Take them to the trailhead. Just keep circling. Think you can do it without getting lost? I'll sneak out the back and bolt the other sheds tight, then go for Darrian. With any luck I'll be back before it gets dark. Nikki, the big thing is not to answer any questions. You have to keep cool, keep your head. They want a reaction for the news, they'll provoke you until you blow. We can't afford another minute of negative publicity. Okay?"

"I got it — now go, go!" I pushed her out and towards the woodshed, trying to sound much cooler than I feel.

In the kitchen I put up water to boil. Let the crew outside squirm. I packed matches, my knife, made sure my gloves were in the pockets of my parka. What route? Farquhar was right, I'd never tested myself on the face of the mountain near the trailhead. Had to keep it simple, diverting. Finally, I gulped a cup of tea, pulled on the parka — I was ready for the piranha outside our door.

* * * * *

"Who are you, Miss? We weren't given the names of student interns at camp. Could you tell us where you're from?" A tall, skinny guy in neon pink sticks a tape recorder under my chin.

The cameraman, in electric orange, switches on a camcorder and suddenly I feel like a shit sample about to be dissected.

"I'm, ah, my name is . . . Franconia Melbonshire . . . from ah, Wheatabaga, New York . . . that's upstate, you know," I say through clenched teeth.

The anchorwoman steps between the guys: "Excuse me, is there a restroom I could use? We've been walking for almost two hours and I've had to go since my third cup of coffee this morning. The snowmobile ride hasn't helped." She flashes her ten-thousand-dollar teeth in my direction.

"Well, actually, we're still quite primitive up here. At this particular facility any old tree will do. We, uh, we close down the latrines after the first snow because they'd only freeze, you know? You'll just have to whiz in the woods like the rest of us." I hope she doesn't notice the color rise in my cheeks or, if she does, she attributes it to modesty.

She takes a step back, then confers with some townie guy, all in red plaid and felt — he's probably the owner of the snowmobile. He grins, then spits a wad of gum suspiciously close to my boot.

"Franci, can I call you Franci? Fine. Franci, we've come all the way up here at considerable trouble and expense just to get an environmental report from you . . . professionals. The eco-folks always complain we don't do enough in the news about pollution, endangered animals, all that sort of thing. Well, here we are, trying to rectify the situation. And it's your big chance to be on TV! What do you say, kid? Just get Dr. Stone out here and let her tell the whole state of Washington what's going on. We want her side of the slaughter last ..." Neon Pink dropped his voice two octaves, down into on-the-air range.

Fear creeps into the morning air. Slaughter? Where? The apes? Darrian? It takes all my control not to run screaming into the woods after Farquhar.

"What slaughter? I think you guys better give me a little background on what *you* think is going on."

"College boys. The Rangers already rounded them up for hunting out of season. Just a bear, I believe. They explained it wasn't an ape — a prank, really. Some fraternity gag." Electric Orange rolls his eyes.

"Yeah, just fucking around, wanted to get a look at the Doc, maybe. Just pledges, just Greek shit." Bubble Gum local scratches his balls through the red and black wool hunting pants.

"No apes? Thank God. You certain of it?" I screw my smile into place as tightly as I can, but my voice is on the edge of breaking.

"No, no Bigfoot, just a yearling black bear. They must have come out because of the false thaw. The Rangers saw the carcass on the hood of the boys' Volvo."

"Didn't even dress the animal, damned fools, only asking to get caught!" Bubble Gum spits his own juices out near the expired wad of gum.

"As much as we can ascertain, there was no gun play in ape territory. But the boys did report seeing large animals moving in that general area yesterday.

We want to confirm, with Dr. Stone, if that could be possible. You must know how hungry the public is for any information about your project, for any footage of Darrian Stone or the animals. It's really been quite some time since she granted her last interview," he continues, his newsy manners all oily and practiced.

"You think wrong, bud. The work up here is very sensitive. I'm sure you're supposed to have a written invitation to climb this high. When Dr. Stone returns I hardly think she's going to be in any mood for an interview. Why didn't you try to make radio contact with us before coming?" Flailing around now, trying to be moderately calm, trying to buy time and knowing they aren't going for it.

"Well, the uh, the Rangers, actually, they said that due to the ice-storm radio contact would be unreliable, at best. They put us in touch with this gentleman and his snowmobiles." Neon Pink steps aside, pointing to Bubble Gum.

"Hey, they got nature tours all over the planet, lady. You can't keep out the press! The public's got a right to know. And you can't keep out the locals, either. We were here before you were born. We got a right to make a living, too, you know." Bubble Gum clenches his fists menacingly.

Suddenly, I realize the anchorwoman hasn't come back. Taking much too long . . . something is wrong.

"You guys, you just stay right here, don't move an inch or so help me, there's going to be hell to pay." I sound more brave than I feel.

Neon Pink and Electric Orange put down the recorders, light cigarettes and watch Bubble Gum glare. I take off behind the cabin. Part of me believes if I got through the front door they'd rush me, push inside. I want them out, off this mountain.

Sure enough, just as I suspected, Ms-Anchor-of-the-Month is trying to pry open a window in the lab. She'd gotten it halfway there when I show up.

Wheeling around, her camera around her neck, she's caught red-handed and knows it. About a foot taller than me, but much thinner, she realizes the unequal match. The way she totters in those designer boots I figure no way is she going to try to wrestle.

"Okay lady, now you can just take a picture of the damage you've done to the window. Put your hand up beside it. Right. Now, give me the camera." I take it from her.

No protest. I'm surprised, wary. I wonder what else is hidden in the folds of her Patagonia jumpsuit?

I click the shutter a few more times, have her freeze-framed in front of the window, showing it clearly broken, jammed with the offending stick still protruding from one corner, her footprints and handprints all over the snow and the sill. I finish the roll, rewind and drop it into my pocket. The camera is shoved into my daypack.

"When Dr. Stone arrives you'll get this back. Till then consider it contraband, understand? I think the police will find this film quite interesting. Shall we rejoin the boys?" Even she knew I wasn't bluffing.

The men haven't budged. They're cocky as ever, though. They know how to play the game. I take more photos — using the videocamera this time. I remove the tape.

"Hell, you all gonna let this punk push you around?" Bubble Gum shakes his head in disgust.

"Look, Dick," begins Neon Pink.

"My name's not Dick," the local growls.

"Right. Dick ... we aren't into confrontational journalism, okay? We *are* professionals, we do things right. Maybe that's hard for you to understand, Dick. Franci's only doing her job and we're only doing ours. We'll play by her rules. I'm sure she's as anxious as we are to set the record straight — right Franci?" He winks at me.

"Right, Dick." I wink back, then walk away.

The cameraman and anchorlady laugh. Running out of chitchat. Have to start walking, keep moving in a big circle, just hope the weather holds a little longer.

"Don't ya want to get the Skee-doos?" Bubble Gum wails.

"No time," I lie, "anyway, the engines will scare the apes, right? Follow me but be very quiet. If an ape comes out of the scrub, screaming, well, just drop to your belly. They'll rip you in half like a grizz if you make them mad. Everyone clear?" Lousy P.R. but I'm desperate.

Pray nobody has a compass and that the clouds hold ... brighter sun and they could figure we're only going around in circles.

Hours pass. Soaked, frozen feet, insults and curses, we hike back to camp via the east route. No one's caught on — yet. As we round the last clump of bushes, Darrian, Farquhar, Julian and five Indians I don't recognize, all carrying rifles, greet us.

"Shee-it!" Bubble Gum stops in his tracks.

"Interesting, same aroma I keep picking up," Darrian says.

"Dr. Stone, Darrian Stone, correct?" Neon Pink jumps forward, pushing me roughly aside. "So pleased to finally catch up with you!" He sticks out his mittened hand.

Darrian fills it with the barrel of her rifle.

Damn. I was convinced the guns in the closet had to be Julian's. She'd never go near a loaded rifle — at least that's what I thought.

"Get out of my camp. Don't ever think of coming here again without written permission, period. The Rangers have no jurisdiction up here. You tell your colleagues and the rest of those assholes looking for some copy, anyone on my mountain — press, poachers, frat boys — anyone hunting anything is going to face me and the National Wilderness Bureau. Got that, mister? The only clearance you have now is to get out!"

Darrian's face is almost purple with rage. Even the whites of her eyes seem dark. Her hair whips around in the rising wind, her new black poncho pulls and flaps around her.

The crew moves back, even the guy in pink, even the local. It would be a cold trip back for them in the coming evening and I'm glad. Neon Pink is going to make some crack but as he turns around the

Indians take a collective step forward in his direction, it's enough to send him scurrying like a rabbit down the trail with the others

"Wait, my camera, your promise!" The anchorwoman turns to call, "Franci, please! Look, why not come back with us, you could do the interview with me. You look like a bright kid. This place is crazy — Dr. Stone is going nuts up here in the woods. If you come back you could do some good — I might even be able to get you a job. Do you know what kind of money we're talking about?"

I yank the camera from my pack, furious that she dares any of her crap and even more so in front of Darrian! I throw the camera like a baseball, right for her face. Blood tinges my vision — for a second it flashes that my face must be as dark as Darrian's.

Darrian doesn't wait for them to turn the bend. She drops her gun, runs back to the cabin. I stop, pick it up, follow after.

Inside, the typer is already sputtering like gunshot. We can hear the staccato screams from behind Darrian's bedroom door — I can imagine the letters.

"Come on in boys, I'll make you some supper!" Julian calls to the Indians politely waiting in the front of the porch.

The men all wipe their feet, smile shyly, come inside.

*　*　*　*　*

Feels like another day when the typer is finally quiet. Indians gone, telling us they'll be back, if we need them. Julian asleep on the couch, finally Farquhar shakes him, wakes him up only to stumble off to his own bed.

Quiet in Darrian's room, but she doesn't come out. The door stays shut.

"Wait for her, will you, Nikki?" Farquhar whispers, moving off to her room.

"Do you think she'll want me to wait up? Really?" Besides the uncertainty, I'm more than a little scared . . . the first one to face her since the departure of the news team. Ugh.

"Yes, I'm sure. And Nikki, you did real good today . . . g'night."

"Goodnight." I smile back, the warmth like a hand against my cheeks, gentled by the compliment.

I turn off the pressure lamps, leave only the fire for light. The red-gold fills the room, fills me like new blood. I'm not tired anymore. It is right for me to wait up for Darrian. They need their sleep. I place the blanket down in front of the hearth . . .

How long? Not chilled but stiff . . . did doze. But the fire is higher than before. I rub my back, then see her. Beside me, propped against the couch, her long legs straight out in front of her, as if she's on guard, on watch. Watching — me.

"Darrian, are you okay?" I move too fast, too clumsily, knocking over her unseen cup of tea.

"Grace." She smiles.

"Dammit!" I don't. "Why don't I just walk around

here with a little sign taped to my forehead —
sorry, sorry, sorry? Jesus, but I am ..." I mop up
the mess with the tail of my shirt.

"Nikki, stop! Please." Darrian reaches out, takes
my hand.

I'm kneeling, above her but still almost eye-level,
my God, I sometimes forget how tall she really is.
My hands are wet and sticky from the spilled
tea ... but not cold. Her touch burns against my
fingers. I can't move, can't breathe.

Like a child playing statue-tag, I'm frozen,
mid-spill. Darrian doesn't drop her grip, she is as
still, only her eyes and their smoldering stare sweep
over me.

My heart pounds, my head answers, all the blood
in my body forced down, focused, past belly, instant
fire, liquid melt, down, down, a kind of weak-kneed
tremble I'd never known outside of bad fiction, "B"
movies, but this is real, my jeans soak, my lips
throb.

"Nikki." Darrian's voice not her voice, not a voice
I've ever heard her use — less, even, than a
whisper, low. "What you did today was hard, maybe
even brave."

I breathe out, my voice pulled by her own. "Had
to let you know, some way, how much you
mean ..." Can't go on, my throat like paper. How
many nights had I played with this scene, only to
cut it off before the end? Too dangerous, even for a
fantasy. Trembling in the dark cave of my room, I'd
wake, the edges of I'd only allow in my dreams,
waking me. Still, Darrian grips my hands.

Long moments, maybe minutes and she is still
staring ... I can see the fire reflected, the golds and

reds masking her forest colors. Hundreds of questions flash in her expression. I see them racing, but I can't interrupt, can't give answers for what she won't ask.

Only feelings are in play, directing everything, now, pushing and pouring over me.

Darrian's forehead wrinkles, as if she's holding a conversation away from our bodies, arguing herself past this minor indiscretion, talking herself out of it only to apologize and then go deeper inside than before, retreating and reinforcing those walls that Farquhar has told me she's constructed around her heart. Alone. No! No! That's the best argument of all to let this happen, maybe exactly why I've been driven to this point of explosion — so she won't be alone again. However unsure or apprehensive I'd been in the past, it was finally clear. I won't back off and I won't allow her to run away. I want this desperate miracle — terrifying as it is.

"Listen to me, Darrian ... you can't stop this, please." I can barely say the words, my lips are like two scalding stones. Still, she holds my hands buried within the grasp of her own.

"Nikki. I've never done this ... oh Nikola, you are my student! Is it because I've lost so much of myself up here?"

These the saddest words I think I've ever heard.

I pull free, angry at pain that could cause this great woman doubt. Who has done this to her? I touch my fingertips to her handsome mouth, wanting to brush away the hateful words ... no more words!

Darrian closes her eyes at the touch. Does not move.

"Darrian, it's my choice. I'm the one who came

here looking for you." I draw my hands through the soft fall of her hair, following the tendrils as they float over her shoulders. Then, as if I'd actually done it a thousand times before (and not just dreamt it) I press into her, fully, into the rough denim of her shirt, the definite rise of her breasts, waiting for her body's own answer — the quick, hardening of nipples, the sure return of flesh, proving what words so easily could deny.

A deep moan, quiet, as quiet as the ash-fall in the fireplace, only for me. God, the longing and burn in this sound — it moves straight through me, making me melt, so wet, as if she'd touched me low, as if she'd touched me there.

This time I take her hand, not caring who is supposed to be the teacher, not needing to be clear. I pull her up with me, pause only a second, a moment to be sure she'll come, then, we move across the room to her door.

She smiles, then it fades, her forehead knitting with questions, but I don't wait. Again I move against her, pressing her back to the door, it is allowed, my God, yes, Darrian, I will this to happen. Sheer force of desire. I'm rewarded for my outrageousness by a second low, deeper moan, all hunger and calling. Again, as if she's inside me, I think for a moment I'll come just standing there with her, listening to this music, overpowered by her wanting me that much.

Inside her room the smell of the lanterns rides the air like incense. The wonderful blue of the stars filters down caught in pools on the floor and her bed ... her bed ... bigger than the guest room's, oh Christ thank you for these favors! Covered by a

97

down comforter, the same color as the starlight, it flows over the edges, calling to us, making us welcome.

Other shapes come into focus. The oversized desk and its avalanche of angry letters, the typewriter, all black and toothy, the dark lantern still holding the scent of its earlier light. Each guidepost gives me answers, proves how close I've come to finding her ... I could be distracted here, want all of these details, her secrets, use them like roadmaps inside. But not distractions, not now. My body refuses them. I'll have to learn her like an explorer, no maps this time.

My feet tingle on the cold boards between rug and bed. I like the feeling — awake, cranking me more alive, so separate and delicious, sharply different from all the other heat in the room. She closes the door gently behind us, then latches it — less a locking in than a locking away from the world — more symbol than necessity. Julian and Farquhar, he is dead asleep and she, she is the one who has known of this night for weeks maybe even before me ... definitely before Darrian. A quick prayer for her generous heart — she who loves Darrian as I do but who must remain separate for her own reasons — thank you my sweet friend. And somewhere, the forest beyond us, banished, that other great love of her life. For now, this is our universe, this single flaming orbit, her entire being is solely here.

I begin to shuck off my sweater, so eager to fall into the snowfield of her bed, my flesh almost steaming in its hunger. Hurry, hurry, so few minutes till dawn.

But she's beside me and again, those strong,

finely veined hands, those long fingers, stopping me, mid-strip: "Slowly, go slowly, sweet one ..." Her voice all tender-hot, now, finally, sure. An epiphany, this tenderness! The word cut from nightflowers; closed against the stars; we would force the petals gently back, expose the center, the dew cupped there, ready: tender.

Her fingers begin tracing circles against my mons, her hands now deep, under my jeans. The hair there already moist from the tide she's created. Her fingers tangle playfully, stroking, pulling me weak, making me brace myself against the wall just trying to stand up, not to fall or to fall only against her, begging for the point I clung to, that sharp place of absolute delight.

My glasses are fog. No need to see, in the blur of the room I know this face, this handsome woman, have memorized her even before the mountain. Now I want to memorize her touch ... carefully, slowly, then.

She moves us toward the bed, pushes me down till I do fall in surrender. Her hands ever between my thighs, caught in the half-stripped jeans, her hands still moving against me, inside of me.

She kneels at the edge, peeling them from me, the scent (my scent!) rising, pungent, almost frightening in its intensity ... such obvious hunger! She drinks it in, letting it wash over her, move her, she tries to control the mounting fire, barely holding back, holding to her own rule of control. Trembling, she breaks me into moan, crying out in that blessed dark:

"My God, Darrian!"

Rough-edged, low, my voice transformed, in the

midst of this I realize this is not the voice of a child nor a teenager in simple heat — this is the voice of a woman. Whatever has come before this night has been mere rehearsal, play. Whatever childhood has remained is banished, shed, forever put away. All for her. It could have happened with no one else. The joy a rising growl, the absolute difference, a sacrament to love here, the reality of what I'd been searching for, my entire life a kind of preparation for this minute and Darrian, Darrian knows it, feels the power of it too.

Her hands begin to quicken, scratching lightly, rising over ribcage and belly, leaving tingling trails in the wake of their travel. The sweater is flung on the floor beside the jeans, the frigid air roils around our sweating bodies ... delicious. I am washed by these sensations, made delirious by her lips, my own throbbing, the want of her mouth, her tongue, the feel and taste and scent of her skin.

My glasses fall somewhere soft, I don't even care, laughing trying not to cry, caring only to pull her down, lower, on top of me full, unable to remain still, unwilling to go slow, to be "good" ... wanting only to wrap around her, move fast and hard against her, the shock of her muscled thigh and bite of her jeans on my swollen cunt makes me shudder, gasp, claw at her clothes.

I strip her, equalizing this power, unable to stop the fire, the maddening need, needing everything at once, flesh to flesh, all touch and sting and motion.

Her shirt sails over us like a banished spirit, with it, her hair tumbles down in benediction, covering my face with its clean scent, soft as mist over me.

Then, the blessing of her breasts, who would have guessed? Such luscious fruit, heavy, silken falling against my smaller chest, another secret, another miracle made mine. Touching against me, the tiny stab of her nipples, hard, dark, ripe as summer seeds, she drags them across my skin. My breath stops. Caught somewhere mid-sigh, never realizing I could feel this much, ache this long, nipple to nipple, barely brushing each other, pleading for the harder berrypress, the pain almost unbearable in this subtle tease — can't stand it, I roll out from her, force her down, move against her, ride her, scalding cunt to scalding cunt, thrust my tongue into her groaning mouth, my pelvis rocking us both in that boat of a bed. I am amazed at the flood, we are waterspirits here on top of this mountain, all salt and seaburn.

I won't let her cry, won't let her stop, will make her come crashing against me, riding this enormous wave we've made, break against the jetty that is my body, her body, our bodies together . . . but I am the one who breaks! Shocked, vainly holding back, wanting to wait for her . . . Can't, everything so wet, all points of flood and light, coming, coming against her heaving bellypush to bellyrush, aware she shares it, the tide mixing in delicious embrace, the clean salt smell that is our tribe's perfume riding the air around us . . . Everything is fire and wet . . . mixing with the lanternscent . . . our breath. 1 want to scream, to let go of the center — have never felt like this — shocked in realizing I don't care if Julian wakes up. Then I bite her gently, muffling my call into her neck, her lips, letting her mouth fill mine, fused, bruised, swollen with delight . . . reeling, my vagina a long throb, still, again, sweet Jesus, again!

Never, ever before — a second time — so fast! Coming again and calling her name in that holy place, coming again simply because she presses those glorious hands deep inside, the energy cracking from her fingertips, and again, I can't be still, can't simply go for the wild ride, have to move, down, down, wanting to know her there, too, wanting to know everything!

She tries to stop me, shy, her lips crying, come back, come back up to her, but behind the words I can feel the delight and fear-tinged hunger, a little dangerous, for her maybe, too much to ask this first time, but I know the halting request, can hear it through the sigh of my name, will not abide.

Amazed at my own need for her, craving for the taste of her there, the scent and touch of her lower lips in my mouth, I want to take suck and be nourished by this dark beauty, this wild Amazon. I begin the glide down, her hands releasing me, knowing I won't allow her to halt me in this act.

She relinquishes the argument, bemused, nervous, she closes her forest eyes in apprehension, the ecstasy there, only barely disguised, she clutches the edges of the sheets, her arms now raised above her head. So open to the night! Her legs move wide, vulnerable. This is her gift to me.

I swim down, past the crashing shore of belly, down, plunging deep, sudden, full-tongued, wrenching a new language from her, seatalk, nightsky, hips rolling under the lightning of my lips, moving with me as I part the royal flesh, the jewel of clitoris pulsing almost purple in its ache. I expect more salt, less sweet, but even here she is honeyed, the womanscent of her like tears, deep in my lungs.

Faster, faster, taking the entire clit into my burning mouth, sucking only slightly harder, listening to her desire, my lessons from her body's response, I cannot stop, pushed faster and farther, my own swelling matching her own, she lifts her hips and begins to move with me, again and again, bucking, clutching and releasing me, fierce in her openness, wild as the mountain outside the cabin, beyond even the naming of this, inside of herself, plunging and groaning, riding me like some ancient, terrible, wondrous beast, her rhythm mine, her body mine, my hands pressed tight to her firm belly, then up the ridge of ribs, raking down, she muffling the startled cry, the instant pleasure, fist to her lips, knowing she can bring down the house with her sounds, holding the mounting scream in her abeyance, holding the prayersong that I am pulling from her, the litany of joy, my hands and lips and tongue and flesh press to her core, boiling whirlpool, the contractions pure spirit, bucking me off, pulling me back, the legs fight to remain open, clenching again and again and again. With her, for me, a third miracle!

Sweet God, where did it come from? This tiny undertow made into a riptide at my center, made furious by her command!

I move up, up to surface, sea thing that I've become, belly to belly, cunt to cunt, our legs wrapped and throbbing still, we ride together entwined, these tides, these currents of our own making, arms locked, lips and teeth and tongues shared, the taste of each now in the other and it is my own scent but hers and the moon's risen, touching the stars, edging them away, filling the room with its arrival, bathing us in a hotter light, and I am exactly where I must be and I know it and the knowing is the final, greatest wonder of all.

Franconia Melbonshire? Wheatabaga, New York!"

"Okay, okay, don't make me feel more ridiculous than I already am." I turn over in the tangled sheets, propped up on one elbow.

"You get two points. How's that?" Darrian reaches a long arm into the frigid air and brushes my shoulder with her fingertips.

"Excellent, actually," I purr.

"Do you think you're up for a hike?" Her voice is almost shy.

"Are you kidding? It's about four a.m.! You aren't thinking of going down to the Ranger Station now, are you?" I moan, realizing there are limits to even my devotion.

"No, silly child, something much, much better. It will be very cold — a hard hike — interested?"

Darrian strokes my hair, tenderly. A word created just for us, for the evening past.

"Where? Darrian, oh God, you aren't playing with me, are you?" It hits me, full force, "The apes?"

"No more teasing, Nikki, not after tonight. Now, get dressed, pack your daypack, remember a canteen." Darrian nudges me to the edge of the bed.

"I'm gone!" Grabbing odds and ends of clothing that have fallen to the floor I stop short of the latched door, then come back to the wrecked bed, back to her.

"Forget something?"

"Darrian." I swallow, hard, wanting to just blurt it out, but feeling as if the vocabulary's changed, the words wrung out. "Darrian, meeting you, being allowed to stay up here, well, I thought that was one of those peak experiences they're all yelling about below . . . no kidding. Now — well, just know, just know who you are to me, it's never been . . . I mean . . . no one . . . no one else . . . not this deep." I bend close to her, touching my lips to hers.

Darrian laughs, finally, through this oh-so-serious-kiss, gently but firmly pushing me towards the door. "Nikki, you are very, very young!"

I open the door, puzzled, euphoric, excited about the next step, even the color of the air as it dances in front of me. Then, as I start to close the door I hear her whisper:

"Thank you."

Two hours of it. Almost blind bushwhacking, first straight up and then sideways, like land crabs. Then she's got me going down a bit, which totally screws up my already poor sense of direction — then back again so high we're even beating the first waves of rosy sun as it comes from the night places.

The apes! The apes! The apes! The apes!

Terror, joy, absolute certainty that one way or another I'm just going to die over this one.

I try to put my boot into every bootprint in front of me.

The problem comes because of our height difference — half the time I miss Darrian's footprint only to slide into the next by a few inches. I end up on my ass every five or six yards only to be "ssshhhed" violently by the good Doctor. I settle for an inelegant hand, knee, elbow, palm approach uphill and a very convincing fanny-slip down. In between it's all stride-n-slide.

Darrian is a mountain goat after all these years up here. She loves it that even though she's the "old lady" she can outdistance me in minutes. Superior power — okay — I can let her have that, but not the admonishment that if I only "stop worrying and keep moving" I'll be just fine. Right.

The apes. The apes. The apes. The apes.

It fills my heart like a Jesus Prayer. Moves my brain, moves my blood past the night wind's sting. I never believed I'd even make it the first time I saw them — when she rescued me — the image of that red-furred arm about twice the length of a human's, the barrel chest and bearded, fanged face ... But this time I'm approaching *with* her, and like everything else from this point on, that fact alone will make all the difference.

At least, that's what I pray.

"C'mon Nikki, I want to get to their feeding areas before the real light. If we get there before they do they'll be less nervous — about you. Hunger has an amazing quality of allowing tolerance for strangers. Now, hurry!"

This is Darrian Stone's essence, then: the morning whipping into amazing colors over us, her cheeks matching the sky's glory, all ruddy and rose; her eyes carrying the deep emeralds of the mossy cliff just under the ice-coat; her hair a tangle of smoke and cloud, framing the face that could have belonged to a teenager on a ski trip. All those years, alone at first, then Farquhar and the other Indians, but still, in her deepest self, still (and maybe more) alone — not any more! I'm the witness to this resurrection — I'm here, beside her, on the top of this mountain, to see the transformation, to know this is who she really is. Gone the old witch with a gun, the scientist held slave to her obsession. Here, this first morning, is Darrian unmasked, unguarded, almost giddy in showing off — for me, for me.

She points to a ledge about fifty feet above us. It's a shelf of rock just now being illuminated by the rising sun. The grays are going purplish and then to blue but still the rocky crag looks ominous. I'm no climber, even at my best, and Darrian brought no belay equipment. But it doesn't seem to bother her, doesn't stop her for more than a minute's pause — she's off and I'm forced to follow. I manage, barely.

The final few feet she simply turns around, somehow anchoring herself, then reaches for me to literally haul me up. Sweat stings my eyes, mixing with tears of relief. Can't even see through the fog of my glasses.

She smiles, thumping me on the back, pure exhilaration — like a "Geographic Special." Then, very unlike a "Geographic Production," Darrian draws me in tight and kisses me long and deep. God — her kiss, hot slow, hard in that high, crinkling cold ... I'm melting again, right into her bones, raging with sudden want for those hands, that spectacular flesh, wanting to make stark love on that rigid outcropping, the height and terrain no longer a worry. Christ, the night's been no dream then. She isn't backing off. Brave, fearsome, almost, she carries us into the morning, my fear of our tryst being only a reaction to the intrusion of the film-crew or fear that this was a whim on her part — a tense experiment exposed to the light and the results destroyed. Fears all washed away by this embrace. I would be whoever she needed me to be, a vow, silent: protector, lover, student, sister-scientist who believes in her, or just a woman totally smitten by these Lone Ranger heroics — whatever she wants, needs, can accept, I can be that. More than our heated night, this trek seals it, the obvious trust searing me through. No words, again, my motor-mouth empty, just her touch, ours, and this memory on the ledge — always that.

Darrian breaks away, connected only by our hands, she moves me from the edge. Hidden behind us, in the brush, a single split boulder, unseen from below, the mouth of a cave. Huge. Anything at all could be hiding there ... I hesitate long enough to stop her.

She turns to look at me, her stare sharp, questioning: "Nikki, relax. You've got to try to trust me now, completely, as much as I trust you.

Whatever I do you have to follow, don't so much as pause to think about it — just do it. Everything depends on this. Do you understand?"

I shake my head, not wanting her to hear the uncertainty in my voice. It isn't a matter of trust, it's a matter of bowels and bladder. My body remembers the last encounter with the apes — and that was in open air. No one ever said I'd have to go underground.

"Okay, here we go! No flashlights, just give your eyes time to adjust. Ready?" Then Darrian steps into the enormous black.

The entrance immediately widens. Darrian doesn't even have to duck. The roof recedes into a pitchy dankness. I can hear the unmistakable sounds of bats . . . their rodent scramblings and the acrid dung smell rising around us. Why aren't they in deep hibernation?

My boots slush down in fresh droppings. We move carefully. The light begins to invade — either my eyes have remarkably adjusted or there is another light source coming from above. Don't pause, even to question, just follow — okay.

Darrian moves quickly to an open space near some fallen boulders about the size of small tractors. Jesus, I didn't even know about such large caverns in this part of the state. Made sense, though, why there had been so few sightings of the apes in all these years. Also why there was such a scarcity of forensic proof — they were cave dwellers!

Light *is* pouring down, so high above I can't see the openings, but enough that small, pale plants are growing, weedy, a strange, mutated form of lichens, close cousins to those outside in the forest, these colors range from frosted olive to navy blue, like a living carpet covering the fallen rocks and moving beyond. Darrian eases her pack and her parka off, then smiles as she strips completely, loving my shock.

When I finally recover from her outrageous behavior (getting naked with four hundred plus pound primates is pretty outrageous, if you ask me), I hear it. My senses already on overload, I'd missed it before, but now, the bell-tinkle of falling water, the sudden warmth, not from above and the outside sun but from below. The ground itself is humid.

"Come on, Nikki! The water — not a sulphur spring but pretty warm, come on, they won't feel threatened if they see you in the water — with me."

Suddenly I feel very, very awkward, almost shy in this odd morning. Just beyond these lit patches of lichen is my ... my lover. Waiting ... for me to get naked and follow her to some underground pool. With a few hundred bat eyes and big old ape faces ogling us from the shadows. I want to run and dive, complete with boots, but prudence suggests a bit more delicacy. No time to pause, worse, don't want to be caught high and dressed and dry while Darrian is safely floating in a warm grotto. I strip.

Darrian chuckles as she sees me emerge with nothing but my glasses for protection. I carry what little dignity's left to the edge of the pool, feeling with bare toes for where the rock dips to water.

"Look, I want to be able to see these guys — give me a break, okay?" I argue, not wanting to have to explain that my real nakedness comes in taking my glasses off.

"Just be careful, it's slippery," Darrian whispers,

her voice brushing the walls and coming back like a breeze.

I am careful, gingerly slip in. Not what I'd call hot, not by a long shot. But, it isn't frigid.

Darrian moves closer, ducking under, taking my hand, then coming up, pulling me out to deeper water.

The light's growing stronger, playing on top of the ripples we create. I can see Darrian's fractured figure just below the surface. Even distorted, it makes me ache.

"It goes to a depth of twenty feet in the center. Really a large, underground pond — see, you can almost look clear to the bottom." Darrian leaves me to swim farther out.

I plunge in, holding onto my specs, my breath sucked by the shock. Resurfacing I am exhilarated. Glorious, she's right! The nervousness of the hike is washed away, I'm not even tired anymore. I breast-stroke out to her, laughing and sputtering. In the same way that she broke me open and made me feel so old, wise, last night, now she's reducing me to kidhood again. This is like Uncle Chris's duckpond in New Hampshire, this is easy, swell.

Just then something bumps against my calf . . . a second lower bump against my heel. I make a grab for Darrian like a drowning child.

"Nikki!" She pulls away, moving me off her neck, clear into my own space. "Nikki, it's just the fish. Don't worry, you're much too big for them. They're only investigating. They keep the water clean in the pool, and keep the apes well fed. She watches as I catch my breath.

I'm okay, a strong swimmer, not panicky. Only

fish, I watch them swim under us, feel the gentle
tides they churn as they glide by, feel the escaping
bubbles. There's thousands below!

"Darrian —" I am cut off by the apparition of a
huge red-orange shape emerging from behind a
column of rock. Clearly a male, but not the one who
charged me, this one is older, with silver-gray
streaks in its beard and chest. It thumps like a
gorilla, two fists pounding its pecs, the echo
bouncing off walls and ceiling, disturbing the bats,
their answering squeaks almost painful.

I swim more towards the center of the pool. I
don't give a rat's ass how long I have to float — no
shore-time for this kid — just want to get closer to
Darrian.

The ape steps into a puddle of morning light. At
that exact second Darrian makes a low, guttural
cough. I spin like a storm-bound buoy, shocked to
hear such an inhuman sound from her. She reaches
out, touches my arm under the water, reassuring me
even as she's reassuring him. Then, these clicking
sounds, her tongue seeming to knock definite
rhythms against her front teeth.

The male understands . . . He comes to the edge
of the water, this time no charge, but a fully upright
walk, like watching a movie about Frankenstein's
monster and Wolfman's cross-bred son. The thing is
easily eight feet tall and way over four hundred
pounds. How many fish to feed this ape? No wonder
the horror stories of Sasquatch. I cling to Darrian's
waist, keeping us afloat, not pulling her down like
my earlier panic, but definitely needing to feel
attached.

The ape goes only as far as the lip of the water.

It squats on a flat boulder, its posture much less human now that it's sitting. Its neck settles onto the heavy shoulders, no longer distended in curiosity. Half-orangutan and half gorilla? No, there is something beyond even those amazing animals here, beyond the obvious empathy I hold for other species. Here there is more than the eyes of an animal, more even, than a great ape — and yet I'd never seen a great ape in the wild, only in pathetic plastic habitats and on Fossey's tapes. Here there were the eyes of something so different from us that it was like looking at a life-form from another planet — an alien with alien intelligence, one wondering what it should ask? I'm speechless and embarrassed that I don't know its mother-tongue . . . clearly Darrian will have to act as our interpreter.

She eases away, squeezing my thigh under the water, letting me know it's okay, all right, just the way it should be. I float, scared of the fishes below and not exactly convinced of a welcome from the shore. If anything happens to Darrian in the next few minutes I'm as good as cut bait.

Darrian glides slick as a water moccasin through the sparkling water. The beauty of her body catches me, pulls me away from my own dark wondering. All of her easy muscle has come not only from climbing the peaks, but of hours spent there, in this pool, swimming among them. Another delicious question answered.

Then, in a display of courage that outranks even her face-off of the charging ape on the mountain, this naked, utterly defenseless woman reaches up and out of the water. A single hand, wrist up, limp, her eyes not even glancing at what might occur. My breath catches, I want to scream for her to get the hell back here where it might be safe. In one single twist of his football-sized hand that ape could have her out of the shallows and on shore like the morning's catch. Or a single snap of those fangs and she would be limbless.

The ape comes forward, doesn't look directly at her either, more towards me, though I can see him glancing casually, through the corner of his eye, at her offered wrist. She makes another series of clicks. How the hell can she stay treading water, let alone vocalize, with this monster about six inches from her head?

Still not looking directly at her, he clicks back. And from behind, in the shadows, movement. Smaller ones, some very small, others closer to his size, all emerge. All click with a few grunts mixed in, all come to the edge where Darrian is clinging to the flattened boulder with her free hand.

And I watch this oh-so-delicate woman, a woman I have torn open the night with, touched and been touched by, now too far from me to save, in absolute surrender to a half-circle of North American Great Apes!

The smallest ones begin to get squirmy, move away to play by the water's edge. The old one, all melancholia and grace, simply reaches out a nonchalant log of an arm and with a gentle brush, touches the offered wrist of Darrian Stone. In a great movement back, she pulls off towards me, almost royally, clearly not in retreat, more like joyful acknowledgment of the message. The apes break their ranks, click and coo and cough, going about various odd jobs now after the morning matin.

Darrian returns to me, nuzzling my neck, wrapping an arm around my waist, all wide grin and raw joy.

"Darrian." I can barely whisper, devastated by awe, an almost unbelieving witness.

She turns around in the liquid sapphire of the water, faces me full, the tears welling up in her eyes.

We spend over an hour in the pool while Darrian reveals, explains about the apes. The apes never actually swim, only come in around the edges, reaching out with surprising swiftness for the unlucky, unwitting fish. Like primates in the higher places in Tibet, they have found this relatively warm spring in the middle of winter and use it as their source of life.

Amazing, these complicated creatures — a lost race. How ancient? Even the Indians couldn't guess. These caverns themselves had remained hidden for centuries — Darrian knew of five, herself, the Deepwoods Tribe suggested hundreds more.

In addition to catching the slow-witted fish, the apes existed in winter on lichens, moss and an occasional aged bat. The elements in the plants and fish, the minerals in the water, all just now beginning to be studied by Darrian. The fish flesh was oily as salmon, full of the calories the large mammals needed to make it through the cold mountain seasons. The plants and water seemed to provide a balance, a delicate balance at best. So much new information. Daily discoveries — no wonder at all why she'd disappear for weeks at a time and come back exhausted, wordless. Who could really put any of this in a comprehensible form —

unless the reader had been here, saw and swam and drank here? More and more I understood Julian and Farquhar and Darrian's intensely quiet sides.

At night the apes went deeper into the caverns — probably for the trapped warmth and to escape the cold drafts. They never soiled the larger caverns where the pools bubbled. Their peaceful eating and social habits were amazing. And I knew, without her telling me, that somewhere as yet undiscovered, there was a cave for their dead.

In all of the literature the one greatest obstacle (until Darrian came with the proof) to definitely demonstrating the actuality of these animals had been lack of skeletal remains. When the Deepwoods Indians came to Darrian to ask for her help they'd brought the first skull. From that point on just enough bone fragments and hair samples had been allowed to "surface" to satisfy even the most skeptical critics. Then, of course, the photographs and the videos. Now, as the century closed, it was the opposite argument that needed to be made, to prove that these animals needed to be left alone — better forgotten, maybe — that was her mission.

The Deepwoods Tribe was committed to that, had been committed to "herding" the apes for decades, as the Europeans advanced into the woods. When the first trappers, then miners and loggers entered the forest, the Indians moved the apes further in, found new caves, and kept the animals there for generations until the memories of the lower, older caves were forgotten.

Darrian had twice witnessed wounded animals (caught in bear traps or shot) carried back to the caves by healthy apes, as if the apes knew instinctively that leaving any evidence would be suicide, as if they knew they were preventing their own genocide.

On occasion, a younger or unlucky ape might wander off, be seen, then the hoopla would begin anew. The Deepwoods people, ever vigilant, would move them all on.

The Tribe's entire myth system was built around the protection of the apes. To them, the apes were messengers that the Great Spirit had sent to remind them of the white man's frailty. Protection of the apes taught the Indians humility, reminding them of their kinship to all living things, and that there were other animal clans even greater than their own, reminded them that as long as they remembered their connections to this other animal people they were not alone in the universe, the Great Spirit had not abandoned them. The Europeans had never known their connection to the immense mysteries of the earth, knew only the bite and burn of powder and guns. This was their weakness. As long as the Deepwoods Tribe kept the vows of the forest, kept to the protection of the apes, they would be fueled by the power of their knowledge. Someday, fueled by this power, they would reclaim their lost lands for all of the animal clans. Because of them and them alone, Darrian had been granted the privilege of this contact. They recognized that a new plan of protection had to be formulated — and she had been sent to help them. Darrian had passed their first tests — and now, the great white scientist was also a believer.

* * * * *

"They watched me a long time, Nikki." Darrian continues the history as we headed back down. "Probably over a year before they came to me. Farquhar and Julian had introduced me to many tribal people, their own families and friends ... but these people were different. Of course I'd already fallen in love with the woods. I'd take my pack and go out for weeks. You know about Joseph, Farquhar's husband ... Well, around then I was spending more and more time in the forest. One evening, on lower Remmel, a young Indian met me in a meadow. Just came out of the trees like a ghost. He motioned me to follow him. For three days we travelled. Something in me made me trust him, maybe it was because of all the good will I'd been given through Farquhar's family, I don't know. He'd leave me alone to make camp at dusk and then be there in the morning when I woke up.

"On the fourth morning we were much farther north, probably over the border, farther than I'd ever hiked. Even the woods were different. It was the way the mist came through the light ... When I came out of my tent that day, instead of the young man, there was this old, silent woman. Her clothes were like something out of one of my anthro texts, but not a ceremonial heirloom, no, clearly this was her everyday clothing. And something else, a deep calm in her eyes, Nikki, a dark, hidden part, a secret maybe tinged with fear. It made me cold. When she saw I was unsettled by the look, she smiled, motioned for me to come sit beside her. Somehow we communicated — sign language, broken French, a little English. It was clear that she wanted me to wear this blindfold she'd brought. She made sure I understood that I wasn't in danger, or even being held accountable for trespassing on tribal land, as I feared. No, she was going to bring me to the people I'd been looking for — how she knew about that, I still don't know. It stunned me that she knew this, so how could I resist?

"I put on the blindfold and allowed this tiny bird of a woman to guide me, slowly, into the high country, past the mountain goats and Bighorns, up to the alpine meadows. Finally we came to a 'village' — I could feel and hear the night coming down. Clearly, when they removed the blindfold, I was in the middle of a nomadic camp — it wasn't their permanent residence. The area was much too harsh to stay in for very long. It was also clear that this was no recorded tribe. I was in the midst of probably the greatest anthropological discovery I'd ever make in this life."

Darrian rearranges her day-pack, then starts back on the path down. I finish lacing my boots (for probably the sixth time in two hours) and begin to just marvel at how easy it is to believe this amazing story, how easy it would be forever to believe anything this woman tells me. Why isn't there a great golden halo around her, or at least some kind of soundtrack playing behind us? How could so much change not be etched in our flesh? And this is part of her everyday existence. When I stand, I am ready to follow her anywhere.

The light is grayer now, the early morning's promise forgotten. Maybe even new snow before night. On lower ground we stop and drink from the canteens, sharing apples. I lean against her back as she continues the saga of the apes and her discovery:

"The Deepwoods Tribe was well aware of the changing times, had made a decision to continue with their lives intact as much as possible — which meant the protection of the apes. The loggers and miners, all equipped with the most sophisticated equipment, were shrinking the forest. It was becoming increasingly difficult to avoid contact. They told me in the camp that first night that they'd had dreams — dreams of a time when it would be necessary to find a European to help them against the Europeans, to help them save the apes.

"They did what they'd never done before, Nikki, they trusted a white with their secrets, with their spirits — because they trusted their own dreams. Maybe I'm not who they dreamt of — I question that, all the time. But I never question that the dreams are real. These are smart, finely tuned people, Nikki — not mystical savages, not romantic icons. They know what they have to do and have plans for how to do it — part of those plans include me.

"I took a pledge, a vow, if you will, that first night with them — because of it there are things I can't tell, not even to you. There will be times when it seems as if I'm going away from you, even while we're together. You'll just have to trust when it occurs that it isn't anything you've said or done — it's about my being with these people, about my promise. It's one of the reasons I've stayed . . . alone. I can't even remember what my life was like before I took this on. But I did take it on, willingly, knowing how it could change my life, knowing once made I couldn't take it back. Maybe if I'd known how ... alone ... how different I'd become ... Maybe if I'd known that you might come along someday ... But none of that matters now. They waited for me to decide, they took me to the caves, to the apes ... There was only one decision after that.

"Today, I wanted you to see what is at the heart of my life, Nikki — so you could understand maybe a little of the things I can't speak of — so you can make your own choice. If you can live with me on these terms, if you want to come with me on this path, as far as I can take you, you know I want you here. But if there's even so much as a single doubt, you have to get ready to leave the mountain ... never come back. And when you leave, you must promise not to tell anyone ... until I tell you it's all right.

"In either case, you should know that you've touched down deep inside this rusty woman, made me feel and see and hope, because of who you are, because, like the Tribe, you came looking for me, and like them, too, I recognized you. I love you, Nikki."

Darrian's hands trace the lines of my face. Her eyes are clouded as the sky over us. Her face is flushed with the effort of telling this long-buried story. Of holding her life out, in her hands to me, the way she offered her wrist to the ape.

She's exposed the bones of truth of the North American Great Ape, and in so doing cut to the marrow of the Deepwoods people and her own initiation, given me the key to all of it, without flinching. That kind of trust — all my life I'd hungered for such a connection, never really believing humans could give that to each other, must always hold back, for their own (my own) protection. Now I was broken open — the evening of surrender, the amazing morning with the apes, all of it rushing over and over me, like the stream we sat beside, like Darrian Stone had rushed over me from the first. I had her heart, and in some ways, had her life — at least as much as she had mine — without any pretense or defense, this proud Amazon risked my knowing and yet allowed me the choice of the responsibility.

Withhold, withhold, information was power, don't show or share too much of your inner side or it may be used against you, keep secrets, hide your deeper feelings, your greatest truths, never give away everything, hadn't my parents always taught me that? All my life I'd watched people bottling themselves up, packaging themselves off, struggling to hide — for what? All the loves given up, lost, all the broken miles I'd come from playing the games in that New England factory town, to the masquerade ball that was Smith, now brushed aside, so much dust, only getting in my eyes, keeping me from really breathing. Compared to what this woman offered it seemed as if I'd woken from a life-long sleep. Yes. Yes.

For the love of Darrian Stone: whatever I had to give.

* * * * *

The chill of the mountain air is broken by the warmth of her hands on my face. Darrian closes her eyes and kisses my lips, full, soft. I feel her tears scalding my cheeks but I can't watch this ... can only kiss her back ... so much, Darrian.

Nightfall when we get back. A radio message from below — the news crew has the governor on their side, they'd return in a couple of weeks, this time with a national broadcast exclusive. No argument. Even though we are privately funded, none of our agencies will fight the governor over so seemingly small a deal — we have to pick our fights. Pick them well.

Darrian tries to call back, dictating the only thing she has control over — the conditions for the shoot. Forty-five minutes later, she comes from the lab, looking exhausted.

I've warmed up the stew Farquhar left for us. The fire is low, the only other light from a single candle on the table. Everyone else in bed.

We eat in silence, the fire occasionally breaking the quiet with a popping hiss. Unhappy about the battle, the governor's unfair intervention, yes, but a deeper happiness — at the core. As Darrian clears away the dishes, I carry the stub of candle into her room.

"Nikki." She closes and latches the door, our new ritual.

"Come to bed, Darrian." My voice comes from that deep place. The slow, achy burn beginning the minute she entered the cool room.

124

Shedding clothes like a worn cocoon, emerging golden under the solitary beam of candlelight, she is the most beautiful woman I've ever known. Her body's sinewy muscles, nothing hard-edged or brutal about their power, only helping to define the softer places. Her body is her spirit made solid . . . here, in this room, I know that secret. Here in this room, safe from all that would carry her away, we are equals. I feel her tremble as she slips beneath the comforter.

"Nikki, all day, all day I've wanted this. Even when we were in the cave it flashed across my mind, what it would be like to make love to you — in the water — weightless — deep, only our heads above the surface, everything inside, everything outside, so wet . . ." Darrian's mouth finds mine, her lips ravenous, mine meeting their hungry press.

Neon newsman was still wearing his flashy jacket when the crew arrived the second time. A different cameraman, though. The woman anchor recognized me, turned away before I had time to say anything.

I decided to wait inside, let Darrian and Julian handle them. Farquhar was firm — she wasn't coming out of her room till they left.

"So glad we could come to some kind of understanding, Ms Stone." Neon slipped off a down mitten and held out a pinkish hand.

I watched, unnoticed, from the cabin windows.

"The only understanding I have is that the Governor pulled rank and ordered me to give you a tour of our facility. I'm honoring that request . . . got it?"

"Ms Stone, what about some ape footage? So far

only *Geographic* has actually filmed you among the apes. Don't you think it's about time your public was rewarded with some six o'clock shots?" Neon grinned a yellow smile.

"No apes. Look, I'm not 'Ms' — that's a magazine. My title is Doctor — Dr. Stone. As head of this research facility I have the legal right to restrict your cameras so that our work here is not disrupted. Every time a human being from below comes into contact with my apes it affects their behavior for months. The disease risk alone is too much to consider. I will personally show you anything you care to see, *in* camp, but I will not take you to the animals."

Darrian was barely keeping the lid on. Even though I was watching from the safety of the cabin I could see the explosion building, could hear Darrian's voice already an octave above normal pitch.

"You know, we could make it quite unpleasant for you, Doctor Stone!" Neon took a step forward.

"It's already unpleasant. Now, follow me and I'll take you to the lab." Darrian turned her back on the bluffing man and started off.

Julian was waiting for the news crew. He followed behind them, subtle insurance.

I moved away from the windows, knew there was paperwork to attend to. Well, at least I was off shit detail for the day. That was something.

Noon. And then we heard them. Something wrong. I knew Darrian's stride. This was her "out of my way I've got business" walk. The door crashed open.

"I knew they'd try to pull something. Just the way that woman held back from the group ... dammit! Isn't she the same one who attempted to break into the lab the last time?" Darrian looked as if she were about to throw punches.

Farquhar, hearing the commotion, came out of her room. My arms were still covered with flour from the bread I was attempting to bake.

"That damned reporter! She's lost! She slipped behind the men when Julian wasn't looking. She waited till I was mouthing The Grand Tour. I'm sure it was premeditated. He played me — that plastic newsboy and his neon suit — played me for the fool I am! Didn't even hear the lab door close! Goddammit!" Darrian pounded one of the bookcases hard enough for several volumes to tumble.

I wiped my hands on the front of my flannel shirt. "How long ago?"

"Maybe as long as half an hour. I don't know for sure. With the new melt her trail won't be easy to follow if she keeps to the rocks. We have to find her before sundown. She'll get hypothermia for sure. The stupid, stupid woman. I swear to you both, this is absolutely the final time — blast the Governor — let him try to pull another stunt like this and I'll get the whole World Wildlife public relations crew on him so fast he won't even know when the next election comes around. Whatever it takes — no more false pride, no more attempting to be a good girl with these fools, I've had it! What's worse is if she so much as breaks a nail out there they'll blow it up out of proportion and blame it on batty Dr. Stone —

say I'm dangerous and deranged, my revenge against the press or some other idiot response." Out of steam, finally, Darrian slumped into her chair.

I crossed over, coming from behind, attempted a hug.

She shrugged me off, her shoulders wrapped in iron, the muscles tight and hard.

Farquhar tried another approach: "Breathe ... just breathe. We're angry, too, but anger isn't going to find the woman. Try to calm down a little." She pulled a chair close to Darrian, touched Darrian's knee. The magic, as usual, worked. Darrian sucked back a few deep gulps of air, held in the tears of frustration I can feel dancing around the edge.

"I'm all right. Really. I'm okay. I don't want to make more of this than needs to be made. We'll split up. Leave the rest of the crew here, to wait, but hide the radio, lock our records tight. I don't want them calling down the mountain. We'll head in different directions, she's no dummy, she knows the apes won't be below us, she'll head up higher. Doesn't have too much of a lead, thank God. Take medi-bags and emergency blankets. We may well end up outside tonight. Tell Julian to go west. I'll climb north. Farquhar east and Nikki, head southeast. The higher terrain is still too rugged for you alone. Okay?"

We nodded. Even her rebuff of my hug didn't mar the feeling of finally being part of the team, of now being someone who can do something. I headed for my room, my gear — angry and elated.

* * * * *

South. Southeast. Months since I've been back this low. Close to where Julian first found my tent. So different. Not even half as wild as it seemed then. Maybe it was true, I had really changed . . . my territory, now. My heart recognizes these places, these individual rocks and trees. My land too — my land too.

I hike till I'm almost at Farquhar's cabin. Clear that no one but me has been around this side of the mountain since the last snow. How had those folks gotten to us? Oh shit! The fucking news crew hadn't come up alone, like they wanted us to believe . . . had to get back, get back to camp and warn Darrian!

Exhausted, breathing like a bull moose, I know it's a lost cause. Night comes back with me into camp. Past eight. I knew I wouldn't make it in time, knew hours ago. All the cabin lights blazing as I slog up the path. Even two lamps winking from the front steps.

The door is open. Looks as if someone had smashed the face of the house and broken its jaw the way the door swings in the calm night breeze.

I peel off my daypack, walking in, unsure of what to expect. Inside, even the fire is blazing. The cabin smells alien: cigarettes and strangers; men's scared sweat and something bitter, biting — disinfectant.

Then, I see the radio. On the middle of the table, hot, crackling, obviously left on for hours. Ghosts fly in and out of range. Part of me wants to rip the damned thing to pieces, scatter the brutalized remains over the mountain — this is what allowed the Governor's call in the first place.

I walk back through the house like a zombie. All of our rooms are closed, no one home. Voices drift from the lab area — lots of disembodied voices coming in from the dark. I take a deep, clean breath and say prayers I haven't thought I still remembered.

Julian and Farquhar flank Darrian as she finishes sewing what looks like a big canvas bag with heavy surgical thread, using a curved, wicked looking needle — all of it on one of the metal tables. The Neon dude smokes a cigarette right inside the lab's door, his eyes darting over me as I push past. Why hasn't Darrian noticed the smoke? The cameraman sits on the cold floor, in a corner, his back to the table, to all of us. Shit — where's the anchorwoman?

Then, in the shadows between the bookcases, I see her. As I suspected, right next to her, the owner of the snowmobiles. He's got a wide gash along the bridge of a swollen nose, his right arm's cradled by a new sling. Clean. Obviously not worn on the way up this morning.

The woman stares at me, her eyes are very, very red, her face puffy but unbruised. If there was any make-up this morning it's gone now. Her forehead is streaked with mud, her newest Patagonia ensemble torn in several places, little spurts of down blowing out each time she exhales. Almost a cartoon. I don't feel like laughing. Our eyes meet, deadlock. I realize

131

for the first time that she's only a little older than I. Funny, I could have sworn she was Darrian's age . . .

Except for the sound of the generator and the needle's track, our silence is frightening. I know enough not to ask.

Neon slinks up behind me, nudging me toward the door. "You just get in?" He coughs, throws his cigarette into the black of the trees, both of us trailing the red eye as it winks and goes out.

I feel the needles of rain as they begin, close my eyes to this unexpected storm, let it hit my face, wash clean some of the grime of this hideous day.

"Kid, look, I feel really bad. We all do. Let me explain. Maybe, maybe you'll listen. We just wanted some hot tape. You know, Doc and the monkeys, Bigfoot at home, whatever. The public loves this Dr. Stone. She doesn't have any idea how cool she is. Very valuable property right now. I don't just mean the gossip sheets, it would be a helluva lot easier if it was just those check-out rags that wanted this story. No, she's legit, star material. The environment is *The Issue* and Darrian Stone is seen as *The Environmentalist*. Fossey, Ed Abbey, Chico Mendes — all dead. The public needs someone breathing, someone upbeat, alive! Do you know what they had out at Christmas?"

Christmas. Wow, it had come and passed and not one of us so much as noticed. Weird relief in that. Not even my parents had gotten through — maybe they never tried. Was I dead to everyone off this mountain? Had I gone that deep into Darrian's world?

"Kid, kid, listen to me — they had Darrian Stone

132

dolls! No lie! Darrian and the apes — in the stores — the apes kind of looked like a hairy *E.T.* or something. That's because no one really knows what the fucking animals look like up close, there's so little access And the dolls, damn, you couldn't get one for love or money! People tearing them out of each other's hands — doesn't she even realize it? Don't any of you? Even you, yet?" Neon grabs me by my elbows, excited again, his face animated with the idea of profit, publicity: his best drugs.

"You prick! This is exactly what she's afraid of!" I struggle away from him, wanting to hit, to hit back hard. "This is what's going to kill her! Maybe kill all of us! What happens when there's nothing left to exploit? You don't save wild things by caging them up or making a movie and popularizing them, sometimes ... oh God help us ... sometimes you just have to walk away and leave them alone!" I pull off into the dark, I won't let him watch me cry — won't give him the sadistic pleasure of any more emotion.

At the lab door, Julian meets me.

"What?" I whisper to him, afraid.

"Come back to the cabin. She's going to need hot food, a bath. You can't do anything here, not while they're around." He takes my arm, pulls me out, toward the light.

Arguing. I hear the loud voices, angry. I want to go back to her, be by her side. Julian's hand is a vise as he grips my sleeve.

The cameraman emerges, shaky, followed by

Neon, then the snowmobile guy and the anchorwoman. Farquhar and Darrian are on their tails, kicking the door shut behind them. Darrian carries the shotgun.

I watch, mute, shocked, as they all head down the path away and out of sight. One barrel blast and I know, even before the oily plume of smoke rises, the snowmobile is wrecked. Then Darrian, furious, glorious, fills the night with her scream:

"Get out of this forest . . . get the hell out of here . . . now!"

The voices fall away like a bad dream. It's quiet. Julian and I go inside the cabin. He puts me to work peeling carrots and potatoes.

Much later, the stew almost finished cooking, Darrian and Farquhar return, their faces smudged with soot. Darrian doesn't speak, only crashes past the kitchen, the sound of her boots thudding down to the bathroom, the door slams.

"I'm going to call in the official report. She can't do it. She'll break. When it's over, I'll help with supper. Nikki, maybe you, maybe you can . . ." Farquhar nods towards Darrian's room. Her face shows two clean lines under each eye, where the soot has washed away. I toss a hand towel from the sink. She puts it to her face, then begins to sob. Immediately Julian and I are there, surrounding her, holding her very, very tight.

"Okay, okay, I've really got to make that call." Farquhar pulls back, wiping her face angrily.

I sit, listening to the report, piecing together the

134

answers I haven't dared ask for. The anchorwoman took a local guide and blasted up on his skimobile into the reserved territory, clearly knowing it was off limits. The machine skidded on the scabby trail, flipping, sending driver over a small ledge and tossing the anchor to the side. She attempted to go back for help but in so doing stumbled upon a family group of apes. The alpha male charged. The anchorwoman had come to camp armed this time — a pistol. She panicked, not realizing it was only a bluff charge. She fired until the gun was empty. The other apes scattered but the male was dead at the scene, shot in the head.

Darrian, already in pursuit, heard the noise and came to the site first. Somehow she got the anchor, the driver and herself back to camp. She went back to the site with equipment and retrieved the body alone.

Half the skull had been blown off at close range. Another bullet pierced the heart. When the rest of the people came back she was performing the autopsy. Recording the accident. She made the news team witness it, film it. The six o'clock report — just as they'd pressed her for, now it was ready to air. She'd called the Rangers to inform them that the team was walking down, to be waiting when they arrived — then she radioed for the Governor.

Farquhar's report is necessary for the World Wildlife, State Wildlife, Leakey Foundation, *Geographic,* and our other supporters — as well as the mainstream media outside of Washington. She clicks off the radio, not wanting to wait for response. Time tomorrow. Now, she only wishes for the day to fold down, be put to rest. Her head nods in exhaustion and numbed pain. She drops it onto her arms and just rocks like a child trying to protect herself from a bad dream.

"Nikki." Farquhar's voice comes from someplace far away. "Nikki, go to her."

"What do I say?" My own hot tears rise in response to hers. Terrified to face Darrian, crazy while waiting for permission, this exact permission to do just that. This murdered animal was a part of herself, her family, her own body, almost destroyed — what did one say? What could *I* say?

Farquhar lifts her dirty face, her eyes shimmering pools, all pain, mirrored there. Her hair falls in coal strings across, black, black as the dead ape's blood. "Stop thinking about yourself! Think of Darrian, dammit, think of Darrian!"

She's right. Chastised, I nod. Reach for her, touch the dirty silk of her head.

"Stop! Not me! I don't need you — go to *her* — she needs you! You're the only one . . . Christ knows I'd do it if she'd let me!" Farquhar's weeping wracks the slim body, moves her so far away I can't follow, can only do what she demands, knowing the cost to her, in that.

The fire throws unhappy shadows against the walls. Monsters loosed, lurking, barely held in check, waiting for a single opening. All my life I've hated these moments after death, never understanding the need for solace sought in the volume of bodies attending a wake or a funeral, always, simply, wanting to be alone then, to deal with my grief and loss privately. To process and probe and finally peel off the sorrow. But alone. I've never known how to really comfort anyone. Usually I slip off, out the back door, whenever asked. But now there is no chance or choice. Not really. Even if Farquhar hadn't asked, I'm the one to go to Darrian, the woman who has held us all, so often — I'm the one to go and hold *her*, this time.

This damned day seems like it has consisted only of walking to hard destinations. My clothes are sticky with sweat, half-dried mud. The salt stings and rasps across my back, my breasts. I feel filthy and so fucking sad.

The bathroom door is still shut. I knock softly, almost hoping there is no answer.

"It's Nikki, may I come in?" I push, the door swings open. Steam fills the small room, sending spirits up from the floor. The scalding water rips, full blast, from the tub's faucets. But the water is going nowhere, just draining out. Then, I see Darrian.

Curled into herself on the floor, like a sick college kid, her hair in snaky ropes, plastered to her face, she just lies there. The room reeks of whiskey.

I reach for the candle and matches I know are in the medicine chest. The light spills into the corners of the steamy room, almost, but not quite, seeming cheery.

"Darrian." I lean over her, trying to keep my voice steady, not wanting her to know what an absolute shock it is finding her like this. I expect her to look up, all snarl and scream, push me away, or worse, crawl into a shadowy corner, gone over the edge, wild.

Instead, slowly, painfully, she pulls up, runs a hand angrily over her head, raking the long hair back.

"Don't let them see me like this ..." She stands, shaking, turning to the sink, running water there, trying to wash her filthy face. She reaches for the soap, brushing the half-empty bottle of Jack Daniels with her knuckles, sending it smashing against the side of the toilet and all over the floor.

"Jesus fucking Christ!" she screams, the sound ripping through me like a chain saw. She holds the sink edge, her hands trembling, her shoulders heaving, the sobs tearing out as if she is dying, right there in front of me.

"Darrian, don't shut us out, don't shut me out — Darrian, I love you!" Inside my throat it's as if I've swallowed glass. I can say no more — everything on this mountain tonight is raw. Raw.

She cries, hard, eventually turning to face me, eventually caving in, letting me hold her, not leaving, not flying out into the wintry night alone, but coming back to us, coming back home.

I moved to the tub, put the stopper in, dump in the one luxury I've hauled in the bottom of my pack — bath oil. And like a baby, she lets me strip the bloody clothes from her, no arguments, gently, so gently, as gently as she removed the bullets from the dead ape, I toss them off, then out, into the hall, I'll burn them later. The smell of jasmine rises around us on the steam.

She offers no protest but no help, either. Like an almost-asleep-toddler, a weary sleep-walker. And I wonder, has anyone ever done this for me? No memory, but familiar. Finally, she is stripped clean of the horror, and I take off my own soiled clothes. Together we enter the water in silence. Outside, the rain rips against the cabin, outside the mountain is washing away its own deep grief. She eases into the tub. The candlelight plays delicately over this beautiful flesh, so elegant, regal, even here, even in the midst of its sorrow.

I sit in front of her, the water rising to the lip of the tub. My glasses are useless against the steam, so I set them aside. The light shatters, the soft focus breaking over us like rain, the water droplets on the panelled walls, on her skin, all filled and echoing the light.

I breathe damply, the empty, teary feeling rushing back. This light is almost cathedral, a catholic, ceremonial gold. I lift one strong hand with my own, raise her tired arm, scrub in delicate circles, trying to ease the tense muscles, push away the pain. Over breastbone and belly, then back to the other long arm, as if we've always done this, as if she has always allowed this sacrament ... She leans against me, my breasts pillowing the hard muscles of her torso, her hair streams back, over us both, as if we are of the same flesh.

Almost neck high in the water. The sobs are easing, released into the perfumed bath, into the fragrant steam. I soap and rinse the smokey hair, let the water run in hot streams ... let my fingers untangle and stroke the knots that still carry the day's horror.

The water is cooling. I climb out, kiss her neck, her shoulders. Watch the silent tears mixing with the bath, wondering if, like the plasma that is clear, coming when a wound has been cleaned and bled, this is where the healing begins?

I hold a towel for her as she comes out, straight, strong. I dry her hair with a second. Inch by blueblack inch, this wet satin is as dark as Farquhar's ... They are of the same clan ... I wonder who will hold Farquhar? Who will wash her hair tonight? The ache that always bubbles up when I think of her, too, doesn't disappoint ... but I can't think of this. It's Darrian, now, Darrian still in danger — hasn't Farquhar made it clear?

The vanity of this sheath of hair — another tender side that makes me love her. Carefully I pull the heavy comb through, guide the way I've known so many women guide it, root to end, a long, smooth glide. She is responding, bit by bit, pulling back against my stroke, sighing with the motion ... done. I put the comb on the sink's edge, pick up the lotion I've brought.

Warming it between my palms, I sit her on the side of the tub, begin to massage her feet. Beloved feet, the toes almost as long as my littlest finger — lightly veined, sculpted, leading to movie star ankles and calves carved from hundreds of miles of climbing this mountain — then up the hollow behind the cap of the knee — higher still, the soft valley of inner thigh — her sighs deepen, rise, her hands tangling in my damp hair.

My own hot ache begins, the desire fierce, bordering obscenity I think, given the cost of the day, but undeniable.

I continue to knead the flesh, slipping and gently brushing against those lower lips, the hair in mossy ringlets, the light reflecting a kind of golden even there.

With each measured motion she breathes in quickly, harder, suddenly pressing her hands to my shoulders, forcing herself to stay open ... Her legs on either side of me as I kneel in front of her, my heart racing with each sound, each scent. Oh the power in this hunger, that it can banish (if only for the moment) such deep sorrow — the power that she allows me this entrance and embrace!

Everything is jasmine and baby oil, the wet heat making our skin prickle, our fever rise. She leans over me, those miraculous, shocking breasts, voluptuously brushing my face: my tongue flicking over each nipple, each nipple answering in instant response, dragging the moan from her, making her cry in a new way now ... It is all soft skin pressed to softer skin, roseate and dark and musky, all delicious shudder and holy violation, our moans rising, rising even as my lips and tongue go lower, drinking her, slowly, fiercely, totally, needing her, even, as she needs me, even, as outside, the mountain needs the rain.

The low drum echoes through the forest like a heart-throb. The sun laps up what remained of the snow, reducing all around to puddles and quiet drip. Other than the drum and the softer echo of the melting, the glade is hushed. Just our pounding veins and the drum's lonely call.

Seven men and seven women circling the platform — four times around in strictest silence. They halt in front of Darrian.

Darrian, Julian, Farquhar: all wearing white buckskin, their hair in braids, all of the same family — they come together, carrying the litter which bears the remains of the great ape, now free of its canvas coffin.

Even with the three of them pulling, it is a huge mass to move. Sweat on their faces, their muscles strain under the virgin leather. I step forward to help and then catch myself, instinctively moving back.

Darrian's face is impassive. She is what they think of her on Remmel Mountain and deeper. Face changed, body different, somehow taller, harder, almost carved from wood or rock.

The others wear forest colors. Sacred beadwork, obvious heirlooms, passed for centuries, the only colors that stand out. Medicine bags abound. I am the only one without a bag, the only uninitiated.

Darrian is given an eagle feather. One woman moving from the circle begins to paint sacred colors on Darrian's face: white, yellow, red, black. She then moves to Julian and Farquhar.

A rock is rolled from the mouth of the cave. In older, safer times a platform probably held the body for years. Those times are gone forever. Now, even the finest hair must be hidden ... like their lives, their spirits.

A deer-hoof rattle keeps rhythm as the body is taken inside the cave. Smoke from a smudge wafts from the mouth, carried on the cold wind. Finally, Darrian, Julian and Farquhar emerge. They do not stay to seal the opening — this is for the Deepwoods Tribe themselves. They circle back in the opposite direction from which they entered.

As she passes me I can see her face-paint is streaked by tears. I follow after, silent, four paces behind. In the forest somewhere, a flute's melancholy lament rises.

* * * * *

Darrian was gone almost a week. I was sick with dread. Farquhar told me it was the usual time she took when the Tribe called her. If she wasn't back by sunrise, the next day, we could worry.

The achy exhaustion of just waiting had beaten me. I went to her room, lighting a single candle, leaving it burning on her desk. So strange to be there without her. I have been sleeping in my own room, unwilling to violate this place with something so pedestrian as celibate slumber ... Darrian would smile at that. But now, can't face the lonely cell of my own room. Not tonight. Will just lie down on top of the comforter, drift for a while, keep watch, wait for the sun ... wait for Darrian.

"Dar —" A hand across my mouth silences my cry.

Her weight presses heavily, but such a welcome press! I can barely make out the face in the dark. Clean of all the ceremonial paint it still, somehow, carries odd shadows — but the body — her body. Even in the middle of this surprising night I would know her. Her eyes seem to be shooting green sparks charging the air around us. It isn't the candle, it's died long ago. No, this light is Darrian's — electric, a little dangerous.

She doesn't speak, not even a hello. Then, moving her palm from my lips, she replaces it with her mouth, her teeth, her tongue full of another kind of greeting. The kisses burn, almost drawing blood, so much, so much time apart ... A little scared but totally aroused, I try to tell her, to pull back and tell her how glad, how relieved, how much I want her . . .

"Show me, Nikki, just show me." Her voice is a low whisper in my ear.

Taking her handsome head between my hands, I roll out from under, flip her on the bottom, hear her breathing get faster, feel her heart pound . . . I will . . . I will . . .

"What are you doing now?" I ask, watching her as she burns bits of white sage and cedar in the small clay bowl by the head of the bed.

"A prayer," she whispers, blowing lightly, making the sparks rise in the dark around us.

"For the apes and Indians?" I ask.

"And, for us," she answers, then, turning, kisses me slow, deep and warm.

Spring.

Only in the deepest shadows of the high woods and along the peaks did the snow stay. Every day Julian and Darrian were out longer. Some days I'd go with them to the caves, taking notes and sketching the apes, a few times even filming them.

The patience with which Darrian made us carry out each minute detail infuriated me. Julian had the natural touch, if not the technical training; Darrian and Farquhar held both. I was learning fast, as much as I could. But there was an odd sense that Darrian was pushing harder than she needed to. Given the time she said we had it didn't seem that she should be so insistent. I could feel wordless underpinnings of worry, but I let them go. In her time ... always ... in her time. My vow.

* * * * *

Three nights in earliest spring there had been someone at the back door.

Three nights in a row Darrian would tell me to go back to sleep, then dress hurriedly, only to return the next morning. When she left I'd leave her bed, go back to my own room. Without her in it, her bed was the loneliest place I knew.

At breakfast nothing was ever said about the rendezvous, but she and Julian would exchange a few glances, then, just up and be off again.

Farquhar wasn't worried. If it was anything serious, we would know — so she said. And so I took her at her word, not wanting to press her anymore than the other two — maybe less. We still hadn't talked about my relationship with Darrian. Where could I even start? Of course she knew, had almost orchestrated it, almost ordered it — or did I just feel that way because it was easier than confronting the possibility that every night that I slept beside Darrian, Farquhar was alone, knowing, torn up inside? Once I'd tried to talk to Darrian, herself, but she became like the mountain — hard, cold, silent. It was the second night of the visitors at the back door. When she returned, it was as if I'd never said a word. Again, someday, in her time. Meanwhile, I was always watching, waiting for a moment of opening with Farquhar, knowing that it would never be resolved between her and Darrian (given the way Darrian treated me when I just brought up the possibility of discussion) but perhaps it could be resolved between Farquhar and me.

She still treated me like a little sister — outwardly there was nothing different. She still was the only one who could calm Darrian when Darrian blew — but behind those doe-eyes and that dancer's grace was a sadness as deep as the cavern pools.

I tried to lose the worry in work: records, catalogues, letters responding to individuals and organizations (so weird to think that I was once one of those letters!), sometimes even minor repairs around camp.

I drew up plans for an herb garden beyond the back porch. I'd repair sleeping bags, clean the lamps, cut wood, all without probing. I'd learned, by now, when to shut up — I'd learned a lot.

Late April.

My first official spring on the mountain. The apes had deserted their winter caves. Blossoming trees and small shrubs were their new delicacies. But delicacies were dangerous as the earliest blooming plants were below the sub-alpine zone. Darrian and Julian were working full time to herd the apes, with the help of the Tribe, back to higher ground. Not an easy task. At least there were no hunters. After the news had hit the wires about the ape murder in winter, a wellspring of new support had come rushing in. People willing to wait for as long as it took for Darrian to talk, people willing to give us a little more time, willing to stay away, off the mountain . . . for a while.

* * * * *

Twice a month I was hiking down with Farquhar to the Ranger Station to pick up the mail and supplies. It was an overnight hike with a stop at her lower cabin.

The first trek back was so strange. Almost like waking from a wonderful dream to find that the reality around you was an ugly set in a run-down theater. As we got lower and lower we began to come upon broken beer bottles, chunks of blackened, melted tinfoil, used diapers coughed back to the surface from the spring melt, pieces of abandoned cars, old firespots, cigarette butts and cans. The sounds of power saws, chains and tractors made me nauseous. The smell of diesel fuel and gas filled the air, masking any flower scents or green smells we took for granted higher up.

Something drastic had happened to me during the winter. I didn't want to be down from camp — down with these other people, the humans making garbage and destroying whatever they touched, wherever they walked. A new awakening in my vision . . . or maybe, a lot of old, hidden guilt.

Even the letters from friends, when they finally arrived, held no pull — same with my family's erratic communiques. I was glad for the distance. They had no idea how far I'd come.

Farquhar kept reminding me to keep perspective. "You're like a newly recovering drunk, Nikki. You can't preach to these people. Our 'purity' comes mostly from necessity. The necessity of our own survival up there, and the necessity of our vision. Any one of us could revert back to lowland ways — even Darrian. Nobody is that pure, Nikki, nobody."

Remembering her words was going to be as hard as first believing them.

My blood family had gone through their expected phases of fear of my being "in the woods." Fear which mellowed to fury and then to plain old anger. This, in turn, changed to pride because I was "working with someone famous," but that also metamorphosized — into a simple resentment. I was too far from their grasp, uncontrollable now, in a big way — and I'd let them all down for "generations to come" by not finishing the year at Smith. Somehow, Cornell had contacted them — after the press went out about the ape murder. I'd considered Cornell as a place to hang out while I decided if grad school could, indeed, be withstood. A letter of inquiry was the extent of it — but they had seized the day and now were hot on my heels — because of Darrian. For me, all of this was simply a distant smile.

Then, the Rangers — my old friends — they'd been reassigned. Desk jobs in Tacoma, rumor had it. Seemed to me like excellent placement.

When we got the mail we never stopped long enough to sort through it, only repacked it and got our supplies. Nerve-wracking down there, wanted only to get back up as fast as we could.

The occasional shocked look of a tourist when I'd pass by told me that I was looking more and more like the others — for this, I was quite gleeful. My grown out, semi-curly hair — which Farquhar always complained was ridiculous — I made her braid. By the time we got down I looked like a hedgehog with a bad perm. In my mind's eye, however, my hair was long and straight and sleek as Darrian's or Farquhar's own. No, I wasn't an Indian, not by a long shot. But I would give anything to become one — anything.

Mid-May.

The news first arrived in mid-May. The mail sack seemed pretty light, but the last run had been especially heavy so I thought it was just a levelling off. We decided to walk all the way back because it was a full-moon night and the weather was like a warm bath. The shadows lapped against us, almost lulling us to sleep as we walked home.

Farquhar broke our easy quiet. "I've got a funny feeling about this mail."

A mule deer snorted in its sleep not far from our path. I was in front. Not wanting to break stride, I just talked over my shoulder, still walking: "What do you mean?"

"Nothing clear ... just a feeling. Maybe we should look through it before we bring it up." Farquhar was half-kidding but also sounding nervous, which I didn't like.

"Right! If Darrian even suspected that we edited her mail you know she'd kill us!" I hoped I sounded lighter than I felt. It was always so eerie when Farquhar "knew" things before the rest of us.

"No, she wouldn't kill, no one left to laugh at her bad primate jokes." Farquhar kicked a pebble at my butt.

"Or do shit slides!" I added.

"Damned right. I can't see Julian stooping to do menial lab labor, can you?"

"You think Darrian would tell us if she was expecting anything serious?" I stopped for a minute, listening to the nightcall of an owl.

"Nikki, she's pretty straight about those things. Sometimes it's like trying to read a brick wall, I know, but believe it or not, she is so much better about it these days. You've done well, little sister."

A lump in the throat at her words — so warm, generous to me when she didn't have to be. It wasn't my doing, Darrian was changing on her own, sharing even more than she did with Julian and Farquhar when I first arrived . . .

A huge shadow moved in front of the moon, momentarily interrupting the light. Spooked owl, its wings silent and powerful as it glided above us.

I was glad for the dark, my cheeks still burning, my heart answering the owl, after Farquhar's words.

The cabin was asleep when we finally arrived. Careful on the noisy floorboards, I put the mailsack outside the bathroom, too tired to empty it on the table. I knew Darrian would find it first thing. Farquhar blew me a coy goodnight kiss. I stifled a giggle. Our return would be a nice surprise to them in the morning.

As I peeled off my steamy hiking boots I thought of Farquhar's cryptic feelings on the way to camp. But even that mite of doubt biting at the edge of my mind couldn't keep me up. I fell into a bone-weary sleep.

* * * * *

In the morning it was Julian's face that told us
the news wasn't good. I joined them for breakfast,
tea already on the table.

"Hi! I missed you!" I sat next to Darrian, giving
her knee a quick squeeze under the table.

"Morning." She smiled back, a little lopsidedly.

I stared back. The small reading glasses perched
on the end of her nose, the eyebrows gone back to a
tight squint — she seemed to be ignoring me.

"I'm glad you both came back last night. It's good
you did." She put the letter she'd been holding on
her plate.

"What's up?" I reached for toast.

"They want to call a meeting." Julian was gazing
out the sun-clad window.

"A bloody symposium!" Darrian growled.

"Who, where?" It sounded a lot less ominous than
anything I'd been imagining. I spread jam in a large,
violet smear across the bread.

"*Geographic, Time, Newsweek,* The Bellingham
Foundation ... and a few of our illustrious sponsors.
They want to invite all the major press and a
roundtable of wildlife ecologists." Darrian dropped
her hands into her lap and lowered her head.

"I don't get it. It sounds, well, really good!" I
looked around the table at the three of them.

"Sounds like shit," mumbled Julian.

"Nikki, they're pulling all of us, all the working
heads of these facilities, away from our field projects
and into bloody classrooms! What will happen during
that week when the news hits the media that we're
all away?" Darrian's eyes shot green sparks.

153

"On the bright side," Farquhar offered, "maybe with all the rest of us staying at Remmel while you're gone you can use the time to blow them out of the water, and not be worried about camp. Nikki's here now, the Indians are close, I mean, if it was just Julian and me we wouldn't be able to cope with anything major, but we aren't alone, Darrian. Besides, the other field scientists will be with you. You know the old saying, 'many voices.'" Farquhar winked at me.

"Ah, yes, 'make mighty music' ... I remember. Still sounds like bull to me. I don't have the time to go! The woods will be crawling with hikers, campers, boy scouts ..."

"Don't be sexist!" Julian finally breaks a smile.

"Girl scouts, then. I have to be *here*. The loggers are only twenty miles from the lowest cave. It's also becoming painfully apparent that the food supply is late this year ... the apes are wandering lower and lower." Darrian poured another cup of tea.

"Acid raid, insect spraying, fire retardants in August last year ... But we knew, Darrian, we knew it was coming, a cumulative effect, no surprise." Farquhar reached over, her hand circling Darrian's larger hand, even as she held her cup.

"It's just that we aren't in position to move yet. I thought we'd have more time." Darrian shook her head.

I dropped my toast.

"Move? Where? When? Why?"

"Master plan." Julian said, quietly.

"I was going to tell you, Nikki, there just hasn't been the right moment. I had to know I, we, could pull it off. It's been in the preparation stages for quite a while. Another winter like this last one and the apes won't recover. Final spring count is one dead and six unaccounted for ... we know what that means. No females pregnant. The apes won't reproduce under stress. Anything, low food supply, snowmobiles in the forest, anything can affect the birth cycles. Fish and moss get them through the coldest months but they need seeds, berries, flowers and roots. We just haven't had enough time or qualified help to begin to study substitutes to supplement their diet ... nor do we want to especially take that track. Once we turn the corner there is no turning back. I need more time! They need more time!"

"I don't know what you want to do?"

"Move them," Julian answered.

"Where?"

"Higher. Maybe Canada, maybe all the way to Alaska, even more inland, if we have to, better suited land, less access, we're too close to the coast, too many people moving west, Nikki. We aren't, just yet, entirely sure." Darrian ran her fingers through her hair.

"What about the governments? Will they allow you to just cross the border like that?" I had visions of Mounties tracking us over the tundra. I thought of Chief Joseph's own sad trek to save the Nez Perces.

"No one has to know. We're close enough to the border and I have my personal permits for research purposes. Anyway, we'll just leave camp set up here. I can stay and make them believe nothing's going on. Give the Indians a good nine months to see if they can establish three family groups farther inland,

and then ..." Darrian was excited, her eyes sparkling, the idea of action fueling her.

"And then we make choices." Julian stood up, walked to the door, left.

"What's he upset about? What choices, Darrian?"

"To follow the Tribe or go back down the mountain." Darrian didn't look at me. The circles under her eyes matched the weariness of her voice. Both had become permanent fixtures. She was losing weight again. I'd noticed it for weeks, but now it was showing dramatically. Her cheeks were lined, hollow. For the first time since I'd arrived on Remmel, Darrian Stone looked old.

"It's easy, we follow the apes!" Farquhar was trying to be bright, but it fell flat.

"Yeah, of course, we just follow the apes." I tried to echo the attempt, puzzled, though, because it seemed a simple solution.

"No, Nikki, you don't understand. This time it won't be to establish another camp. If we go after the apes, with the Tribe, there will be no coming back, not ever." Darrian stared at the floating tea leaves in her cup, maybe trying to read an escape route there.

"That's crazy! The whole planet would be out looking for you, Darrian! You know what those reporters said — it would mean more press, more hunters, more Rangers in the forest. It would be worse for the woods and the animals than if we just toughed it out here."

I looked from Darrian to Farquhar. Neither would meet my gaze.

The panic had already risen, thoughts of elephants fenced into compounds in Africa, all in the name of conversation, now like fish in a huge barrel for the poachers they still fell prey to. Or Dian Fossey's beloved gorillas in Rwanda — how much better were they now as they contracted measles and pneumonia from tourists? It could go either way. It just seemed that whenever people got on the bandwagon with the animals, whatever the side, the animals were ultimately the losers. People with condors, hunters, people with black rhinos, with grizzly bears first fed in Yellowstone, then retaught natural ways, only to be fed by campers and now being herded out of Yellowstone for good, maybe — it never worked. When people got involved it never meant simply letting the animals alone. Ultimately confinement, call it management, call it conservation, no matter how large you made the cage, it was still a prison. Maybe, oh Jesus, what if Darrian was dead-on right? What would I do — forever?

"We'd let people know we were on expedition, keep sending back updates to assuage curiosity or concern, but slowly, we'd taper off, pull back farther. In three or four years we could get deep enough that there would be hardly any chance of people finding us, even if they tried. Especially if the caverns continue north, the way the Indians suspect. By then, the species could recover enough that we might come back, if we had to ... if we wanted to." Darrian finally looked at me, a slow, funny smile playing across her face.

"Sounds like a decision, not a plan anymore." Surprisingly, Farquhar pushed back from the table, angry.

"Wait, Farquhar, please, sit. Hold on. Both of you, just wait. Farquhar, you are my ... my right hand, you know that. Nothing has been finalized. Julian and I have just been checking the forest for our options. You and Nikki, you have ... different choices to make. Farquhar, my dear woman, we've come so far ... I have no reservations if you and Nikki or you alone want to stay here, run base camp, deal with the outside. With all the information we've accumulated these past years at least three books could, should be written — articles, interviews, lectures, public debates, a foundation, a formal body, finally established, independent, in our name. Of course you'd always know where we were. I'm not asking you to leave everyone you've ever known or loved and come off with me — nor you, Nikki, either. You've already given me perhaps too much ... your lives. I've never known what to do about that. Now, well, I can't go down. To be relegated to a simple tour guide or worse, a college professor, well, I'd rather be shot. If it comes to that then I will go off, like an old ape. Julian, too, has opted for that choice. Farquhar, Nikki, you have to make your own decisions." Darrian's voice had gentled, as if she were talking to her children. Maybe that's what we were.

"Dammit, Stone!" Farquhar's face darkened. "You *have* made a decision — for all of us! You're going native — bushy — that's what they'll finally say! And us, running Remmel or any goddamned foundation below without you — it's all the same! You taught me the only thing that matters is saving the lives of these animals and the people who have always protected them — it was our part of the planet, our contribution, you said. I believed you, Darrian! I've loved you so fucking hard all these

158

years because of it! Now you're going to walk out, talking all this mystic in the woods crap. You aren't Indian, Darrian, no matter what you learn or how hard you try — you will always be the white woman playing shaman! This is as much pure shit as the movies hand us! Or your own history books! There are other ways, ways we can stay together, keep this place together, protect the animals and be together. No reason anything has to change! You say I have a vote, a decision of my own, but without you, Darrian Stone, what decision is left for me? What is it? You want them to remember you as this great, white holy woman? Gone off in the mountains to die with her apes? You want them to make a fucking TV special out of your life?" Farquhar's voice was a ragged whisper, her face held pure hate — almost purple in this rage that had come from seemingly nowhere. I was terrified.

Then, I saw the effect on Darrian.

Darrian moved back from the table as if she were seventy. Her face was soft, but incredibly tired, so, so sad. She came to Farquhar, her arms outstretched to the younger woman.

"Please," Darrian called, the most direct invitation she'd ever uttered.

Farquhar, her lips quivering, her hands curled into ready fists, fighting the volcano that had just erupted, the locked away emotion of years back, years when she had first declared her love for this woman, years when Darrian had been too frightened of what their life together would cost Farquhar — family, another life, being seen ever through the screen of Darrian Stone, the racist shit they'd have to endure — so much lost heart in the center of

159

that confusion, and always, always Farquhar lived knowing that Darrian did love her and never would it be consummated. Now, it came clear to me in her fury and hell-fire response that as close as Darrian could let her come, this might be taken back, too.

"Please." Darrian's voice was barely a whisper, the tears spilling on her face.

Farquhar hesitated, and then, in a single, sudden breath, she folded directly into the center of those strong arms, sobbing out the feelings of betrayal, of fear, of absolute love.

"Ssh, I know, I know ... Every day, my darling friend, I live with it, too. Maybe, maybe you are right. Maybe there's another answer. Shh, shh. I'll go — the symposium — pick their brains, okay, maybe pick their pockets ... Shhh now, Farquhar, oh sweet one, shh." Darrian held her close, deep inside, burying the slim woman against herself.

Christ, how could I witness this? Fuck the world that kept them from each other. I wasn't even a substitute — no, this went way past that. And maybe I was privileged to see it. This connection was like nothing I'd ever seen or could possibly know. Separate, so separate from the one I held with Darrian. Why there was no jealousy from Farquhar, why they both could go on with each other — this was the world I wanted, shared with these kinds of people. Wherever they would be, that was where I must go — my real Tribe. I stood in silent testimony, watching, watching.

"Promise me, you old goat, promise you won't go off and leave us, won't sneak off without us!" Farquhar, sniffing, coughing a bit, pulled back to look directly into Darrian's eyes.

"You ask for too much." Darrian attempted a smile.

"I don't ask for anything I'm not willing to give!" Farquhar buried her face against Darrian's shoulder, crying softly.

Darrian sighed, stroking the long, silky mane. Together the way they fit — instead of me — in a better place, but not here. Not ever here . . . the sorrow in that staggered me.

"Farquhar? All right, I . . . promise." Darrian sounded defeated.

My blood ran to ice, made me unable to move from my chair.

"Darrian . . . thank you. You'll see, we'll be all right, everything will be all right . . . When do you have to leave for the symposium?" Farquhar had regained herself, still in pieces, but mostly gathered up.

"Beginning of next week. Will you and Nikki be all right? Keep an eye on Julian while I'm away?"

"Will he be deepwoods?" I asked, my voice all trembly, too.

"During the night, but in the day he'll be here. I may be down for as long as a month. After the symposium itself a few of our sponsors want me to meet with them, give some interviews, no doubt, get their mileage while they can. There's even talk about testifying at an international hearing at Columbia on poaching. What can we say, if I go down — no excuses then. They hold our purse strings. Guess I'll have to shave my legs . . ."

The color was returning to normal in both of their faces. I felt my lungs begin to unfreeze.

Darrian's decision, after all these years on

Remmel, well, it didn't jive. There was something else, not exactly hidden, but something weighing on her that she wasn't letting us know — not yet. What Farquhar was asking for wasn't unreasonable. If I'd been brave I would have asked myself. Darrian wasn't being the meticulous, slow-moving, maddeningly careful scientist that I knew and loved — this seemed almost reactionary. Misplaced.

The feeling of dread I'd felt carrying the mail sack was back. Either something was far worse with the apes or there was an unknown factor. Maybe I was feeling like Farquhar, finally settled, with a decent staff, positive press for the first time in eighteen months, even some new money filtering in — why move, why now? And the choice of leaving her or staying was moot. Like Farquhar, I would follow Darrian Stone to hell and back before leaving this mountain without her. In this sense, then, Farquhar was *exactly* right: the decision, indeed, had already been made.

I despised goodbyes, especially shaky ones. So, when Julian said he wanted to walk Darrian down, I offered no argument.

"Stop it, please!" Darrian turned from the tiny bedroom mirror and took my arm.

"What?" I pleaded innocence.

"I know what you're thinking." She smiled, the light in her look like dappled sun in the meadow above us, warm, inviting.

"I'm not ... thinking anything! Just that I like

the way you look in tight levis. Make sure you buy a few dozen more on the way back, okay?"

"Nikki, sit down here, on the bed, just for a second? Listen, I know what it's like to watch someone you love walk out of this camp. I *am* coming back, as soon as possible, and I'm coming back alone. My wish, my prayer, is that you will still be here when I return, tight jeans or not. Hey, that was supposed to be funny ... Look, the symposium, all the rest, it's been done before, remember. I'm not a neophyte, whether you see it or not — I've been around the block a few times, as they say. Every time I've done it, though, I swear it will be the last. So hard to leave Remmel — to leave you. I know you don't believe that — maybe I am to blame. I try to show you but I know how difficult I can be, too. Nikki, you're just going to have to keep trusting me, please?"

Darrian pulled me tight and kissed me, for the last time, on her bed. Whatever occurred between this kiss and her return, we would have no more intimacy. I felt like a novitiate taking my vows.

"You make me weak, sometimes," I whispered into her neck, the familiar rush flooding from heart to head and then belly.

"Good. We're even. Now, off, before the rumors start to fly!" She pushed me from the bed, towards her door.

"Darrian, you better write — a lot! I'm going down at least once a week for the mail. I mean it." I did.

"No promises. Hey, Nikki — I do love you." Then she stood up, her best workshirt tucked neatly into those new, ass-clutching jeans, her hiking boots dazzling with the gift of scarlet laces we'd ordered for her from down below. The gray in her hair had been spreading all winter — like the snow — and now it made her summer tan golden in contrast. Her hair floated lightly, around her shoulders and down her back, carried by the soft breezes flooding the room. Her room ... some nights, ours. Christ, she was the loveliest woman I knew and her leaving us made me ache. Just ache.

So they trekked off, waving back only once. We watched from the cabin till they were out of sight — Darrian a full head taller than the older Indian, but both so straight and strong under their packs.

Farquhar gave me a shoulder squeeze, then laughed. I thumped her on the back. Like adolescent boys after a winning game, we weren't quite sure what to do with all of this emotion. Had to admit, though, some relief was there, coming from the fact that our beloved Dr. Stone was headed *down* the mountain — and not in the opposite direction.

Three weeks and finally we hear something. The agonizing wait is broken by the static-loving radio. She'd made it out just fine ...

Letters followed irregularly, as if she didn't want to put anything on paper — or even call for fear of being misunderstood — more darkly, intercepted.

Farquhar explained I wasn't being paranoid in realizing this. The caution was real, but I didn't like it.

Darrian's leaving became a time of clarification, for me at least, a time of digesting the belief that I truly was one of them, not a visitor who didn't know the length of her visa. One of "them" — more than a "couple" — that was another piece to accept. No, this meant that I was part of their facility, the honest mountain research, but also, in a strange, at-the-edges way, part of the Deepwoods people, too. Maybe most of all, part of the forest. Wild. Like my parents' worst nightmare.

Each day I woke with the clarity of our cause. That, and the hunger for Darrian's return.

Fifth week; a late call on the radio. Darrian's voice breaks mid-sentence.

"What? I can't understand, please repeat, over," I transmit back, Julian and Farquhar standing over the crackling set, equally confused by the garbage we're receiving.

"... another three weeks here ... will be back .. . over." Darrian's signal is feeble at best and she's speaking softly, as if she doesn't want anyone else to hear or to wake anyone up.

"Try again, please. What about three weeks, what do you want us to do in three weeks? Over." I understood exactly what she was saying but I wasn't going to accept it without confirmation. My heart fell into my boots.

"Nikki, I have to stay ... three more weeks ... Part of ... in July ... can't speak ... will write, promise. Over." She was gone.

"Understood. Take care. Over and out." I handed the mike to Julian. He shut us down for the night.

Fourth of July. Completely slipped my mind till the gunfire hit the cabin.

I fall from the couch, fall out of an afternoon nap onto the floor. Too scared to scream, besides, don't want Farquhar rushing in and running straight into a bullet. She's on the back porch, her headphones on tight, listening to music.

Inch my way, belly down, iguana-style, my heart's chugging as slivers from the floorboards pierce my elbows and knees.

Second round. Hits the front screen-door, careening through as if it was cardboard, six or seven bullets lodging in volumes in the bookcase ... Keep crawling ... Ammo's large enough to do serious damage ... Jesus, where is Julian? I scramble, deranged snake, hissing for Farquhar as I hit the back porch, hissing because I can't unclench my jaw. Then, from outside, loud laughter, drunken men's voices.

Farquhar catches me on the floor out of the corner of her eye, her face positively astonished.

"Get down!" I finally manage to scream.

Through the blaring music, she understands, slams to the floor in one fluid drop. Through the lost headphones I can hear the moody strains of Beethoven, even as another round comes zinging over our heads. The sick sound of splintering wood and shattered glass galvanizes us into action.

"The guns! Nikki, the closet!"

I roll out, into a crouch in the hallway, make my way down. She's two steps behind.

We make it to the closet where the gear is stored. I pull out the shotgun Darrian used to kill the snowmobile. I hand Farquhar one of the .22's. Darrian won't allow any of the rifles to be stored while loaded, so we know they're empty. Ah, but my father's long ago lessons, his thwarted attempts to teach me how to shoot deer, they suddenly spring into the forefront of my memory — amazing what fear will do. I load them.

We shimmy into the front room. There's a lull. Then, like a wet hand grenade, a foaming beer can hits the smashed screen door. The suds spray us down, sick spit, then followed by two more. Possibly "the enemy" had run out of ammunition.

I pray, please God, no more bullets. We move to either side of the front door. Through the splintered frame I can see men ... three. Maybe twenty, thirty years old, scraggy, obviously plastered.

Their rifles are propped against a lodgepole pine, two feet from where they're still guzzling brew. Doesn't seem likely that anyone is hiding in the bushes, not with this crew. Farquhar signals. We stand in unison, then I kick open the door, she still hidden behind me, off to one side. I can feel the barrel of her gun directly aimed at the men. I wonder what kind of shot she is. Maybe if they don't see both of us we can bluff our way out. Machismo is our worst enemy.

"Don't any of you filthy bastards move!" I try to sound pissed off in the middle of my terror.

"Oh my, Lordy, what have we here? One of the little dykes on the hill? Did we wake you, missy? So sorry, we just came up to invite you gals to a real celebration. Heard the big bull-dagger's out of town for a while and you might be lonely. Soooo we invited ourselves up! Not too much for you to do with that Red Faggot, is there? We saw you come into the Rangers' Station last week, bet you don't remember, right? Couldn't give us the right time of day. Well, I bet you're going to give us a whole lot more now, huh? Stuck up cunt! Tell your Apple girlfriend to come on out! She sure don't look like a squaw!" The oldest guy leers, taking a step closer.

I don't see Farquhar fire, only hear the shot. A fountain of blood spurts out of the drunk's sneaker where his big toe should have been. Then, his screams. Something inside of me wants to shut him up — permanently. Even raise the cocked shotgun. This snaps him sober. Gives up on his toe. The two buddies stop laughing long enough to notice I'm aiming at them. Didn't even give warning.

Through a mist of scarlet, feeling my blood move like steam in my veins, I pull back and let the first barrel fly. It's followed by the second.

The three guns propped against the pine are no more! The explosion of stocks, the screaming men; each sweeter than Farquhar's abandoned Beethoven.

They flee, hobbling, cursing, crashing through the scorched underbrush. Gone.

I drop the now empty gun in the dirt and sit down, hard.

Farquhar walks out quietly. The twenty-two is crooked careful as a newborn in her arm.

"Scum suckers. I should have aimed higher!" She spits.

"Maybe," I agree, weakly," May-beeee."

"Think they'll come back?" She sits beside me. Around us the birds still haven't recovered but the insects begin their sizzling whir and chirp.

"Not today. But there's going to be hell to pay. We better radio down ... to the Sheriff." I get up, my knees shaking as if I'm on a deck out in a storm.

"What about calling Darrian?"

"No, Farquhar! Nothing — not a single word. Wait until she calls us, please! Maybe, maybe that way she won't have to come back early, won't have to cancel the rest of the trip. If she does that and then has to rearrange another trek down she won't be able to do it! No, I think, maybe, maybe we're okay if we just take care of it ourselves. All right?"

Farquhar squints at me long and hard. She takes a step towards me. With her fingertips she wipes away the blood from my bitten lower lip.

"I think we better find Julian," she says.

"Julian's found." He moves from behind the big spruce, moves with four other Deepwoods Indians, each well-armed.

"Guess you didn't need us, huh?" Julian's face is drawn tight.

"Right." I run to him, so fucking relieved, hug him briefly, elated he's back — feels like the "grown-ups" have finally arrived.

169

"Nikki, you know we have to tell Darrian." He doesn't meet my smile, keeps glancing beyond me, off into the woods.

"Maybe those guys were all bluff — just the liquor talking? If they try to say we shot first we've got the evidence ... they won't risk it. Let's wait." Something inside me wasn't ready for Darrian's return; wanted her as far away as possible right now.

"No, Nikki. I got to pull rank. Sorry. Anyway, those guys know other guys and they all got rifles. Maybe not for us, in camp, but for the apes. Or maybe they'll climb up to the Indian camps. They been waiting all winter for a chance like this and they ain't going to stop."

We move into the cabin, begin to pick up the pieces. The Indians take off back to their own camp, nervous about what Julian's pointed out. The three of us work in silence. Finally, Farquhar sits down on the couch, a strange look in her eyes.

"Julian, what if Nikki's right? Darrian is trying to raise the money we need. If she comes back before she keeps her commitments and then our funding gets pulled, well, it will be as if someone's shot the apes! Maybe we can hold it together a little bit longer."

"Nikki, Farquhar, you really think Darrian ain't already going to know?" Julian shakes his head in disbelief.

I put my hammer on the floor, spit out the nails I've held by my teeth. "What?"

"Hey, Nikki, Darrian *is* this mountain. She don't have to be here to know what's going on." Julian moves toward the still-broken door.

"Come on, Julian!" What was this crap? Really almost shocking, coming from him.

"We wait till nightfall, that's it — fair?" He looks first at Farquhar, then back to me. Waits for us to respond.

Farquhar sighs, nods — a signal for me to give it up, to give in.

At least for now.

I nod: yes.

Of course, Julian won. Darrian radioed us — late.

We were up, waiting. Julian was also waiting for the men to return — Farquhar settling for listening for the Sheriff.

Julian told me to pick it up.

"Tell me what's happening! Over." Darrian's voice was past strained.

"How did you know? Over." I was incredulous.

"A call. Rangers. The Sheriff. Someone shot at Remmel. Are you all right? All of you? Over." The radio was flat sounding, mechanical.

"Yes. Just some drunk fools. Farquhar shot one of them in the toe. Over."

"Good for her! Over." Darrian seemed to gain strength with the news.

"That's what I said. But what's the word from the Sheriff to you? Over." I was anxious — they could, technically, call us all down for questioning.

"Tomorrow. Early. Full investigation — on our behalf — that's what they're saying. The man shot is a developer's son. There's going to be some hassle, but I believe the evidence will support your story. Over." Darrian was slipping away.

"Darrian! Are you coming back? Over." I didn't want to sound desperate, but like a homesick kid, I wanted her back.

"Sorry. Truly. Intended to call earlier ... messy hang-ups ... paperwork ... Looks ... another four weeks ... Don't worry ... I'll be ... close. Hang on ... I'm raising hell to get ... more protection This ... breaking up on me here ... I .. ." Her voice faded like a ghost.

"Darrian? Darrian? Over." I hollered into the mike.

"She's lost, Nikki." Julian switched it off.

"No! The signal might come back! Why can't we call her? Why's she so cool about this? What if they do go up for the apes now, if they hear she's going to be away another whole month? They know how many of us are up here — they know and won't listen to us without her!" Hard to breathe, panic coming in like a fist to my gut.

"Easy, easy. Hey — I forgot — this is your first summer, isn't it?" Farquhar is there, touching my temples with her firm fingertips, then my cheeks with the backs of her hands. Farquhar of the instantaneous medicine ... I calm down. My mind quiets, even though my heart is still thudding.

"This isn't the first time we've been harassed. The Sheriff will most likely come up in the morning, take lots of notes, maybe, because it's the first time anyone has shot into the cabin, take a few wood chip samples, measure trajectories, check our guns. The drunks will get tickets — fines — no jail. Maybe the Sheriff will beef up our perimeter for a while, maybe not. The Rangers will be alerted, for what it's worth. Darrian knows this routine, Nikki, most likely she's been talking for hours. Julian was right — I shouldn't have doubted — like always, she knows what's been going on here, no surprise. If there was a real threat, she'd be on the first plane back — honest Injun." Farquhar held up her right hand.

I didn't feel so sure.

"Let's just wait. And see." Julian raised his eyebrows.

"Fine with me." Farquhar waited for me to answer.

"Fine." I said it but it didn't feel fine at all.

Less than an hour and the Sheriff was finished. Most of that was spent drinking coffee that Julian had burned — on purpose.

I gave a statement and then sulked in the lab until they left. Farquhar's knock broke some of my gloom.

"It's over?" Didn't even raise my eyes from the microscope. Shit seemed the perfect occupation for the day.

"For now. Not fun, is it?" She sat across the lab table, twiddling an eye-dropper. I used the eye-dropper to prepare slides for mounting.

"What isn't?" This time I pushed the microscope aside.

"Being treated like an Indian." She was playing with a single droplet of water stuck in the tubing, kept moving the drop up and down, seemingly mesmerized by the inane activity.

I watched, wondering what she was thinking. Harder these days to read her, as if there was so much already riding along our surfaces that there was no time for the old ways of being ... maybe. Her hair was in a long pony-tail. It had grown very long through the winter, now was almost to her lower back. When the light hit it just right, shimmers of blue-black would flash, fast as a raven's wing. The light blue of her faded shirt made the copper tones in her face look as if she were burnished. How rare to know someone with such grace, so intensely controlled, but never fake — no, Farquhar had always been real, frighteningly real sometimes. She made me feel like there was so much more I was supposed to do, made me push — not directly, the way Darrian did, her expectations and lessons were obvious. Farquhar's were deeply different. With her I almost always had to go away for a while and think about what had gone down — why I'd done what I'd done. The lessons came, with Farquhar, after the deeds. With Darrian, it was before. Why? Where was she taking me, now?

"Since I was a little girl, Nikki, I've been cursed at, threatened, roughed up, a few times even shot at ... it isn't fun." She dropped the glass and rubber tool, looking deeply into me. I could feel her stare like a touch.

"I'm sorry." White liberal guilt raises its myopic head. What the hell can I say? Of course I knew this.

"I don't want you to be sorry — just want you to

know how it is with us. Makah, Creek, Quinault, Hopi — doesn't matter. We all grew up around white boys with guns. Someday, maybe you'll understand, even more than today ... understand why it's the way it is between Darrian and me. That's all." Then, just as offhandedly as she'd come in, she got up from the lab chair and quietly left, left me open-mouthed, face burning, wanting to cry. I loved her, almost like I loved Darrian. Fiercely. In the end, though, could I even be sure she liked me? Was there already too much to pass by? Jesus, when was there going to be an easier time?

September.
The rains began in earnest, the nights cooled and misty. Apes were beginning to sleep in the caves again. Summer was almost lost.

Farquhar's cry came above the storm's roar. I bolted into the cabin from the lab, stopping only long enough to check to see that the shotgun was loaded — we'd been keeping it by the back door, as of late. Again, her cry. The gun was ready. I moved cautiously across the front room, prepared to fire straight through the fucking door this time if she was in danger.

As I looked through the window a bolt of lightning lit the front of the cabin. There, coming up the path, the storm only serving as backdrop, was Darrian!

Farquhar met her in the mud, half lifting the taller woman off the ground in an enormous hug. Another crack of lightning, this time showing off Darrian's ecstatic face. The smile was wide, thirsty for home ... but there was more. She'd grown almost gaunt since that long ago spring when she'd left us.

Trying to shush my unquiet heart, still the hammering to a slower pace, wipe away the tears. Shock, its steady hum like a high-power line in my head, surprise that she hadn't warned us, all crowding in, begging for my attention. Push everything past the fact that she was home. Home!

I waited a few moments, knowing that even in the middle of Farquhar's embrace Darrian was glancing over her shoulder. The rain pelted over them. I waited still, in the shadows of the porch, between the lightning flashes. As close as they were there was a bridge only I could cross ... Finally, it seemed right ... finally, it was my turn to welcome Darrian home.

"God, it's good you're back!" I kiss her on the cheek, shy, then fall right into the hunger of her emerald eyes. Only for a second, maybe the lightning ... a speck, a flash, something different in her face, then it's gone. Can't read it in the raggedy light. Too fast, I know her well enough to know it won't be back. She squeezes my hands, turns back to Farquhar, we three move up toward the cabin like some monstrous bug.

On the porch steps I notice Darrian leaning on

177

Farquhar as she climbs. Okay, the trip up must have been brutal, especially after a summer spent indoors ... not exactly the rigors of Remmel. Just give her time, for Christ's sake, nothing to worry about, hadn't she given me that much every chance I asked?

"The thought of quietly sneaking up on you all seemed so delicious ... couldn't resist the surprise. I must say, you two look very, very well. From some of Nikki's letters I thought I might find skeletons in an abandoned camp." Darrian winks.

"Never abandoned!" Farquhar links her arm through Darrian's on the final step. Again, the minute limp, the slowness she hadn't left with ... and her hair! Almost as silver as the lightning! Clearly the summer has been hard, on and off the mountain.

"So, where's that old Indian hiding?" Darrian's roar fills our cabin.

Julian poured tea all around as we sat in front of the fire. He'd been off all day counting family groups in the uppermost caves. Three more animals lost. The news was very bad ... this time, he found the bodies. It was no natural death taking them.

Darrian's face was like a piece of flint in the firelight. No tears — a different exhaustion had crept into her eyes.

"I always expect fall casualties, lousy deer hunters with shit for aim, but not this early. Nikki was right, it's been a horrible season."

"Darrian, it's all the new logging roads — they

keep increasing access into the deep woods."
Farquhar held Darrian's hand, almost as if Darrian
would get up and walk away from us for good if she
wasn't held down.

Julian took a deep swig of tea. "Some of our
lower signs get knocked off in construction, the
damned bastards don't bother to put them back up."
He wiped his lower lip with the back of a calloused
hand. Tonight he looked younger, and angrier, than
Darrian.

Darrian stood up, stretched, got another log and
threw it onto the already blazing fire. I couldn't take
my eyes off her. My obvious stare must have been
as mildly annoying as Farquhar's constant touch.
Darrian put up with both of them.

"We'll discuss the details tomorrow. I want to go
over all of your reports, the daily log, everything.
Tell you the news from below. Let's say, for tonight,
next year's funding comes with many new strings
attached. My new found notoriety has made quite a
difference, but I'm not convinced it's in the best
interests of the apes. Tonight I just want to be here
with you ... be back home. So, then, a toast: to a
team of outstanding researchers, my beloved family!"
Darrian picked up her tea mug.

"To us!" Farquhar laughed.

"To all Indians and apes." Julian's smile was just
a wee bit sad.

"Amen," Darrian added, "amen."

Julian and Farquhar have left us alone, out on
the back porch, listening to the rain as it rides down

the cordillera. Just beyond, owls call, diving for mice. A misted moon rises over the Douglas firs, sending shadows all the way back to the porch.

"Long fingers," Darrian muses, rocking in an old chair.

"Friendly, they're glad you're back," I whisper, reaching over to touch her knee, our old comfort and spark rekindling.

"I can feel it. You know, it's funny, I don't think I've consciously thought about it in this way before, but it occurs to me, this will be my home, Nikki . . . From now on . . . this is it." Darrian's voice is resolved as the night beyond the shadows.

"What do you mean?"

"I'm not going down there again, not ever . . . Except if they drag me in a pine box."

"Dammit Darrian! You just got home — don't talk like that!" I get out of my chair, come behind her, my hands beginning to knead the muscles of her shoulders and neck. I'll rub out any of that lowland thought — move the results of bad air and poor people right out of her body with my own two hands.

"Darrian, it's only natural to think like this, you've been running on empty down there all summer — alone." A chill was creeping in on the moonlight. I fight down a shiver.

"Don't panic, my histrionic friend! I simply mean I'm not willing to run a dog and pony show. I won't be humiliated like that again, not ever, not for any sum. They ruin us, Nikki. They get us crazy, thinking they can dictate terms, remove us from our research areas. Even Goodall, maybe the best of us with the public and the press, they even hurt her.

I'm not Jane. I'm only ... me. A poor actress, indeed. No, no more singing and dancing. We'll find another way. A few sources I've been reluctant to tap — their money is needed in lots of places — friends in southern California, on the East Coast ... I don't know just yet ... possibilities. I do know, however, that I won't be going back down." Darrian closes her eyes as I work my fingers more deeply into the tight muscles of her shoulders.

My voice can't conceal it anymore, even in the midst of money talk, uncertain futures, even in the middle of bad politics and maximum concern, the hunger rises, burns my belly, constricts my throat. I drop my hands, leaning over that newly silvered head, my lips brush her earlobe, whisper:

"Darrian ... come to bed."

Almost embarrassed, shy, she opens her eyes, smiling. They catch the shrouded moon, shimmer like a still pond at midnight. She takes my proffered hand, uses it to steady herself as she moves out of the chair stiffly ... giggles at the incongruity; her, the aging adventurer, all ache around the edges, allowing this rising upstart to lead her directly to her own room. As for me, she is my altar, my new sacrament, the woman I will always wait for — I am just so damned glad she's come back to us, that she's come home.

"The room is wrecked," Darrian sighs, her butt pressed tight against my stomach, the small of her back nestled against my breasts. She has lost a lot of weight, but none of her old ways.

"Not just the room, you witch!" I reach an arm over her, spooning, crazy in love.

"Aah then, just as I planned! Goodnight darling Nikki."

"Goodnight, love."

Winter came in angry, ready to take a stand. The apes were much higher, deeper. The cave Darrian had first taken me to was long since abandoned. It took us hard hiking for three weeks before we located the new caverns.

We would trek everyday. Julian stayed in camp to do repairs, call in reports, answer mail — at least that was his excuse. There was more, but I never pushed. For me, it was enough simply to have the luxury of being alone, in the forest, with Darrian.

Farquhar had been given a gift when Darrian came back: all of Darrian's field research to organize into the first book — with Farquhar's name as author. Farquhar had protested, overwhelmed by the magnitude of the gift.

"It's your work as well as mine," countered Darrian. "Your name should be on it. My God, every other researcher in America orders his or her researchers to keep their names off the primary material — there's always hard feelings, a fight. I get the one research assistant who wants to create a rift because I'm insisting she take the credit she deserves! Is there no winning? It isn't a gift, my friend, not by a long shot. This is your work — without you and your family do you think I'd even be here on Remmel?"

"Darrian ... I don't ..." Farquhar swallowed hard, trying to be decorous.

"You know, years ago, they warned me that it would be like this working with emotional women." Darrian looked at Julian.

"Don't look at me. You're as bad as any man I know." Julian chuckled.

Darrian threw a book of anatomy at him from across the room.

We all knew giving Farquhar the authorship was the signal for another turn on this walk ... but to where?

Her face had grown even more drawn since she came back to camp. As the gold of the summer faded, the dark circles were clear under each eye. The silver in her hair was bleaching to snow, almost as if she'd been struck by the lightning in the storm the night of her return. Now, her reading glasses were a constant, always on or around her neck.

She reminded me, in my weaker moments, of nothing so much as a berserk librarian, all serious bristle — then she'd catch herself and the college woman would return, coy and full of smart-ass sex. It was the rare second that the stress would truly come to the surface. Always, it was about funding and the future of the apes.

I wondered if her phenomenal resistance to all of our coughs and colds and illnesses would hold through this wild season or if she would have to begin to limit her hikes up into the high territory the way the rest of us must.

Then, someone would turn on a pressure lamp or add another log to the fire — all wrinkles would be washed away from her face — her hair would seem spun by Rapunzel — the old piss and vinegar in her voice returned — and I would pack away the worries. Darrian Stone was this mountain. Julian had told me himself ... and Julian had never lied.

The cave was smaller than the last, forcing me to duck as we entered.

Farquhar had less and less time free, what with the book, to roam with us. The lab was completely torn apart, taken over by a snowstorm of graphs, photos, notes, and forensic materials. It was a relief to get out of there each morning and up to the cool, clear timber.

We'd stopped for a sip of tea when I asked: "What made you finally decide to give the book away?"

"Are you jealous?" Darrian lowered the canteen, looked at me closely.

"Of course not! I don't even have a master's degree. This is your mountain . . . and theirs. It's her project, you were absolutely right when you said that. Still, don't you think it would get more closely reviewed and accepted if it had your name as well as hers on it?" I put my hand on her shoulder, trying to communicate beyond my words, so there would be no misunderstanding. It was Farquhar's right . . . a kind of premature legacy maybe.

Darrian's breathing was a little wheezy. The climb had been labored, the weather mushy — sleet mixed with snow. "If it was coming out today, maybe, but enough time has passed that Farquhar has built her own reputation. By the time of publication of the book she'll be fully recognized in her own right. I'm positive of that. Someone besides me, Nikki, has to . . . to push. Someday, our own foundation, perhaps. At the very least we might be able to buy a piece of the land rights. If Farquhar hustles, gets the work out, she'll have the necessary credentials, a name beyond my assistant, she'd be the natural replacement for me. It would be a much easier fight." Darrian's sudden cough was deep, dry.

I took my hand off her shoulder, patted her back, offered my canteen. "You really should be taking those vitamins you came back with. You aren't getting any younger, you know." I was sorry the minute it came out.

"Oh, and I suppose you've had nothing to do with my sudden aging, eh? You little brat! Listen, the day I can't out-swim, out-hike or out-climb you is the day you get to make geriatric jokes. Until then —" Another series of hacking coughs cut her off.

"When we get back you're going to bed. It really sounds like bronchitis, Darrian."

"Let's swim." Ignoring me, winding her hair into a long, neat braid, she started to get up and go off.

"Come on! Get serious! It's too cold, even in

here!" She made me crazy when she got like this, changing the obvious subject, pretending there wasn't pain when it was clear there was. I grabbed her arm and held on. This time, she didn't fight back.

"Maybe, this once, you're right." She sat again, letting the avalanche of white loose from its braid.

"You know, I really like your hair, the way it's changed, kind of like an emblem or something. Makes you look ... Indian." My voice caressed her, made her face grow soft, as I'd hoped it would. I was trying to learn Farquhar's medicine.

"Nikki, will you promise me something?" She stopped pulling nervous fingers through her hair, then took both of my hands into her own.

"You know I'd promise you anything." I watched the flash of forest come back into her tired eyes, almost like the night in the storm, between the lightning cracks.

"Nikki, you don't feel that I've ... taken advantage of you, do you? At any time, I mean, while you've been here?"

"What are you saying? Darrian, look, I'm sorry about the stupid joke I made. Are you upset about your hair? I really like it. I mean it. Anyway, it's got nothing to do with age, it's the stress, I've read a thousand articles at school about ..." A slow bubble of panic was beginning its insidious rise. Where was she going with this?

"Oh darling, it wasn't your joke. It's only that someday someone will ask you, they'll say I was crazy, sick, out of my mind up here — that you were used. I want to be sure I haven't been kidding myself, Nikki — or you, that's all."

Her eyes were full of pain; not since the night of the great ape's murder had I see her like this.

"No one will ever say that. And you'll be right there to prove it isn't true. Together, we'll be together, Darrian. Face off — a fair fight — just let them try. I don't give a shit what they call us — dykes — apple polishers — whatever — not even with my family. No one below has ever meant to me what you do. All my life, all my life I've been trying, trying to understand what I was longing for, I didn't know how to get rid of those huge empty places. No one ... no one ... All my life I've been frozen, I never knew it, whatever Spirit there is, that Spirit led me to you, let me see you, really see you and recognize you and finally come to you. I was the one who came looking — all you did was take a chance, you let me in. My mentor, my teacher — but you are also my lover. You are the person I want to spend my life with, Darrian, on or off this mountain." I pulled her to me, roughly, feeling my heart pound, knowing its partner was so close, recognizing, even as my mind, my spirit recognized the other brilliant one, so close.

"You are my lover ..."

Halfway through winter, past my second Christmas, past the Solstice, more hunters' and ski mobile tracks in the woods. Darrian was grinding her teeth in her sleep. All of us felt tight as piano wire. And then, half lark, half in earnest, she sent the word about "the virus."

I knew she was trying to buy the apes some time, hoping an undisturbed winter would allow them to reproduce, at least one or two young to replace some of last year's losses. In a way, maybe, she was even teasing the popular press. Figured anyone worth their salt would research enough to know that no such "virus" was possible. So she radioed out that the mountains around Remmel and to the north were infected, and that a quarantine was needed to keep the infection from spreading.

We were all shocked, probably most of all, when a few zoological societies responded seriously. Caught with our proverbial pants down, we should have stopped it there, but Darrian, believing even a couple of months of this charade would make a difference, went along with the feeble ruse.

She took stool samples, leached human viruses and bacteria into them somehow, and sent these "packages" down. Pure bush-league. Had people not been so full of ape mania, the farce would have been discovered instantly and those serious scientists would have recognized the sad ploy, maybe been a little put off, but would have understood. Instead, the "virus" and the "quarantine" got front page headlines. Now, we were trapped, as much as the apes.

Darrian, feeling the net getting tighter, attempted a salvage, a weak retraction. Claiming a lab mistake, contaminated slides, whatever, she tried to get it all taken back — instead, shockingly, no one seemed willing to listen.

It was the most sensational thing to come off Remmel since her own descent in the summer. Every day we received letters from scientists, doctors, college kids, even the Boy Scouts — all wanting to volunteer. Vaccinations, antibiotic laced bait, whatever it took. Fundraisers called in, wanting to know if money could be raised to evacuate the apes en masse. Even the State tourist bureau wanted to send a rep up. All we could do was sit on our thumbs and pray it would die down. Let Darrian lose face, handle the lowland folks best she could, maybe it would all drift away.

Weeks went by, with only the weather on our side, the worst storm season in a decade. Our work took on a feverish quality. I dismissed the unreality, thought only that immersion in activity was the prescription Darrian had prepared — as usual, not telling us outright, but through her example. Maybe now, because I was part of them, I just felt it more acutely — a simple matter of refocusing. I had to relax, remember, remember to breathe.

Then the letter arrived.

A knock on the front door. Shocking ... Julian opens it to find a Ranger in the sleety rain. Hand delivery. Very official business. Julian won't let the miserable-looking guy inside. We can hear him muttering all the way down the icing path. Darrian is called in from the lab.

She doesn't even sit down before opening it.

A long time. Like three wolf cubs waiting for Mama to tell us it's all right to move, we wait for her. She's so quiet. Then she moves to her chair by the windows. Sitting, she re-reads the letter. Finally, it drops from her fingers, drifts onto her lap, a dead moth, huge, frightening, even in its demise. Darrian stares out towards the east, silent.

"Darrian?" Farquhar breaks the intolerable stillness.

No answer.

Gingerly, Farquhar reaches for the letter, plucking the single sheet from Darrian's unmoving lap.

"Oh my God — no! There's got to be a mistake!" Farquhar crushes the paper into a ball and throws it against the mantle, her face a mask of disbelief.

I look from Farquhar to Darrian. "What is it! What's going on?"

"Those stinking bastards! You have to call down there, Darrian, this is a mistake, a horrible mistake! Appeal it, God-dammit! Contact our support . . . a phone campaign . . . today! Letters to everyone, all the other organizations, no way is this going to fly!" Farquhar is out the back door, full stride, heading for the radio.

Julian picks up the paper ball. His dark hands are like two heavy stones as he smooths it against his thigh. The afternoon light is all blues and grays. Julian squints as he reads by the fireplace, his lips move, following what his eyes see. Finished, he hands it to me, his face an impassive oak.

When I make it through, I drop the hideous thing into the flames.

"They've found out the truth about the virus." Darrian's voice was shockingly strong.

"How?" I watched the paper curl, brown, burst into a kamikaze fireball.

"Nikki, we weren't careful, I wasn't careful — stupid. So stupid. I knew it was only a matter of time. When they wouldn't listen to my explanations

— half-assed as they were — I knew it would ride like this till the end and then they'd come looking for me."

Darrian rocked herself by the windows, watching the wet woods ice over. "Anyone with the slightest doubt, or wanting there to be a doubt, would have conducted serious tests, would have heard what I was trying to say — maybe even felt a little sorry for our cabin fever here. No, they didn't want science, they wanted hype. A wild card at best ... it's turned on us."

"To hell with them all, Darrian!" Julian exclaimed. "I say it's the logging companies lobbying Olympia — they've been eyeing this place for too long not to jump in when they see a crack. Do it all the time to the Indians — you're just one of us. All those fancy foundations and their high-falutin' grants, just a smokescreen, just a bunch of white men trying to make a buck. They found a chance in you and the apes, now they're moving in for the kill. To hell with them — it's been time to fight for too long, no more excuses!" Julian was pacing like an old bear with a toothache.

"Careful — have to be extremely careful, Julian. They expect a reaction. They want to push us half-blind into confrontation — that's the reason for the special delivery. A perfect excuse then for the government to intervene — an invitation to come up. They know the cold is on our side ... or maybe somebody did sell us out. Academia has never been my favorite part of the jungle." Darrian turned her chair to look at us directly.

Fight was filling her, she looked ten years

younger, she looked like the tape of herself. The transformation was startling.

"We know it wasn't an Indian," Julian growls.

"Of course not. You're right — it's about profit. Maybe they just want me down there in court to use up our time, wait for spring when it will be easier for them. Who knows what got kicked up when I was down there last summer? Maybe it's time to give Jayne Carlyle in Los Angeles a call. She's a good attorney, knows how to use the press. We could see where we stand at the end of the week." Darrian stretches, as if this is no more bothersome than a bounced check, something to cover, a technical error in our bookkeeping. It's as if something very calm, something very deep in her memory has taken over and she's awoken from a great sleep.

"Darrian! Darrian that's just gonna be more legal bullshit!" Julian spits into the fire. "Too much bullshit already. What's that lawyer lady gonna do for us in Mickey-Mouse-land?"

"Maybe she can get the good guys here, Julian, a few good people might make all the difference. Maybe she'll organize a posse." Darrian touches his shoulder as she passes us, heading after Farquhar.

"Yeah, well you know what always happens to the Indians when the cowboys show up," Julian yells after her, dropping heavily into the lap of the couch.

I sit beside him, don't know what else to do. The air is knocked out of me, I'm hollow as the caves above us. Only I feel more dead.

Darrian removed as head of Remmel.

"A World Tribunal of ecologists, politicians,

corporations ... Time to make public this international resource ... In your place Dr. Henry Brogan of Cornell University ... If you refuse to comply we will send an escort to serve restraining orders and have you and your staff removed from the mountain..."

Not in my wildest nightmares — the sweat trickles down my backbone.

"This lawyer shit ain't gonna take, Nikki," Julian says. "I know. I feel it. I watched it happen to my grandparents, my mother, even my nephew Joseph."

"Joseph? Farquhar's husband was your nephew?"

"It's how I met Darrian. Lots of promises given to us, lots of stuff dangled in front of us — then the good guys leave and all the promises are forgotten. It killed my whole family, now it's gonna kill Darrian. You can't play with these people, try to fool them — even if you're trying to do some good. The only thing you can do is fight. Then, if you die, you die trying." Julian's face looks haunted, all shadows and light dancing across.

"Nobody's going to die! I won't let even you try it, old man! We'll move the apes, she's already talked about a plan. We'll get the foundation started, that lawyer in L.A. — she'll stop the injunction. Other people below, not part of the universities or big business, just people, they support us. They know she's the only one who could do the work here, keep the balance. Okay, so maybe we have to be more open, just a bit, a few more specials for TV every couple of years — maybe even more researchers — but we control it, Julian, it's legally in our hands! We'll keep everyone but the

Deepwoods Tribe and ourselves out of the caves. We'll be the only ones in direct contact with the apes — we can try, Julian, we have to try!" I pound the worn skin of the sofa with both fists.

Hold on, hold on, don't lose it in front of this man you love like an uncle — he needs you to be strong — hold on!

"Maybe, Nikki. Maybe." Julian's impassive face chills me to silence.

Late, Too late. Word's gone down as far as Los Angeles, as far as attorney Carlyle herself. Gears in motion. The machine cranked up, ready, rolled into place, but it isn't enough. By the end of the week we know they've moved in on us, under cover of another storm, surprising us with their stealth, a military bivouac ready, watching, the Governor's blessings upon their heads.

Julian comes tumbling in before dawn, after being all night up with the apes.

"They wouldn't let me out!" His face black with choked fear and rage. "All around us, except for above . . . can't tell exactly how many, lots of rifles — won't let us down for any supplies . . . no mail . . ." He coughs harshly, spitting into his handkerchief.

"State police . . ." Darrian's voice like the voice of a ghost.

"Dammit! Damn them!" Farquhar shrinks against the bookcase, as if she's remembering the last rifles up here.

I read *Wounded Knee,* I read *Attica,* I read *Ganiankah* in their faces.

"There's time." Darrian is too calm.

"There is no time!" shrieks Julian, hacking as if he's going to cut himself in half with the coughs.

"Julian. There is still time." When Darrian turns, her face is not her face — it is a face completely unlined, hard, heavy smooth. The eyes clear and cold as any cut jewel, burning with interior ice. Her voice is the striking hiss of a viper. "They won't come in. Not yet. They're waiting for our move. They won't move first. We have to sit, we have to wait for Jayne's people."

Julian won't look at her. Afraid, maybe, of what he'll really see.

"And then?" he asks.

"Then it will be time, Julian. Then it will be time." Darrian walks to her room, pulling the door closed on us — on me.

"We — I — don't dare follow.

I hear the poppoppop and sit up, the sound too familiar! Only the fire. The sappy wood spitting as it burns down. My heart is a racing marmot, my shirt soaked with sweat.

I'd fallen asleep on the couch, waiting for Darrian. Now, her bedroom is open but it's dark and quiet inside. Julian is gone, too.

Have to pee. The bathroom is cold. I light a candle and examine my face in the mirror, sure it has aged in these last few hours.

For a second! But I blink and it's gone — Darrian's face staring back at me. I shake off the illusion, wash up, go to my room for fresh clothes.

My sweater is halfway over my head when Farquhar comes in, scaring me badly. Her hair is in two braids. Clothes I've never seen before — leather, suede — traditional dress?

"I've come for you, Nikki. Wear your warmest things. It's bitter outside." She hugs me, hard, the scent of warmed leather, nervous sweat, clean hair and woodsmoke all rise like perfume from her skin. The press of her abalone beads on the medicine bag around her neck marks my cheek like a tattoo.

I shake as I finish dressing. Don't think. Don't wonder. Don't worry. Dress — heavy boots, like the first time here; wool socks, down jacket — pull all of it from the little closet ... Somehow I understand: I'm dressing for war.

The night breaks into a thousand shards of glass, stars so brittle, so sharp I feel I can chip them off the black velvet of the sky. The wind cuts at our faces, finding every chink in the cloth armor I've got on. A brutal night, a hunted place. Even my breath moves in tiny spirit huffs away from my mouth — haunted.

Try to keep my glasses clear, but it's hard going the pace Farquhar sets. Icicles hang in long fangs from the pines and fir, mounds of frost heave up, impersonating boulders in our path, the knife edges of rocks bite my ankles and knees when I stumble, and I stumble, following, ever faster.

I know nothing. Feel only that wherever we are going we will find Darrian. It's all I need.

Farquhar is a shadow in buckskin as she moves through the skeletal trees. I'm not afraid, only out of breath, sweating and chilled at the same time, the shivering tearing through me as much from apprehension as the weather. But I won't say I am afraid.

Higher and higher we climb, beyond where the trees seem to trip the stars. Below, on an outcropping of rock, their nightlights bright against the butt of the mountain, a semi-circle of little men and machines ... meaning nothing, only to themselves their consequence of worth.

Higher still. Above them, their faces disappearing like grains of sand below the climbing eagle. And then, under our feet, the ground levels. We come to an alpine meadow, heavy with frost, hard as macadam, each step is treacherous.

I walk behind Farquhar as I've walked behind Darrian, one foot at a time, mimicking her stride. In this way we make our path across the barren, open place and fall into the line of trees.

Farquhar stops suddenly. She looks up. I follow her gaze, discover an opening above us in the steep rock, its black maw a deeper shade than the night surrounding it. This is where we will find Darrian. I know.

Hand and toe, like going eons back to my first climb, I scramble to keep up with the lithe dancer

Farquhar. Then, like a match extinguished, she's gone!

There is no choice: enter the hole. I bang my head a solid whack as I move, groping, through the entrance. Seeing brilliant flashes, like in a cartoon, I try to steady myself.

The tunnel is deep, descending. Fear rises in my bowels. My head aches, my thigh muscles scream for me to stop, my heart's on hyper-drive, but no break, I can't ask, won't, not even for water, not even for explanation. I can half run and tumble, hearing, ahead, what seems to be the droning of very large, ominous insects.

Farquhar moves to the side of me and suddenly there is the brilliance of fire. My eyes close against the invading light. I can feel we are standing on a ledge. The droning, much louder now, is coming from below us. Finally, adjusting to the light, I see the walls are encrusted with quartz or mica: the fire is reflected up from hundreds of feet below.

Farquhar pulls me down on my belly, beside her. The sounds drift up slowly, separating on the brisk air, individual notes, chants . . . like nothing I've ever heard. Half-tones maybe . . . vibrations emitted from human throats ricochetting on the firelit walls.

Below, in a circle, dancers . . . one with hair the color of lightning through her braids . . . She whirls and spins . . . long moments before the recognition sifts in . . . and then, though I can't really make out her face, I feel her, feel her look up, high, past the roaring fire, high to where the sparks rise and disappear, up to the edge of the outcrop, looking for me . . . into me . . . I feel her here . . . my love, my heart . . . Darrian . . . dancing, chanting, more than honored guest . . . and yet, still, she looks for me.

Beyond time, watching in the cold dark, how long? The sweet smoke I've inhaled has altered my sense of time. My breathing stops, starts, dances around the pulse of my heart. Darrian! Where is Darrian? And then she is again looking for us, into us, into me . . . Her haunted eyes . . . the fire of emeralds sparking up . . . The drum slows . . . solo . . . A woman rises, old or younger, I can't tell . . . Moves to Darrian's flank. There is an exchange, something given . . . unrecognizable . . . She turns away . . . away from us . . .

"We must go. She wanted you here, for this much." Farquhar can't say more, simply takes my hand, begins to lead me away from the edge, away from the smoking dance and throbbing drum.

I'm stoned . . . or not. Can't be sure. The questions melt as there is no more need for questions. The air is acid outside, burning everything exposed . . . Hits me in the face, my hands, and then deeper, my lungs. The stars sing over us. Farquhar is smiling, still clutching my hand. We say nothing. Nothing. We say nothing to each other the entire way back.

The radio is quiet, not even the cackle of static. The winter birds have abandoned camp. Everything holds its breath. We wait.

Darrian sits with gun propped in her lap.

On the sunporch Julian rocks in one of the weather-beaten chairs, his rifle loaded, ready.

Farquhar is on watch by the windows but there is no movement outside.

The sun rises coldly, as if all life has been sucked from its husk. A fog bank moves in, covering the half-light. Even the clouds are tinged with blood. We wait.

"Something coming over the radio." Julian is sharp as a firecracker and as jumpy.

I'm awake, shocked that I could have dozed.

Darrian is already moving down the hallway.

Evil. Officious. The voices crackle, coming from hell. We crowd the radio, desperate for reprieve.

There will be no call from the Governor.

Over. It's done.

They want Darrian off the mountain by nightfall. They want the rest of us later — no sudden moves — an easy surrender. No room for negotiation. We are pinned. All firepower, all manpower, whatever it takes, we are too far away for outside witnesses. The press hasn't arrived. There will be no posse.

Darrian attempts a relay to L.A. but the breaking storm front prevents the call from going through. Does anyone off this mountain know what's going down?

Did Darrian know it would be like this? Go this far? Part of me wakes, the part that didn't believe the bluff, more pissant politics. Who did they think we were? What did they expect to find, coming after us like this?

At the last minute Darrian would drop back, give in, call it off ... Maybe, maybe she'd have to sign some forms for the government, okay ... By then our counsel would have arrived ... By then the TV news and the papers ... One look at Darrian, all calm fire and intelligence, and it would stop the rumors dead! She wasn't crazy — hadn't gone mad. There were no berserk Indians or armed apes. The only hostages were the three of us in this cabin. It was the guys with the guns holding us. Why hadn't anyone admitted this was the wrong script?

I made a grab for the microphone. Someone had to be listening, one of the State Troopers had to be for real, just one guy, one person realizing this was a fucking mistake. Someone had to stop before a gun went off in the shadows, some trembling, tired finger ... Then ... then I just put the microphone down.

Awake. Fully, awfully awake. There was no one listening. This was the only script.

I move away, feel their eyes on my back, in absolute retreat, weak, I'm weak, walk to the kitchen. Outside, the thrumming of the rain begins.

"Nikki." Darrian stands in the small doorway, filling it. "We have to talk, all of us, right now. Please, will you come?" She doesn't step closer.

Can't speak. All our nights, all our nights come crashing in, all our nights together ... Who is she? My mentor, my guide? Lover or sister or mother or shaman? So often I've been outside, watching, waiting for her ... Now she's crossed a line I never knew existed. Darrian Stone was never coming down from this mountain. I was all alone.

"Nikki. Please. We want you." Farquhar pushes past Darrian, turns me around to face her.

Can't speak. No way to get out of this. Not some damned college demonstration where it ends with the cops slapping your wrists and a rowdy night with friends in the local jail. Darrian's no Billy Jack. No cameras to film her solid, bravery-filled trek down the mountain, complete with soundtrack. Fuck, the idiot Governor won't even pick up his fucking phone.

"Nikki, once I told you there'd be a day when you would show whose side you were on. The choice was for or against us, for or against the spirits of this place. Nikki, this is the day. This is your choice. You are the one white girl who could walk away, now, and make it down. Choose, little sister." Farquhar holds my face in her hands, she lets me go.

All of our time together fast-forwards in my head: Julian finding me, almost frozen, in my tent; Farquhar's first touch; Darrian; the caves; the entombment of the murdered ape; the Fourth of July shooting; news crews and a bad joke gone to hell; all of the dinners eaten, the hikes trekked, the work done; simple chores of chopping wood, getting

stronger, talking of our lives; our lives before
Remmel, our lives before Darrian ... what real life?
The aching truth that she had given me my life.
"Farquhar, you're wrong. There is no choice."

Four o'clock.
Sun down like a comet, behind the rainclouds,
everything sulphurous, evil. A raggedy wind blows.
Darrian certain they won't move, not in the rain and
dark. They're still dealing with their own myths
about this place. They'd bragged sundown, but this
is no spaghetti western, Darrian is sure we have till
the morning.
We do the small, final things people do when
they are pretending nothing huge and hulking is
hovering over their home. We make stew, bake
bread, hold hands around the table for this, our final
meal together. No speeches. Darrian holds Farquhar's
and my hand, Julian she holds in her eyes.
The fire crackles good-naturedly. All of these
sights, aromas, touches: synonyms for safe.
Woodsmoke, pine, rainscent, warm flannel,
scratchy wool, the oily metal of our friendly guns as
they lean against the table, ready, even the faint,
acrid trace of fear on our skin ... this is home.
We eat little, pretending to eat more. Remember
to put out the little bowl on the steps. Then,
Darrian speaks:
"This is our stand, no options, anyone trying to
get down in the dark will be stopped by the men, it

isn't a viable exit anymore. We can go Deepwoods with the Tribe, with the apes ... up north ... but it means never coming back. Never." She looks around at each of us.

"Why not wait till it just cools, then we might be able to come back and tell our side!" I still cling to that spidery hope.

"There will be nothing to come back to, Nikki. We're going to burn Remmel before the night is through." Darrian can't look at me.

"No! Not after all the work! You talked about our, our foundation, Farquhar's book, you, me and Julian, together! What about that woman in Los Angeles — the lawyer? No, I won't let you do it!" Rage, filling me, blanking out the fear, masking the horror of the death squad below.

"Nikki." Julian's voice is a knife cutting me off, cold.

"Nikki, this is one choice no one can make but me. All summer I struggled, reading the signs, hoping it would turn around, different possibilities arise. All summer, with every letter you sent, I could see what was happening. Off mountain the public expected, ultimately, a game park, a fence around the animals, around the Indians who protect them — turning them into tour guides. Maybe it's true, the final proof I've gone bushy. I see, now, I should never have come to Remmel in the first place ... or maybe left long ago. The only hope is to drive the apes north ... deeper, away from people, pray the Tribe can continue so far from home. I was so wrong, I thought science could save them, maybe save us all. If the Tribe can find caverns in Canada, maybe, another twenty years, the apes can recover . . . maybe."

"What the fuck is twenty years?" I pound the table in absolute impotence.

"It's as much as I can give them, dammit. Don't you see? Two generations, they have that much freedom, and maybe after what we do here, tonight, someone will come looking for real solutions, maybe we can raise enough questions tonight so they have to look, look hard, sift through to honest answers . . . A lasting impact, not some stop-gap measure . . . At the very least, Nikki, the animals will be free!"

The shock of Darrian's tears shuts me up faster than any argument. Julian looks away. Farquhar, already there, cradling the older woman tight. And I, the supposed rider of her heart, sounding like the basest traitor, what do I do but pound dead wood and demand yet more. The lump in my throat feels cancerous.

"It's final, then. We burn the compound. All records, all evidence, blueprints, specimens. If you want to leave for the caverns you must go soon. The Tribe will take you up and over the mountain tonight. Once the fire is detected it will be too late. The men will come blasting in from below. If you want to go back to the city you'll have to go out through the Coleville Reservation. We have friends there. They can get you as far as California. You'll be underground, but maybe, maybe that can work. By the time the press gets the story it will have a high profile. Jayne, in L.A., she'll be your contact. When it's time to surface she'll know what to do, have some good come out of it. But you'll never be able to come back here. The apes, the Tribe, all vanished ... These are the options, Nikki. Farquhar." Darrian is almost whispering.

"What about you? When do you leave?" Farquhar is struggling not to cry, her face buried against Darrian's head.

"I don't."

"What? Darrian, I don't understand. You are going with the Tribe. I'm going with you. Fuck the off-mountain people, there's nothing down there, nothing for me anywhere without you."

And then I know it's true, what I'm going to do — I'm going to live, in her mountains, with all of them, forever.

Julian pushes away. He pulls down his jacket from a peg by the door. Out of one pocket he fishes a red bandanna. Comes back to the table, ties it around my neck, rests his big hands on my shoulders. Over my head he nods to Farquhar, I can feel him, then to Darrian. Without another word he takes one of the rifles and walks down the hallway, to the back door, shuts it firmly behind him.

"What? What?" Something is happening and I haven't a clue!

"Nikki, dear one, Farquhar ... sit with me. Only a little time, now." Darrian goes to her rocking chair.

We sit on the floor, close, close as we can get, like children waiting for a story ... waiting for something.

How little I know her. How much I love her ... My stomach is churning, the dry, throaty feeling is hard. I want to ask her about when she was my age ... Did she ever feel like this, the uncertainty, the awkwardness, does it ever go away? I want to ask her about her family, growing up, other lovers, women or men, I can handle that, secure enough now, with her, with us, want to ask her why she came here in the first place, years back, before Farquhar — about Farquhar. I know it isn't time now, so many stories waiting to be told in some future dark, tangled around each other, an easier place than this. My glasses are misting, everything is out of focus . . .

"When Fossey was killed in Rwanda, it saved the mountain gorillas. It saved them in a surer way than any amount of work she might have accomplished had she stayed alive. She was a risk to the political powers . . . unmanageable. In the same way I've become unmanageable."

Farquhar is sobbing, her face pressed to Darrian's lap, the earlier tears now raging.

"I took the drug before dinner. No traces. Last night, at the ceremony, power medicine given as my final gift, clean and quick. Now, you must listen because there is really so very little time left — you have to follow each detail." Her voice already fading, not my imagination, no, she is already backing away . . . I could feel her moving away from us.

"I can't . . ." Waves of nausea wash over me.

"Nikki! Look at me! If you have ever really loved me you will do *exactly* this! And you will do more, because, because it is what we have loved in each other. All our work, our belief, it isn't the only way for me, it is the best way. I've got nothing left to give but this moment. I learned from the women who came before me. Now it's my turn, passing it to you. Be glad, my sweet, be glad for me!"

Darrian caresses my burning face. Her long, strong hands, my flesh knows this touch, this press, my lips remember this flesh.

"Not here, we'll take you to the caves, an antidote, we'll carry you — Darrian, your dream, our dream together, to be free, together!" Farquhar's gasp, a plea, the gasp of a child at a dying parent's bed.

"I'm already dying ... there's no antidote for death. Oh we have come so far, learned so much here ... Without you my life would have been spent in a musty library or a dead classroom ... a hundred little deaths each year. We have had a life, my darling Farquhar, we have had a life and our freedom, together. Carry it with you, help Nikki with the truth. Julian is in the woods, now, safe, with the Tribe — it's enough! For you, you two, be with each other, for each other — my last gift. This summer, down in the city, they found cancer. I suppose it was leaked, my medical records, why everyone is making a grab for this place now — they know, not any time left at all. I won't give it to them, though — in a little while, I'll fly straight off this mountain. Look up, my loves, see me in the night sky ... Know I could do it because I know you both are strong, so strong ... Teach what can be taught, save the rest, together. You carry me with you, in you ... Farquhar, teach Nikki, my body just an emptying bag, now, my spirit almost out ... Nikki, Nikki, it's up to you ... this final, hard thing ... It has to be you I ask ... the hardest favor of all. If they think there was a murder up here ... If they find the fire and all of you gone, it will get ... get front page ... full investigation ... five o'clock news ... Even if

211

they find the cancer, that's extraneous . . . As long
as they see I couldn't have shot myself, no suicide,
no confirmation that I've gone over the edge . . . This
drug, no trace, not even in an autopsy . . . I've
thought long and hard . . . The best way . . . across
the room, the rifle, Nikki, in a little bit . . . The
moment you know I've really gone . . . Across the
room, one shot . . . Make it straight, little one, make
it count . . . When they find the body . . . it will look
like foul play. Confuse them. Send them in the
wrong directions . . . Give Julian, the Tribe, the apes,
just a little more time . . . enough time to get to the
newest caves . . . While everyone looks for a
murderer, no one will . . . no one will look for apes .
. . A head start, Nikki, you can give them that . . .
Just an empty sack you're hitting . . . not me . . . I'll
be gone, watching you . . . Send fireworks in my
honor, my sweet, sweet love . . . Find Jayne, off
mountain, she'll know what to do . . . If you get
caught . . . she can help . . . Buy them time, Nikki,
you can do it . . . if I ask . . ." Darrian fights to hold
her arms open.

Her voice nothing more than a feather, barely
moving in the night air . . . leaving us, nothing we
can do, can't hold her . . .

"Hold her!" I scream.

"No, Nikki." Darrian's voice less than a whisper.
"Let me go . . . Nikki, if you cry, it will be . . . too
hard . . . You can call me back, you who are the
best gift the woods . . . ever brought . . . to me . . .
my best secret . . . Let me go . . . You have to be . . .
the one with the gun . . . love . . ."

I hold, hold, press the falling body hard, press
my heart to her heart, feel her slip, the eyes too

heavy, Farquhar on the floor, sobbing, sobbing, Darrian trying to leave, the fight there, fighting us both, and I can't ... cannot let her go ... no ... not fair ... kiss her hard, breathe, breathe, dammit, bite and scratch and fight me, hate me even, for this, come back come back ... I know (the vow ... the only promise I've ever made worth keeping in my life ... my life, my life is going, my soul going with her ... can't follow ... let her loose ... feel it, a whisper, her whisper, deep, inside me, then, the sound of a mighty bird, sudden wind in the chimney, a roar, sparks stinging the air around our heads, I am being torn apart ... this is what it is not to die but to be left ... Darrian, Darrian ... I let go, move back, pick up the gun ...

"Gone." Farquhar exhales the word. Rises, moves across the room, too, not looking back at the imposter who sits in Darrian's chair.

Pausing only a second, a heartbeat, Farquhar reaches under her shirt, strips the medicine bag from around her neck ... Kissing it, she slips it silently over my head.

"Farquhar ..." Blinded by my tears, all sense of time gone ... We kiss, hard, our lips taste of salt and blood ... Then pull back, she moving to the heart, making a torch out of a branch and the Indian rug on the floor ... lighting it ... Then, Darrian's name a scream on her lips, she empties lantern fuel out on the back porch ... the fire leaps behind her.

My eyes sting from the oily smoke, the flames hissing angrily outside in the storm, the flash and small explosion first from the lab, then the records shed ... Wait, another second, my tears washing my vision clean ... A single shot ... across the room, aim straight ... her words ... They'll get to this house before the body's ash ... before the lifeless rags catch ... Wrap Julian's bandanna across my nose and mouth ... outlaw red ... I am ... I raise the gun ... think only a second ... A tiny vision ... the first time I saw you seated in that chair, the center of the sun ... my love, now, above us, dancing banshee in the dark, riding the stars ... watch, watch, remembering everything my New England father taught ... Bracing for the recoil, squeezing gently, evenly, surely, surely as anything I've ever done ...

Epilogue

"Darrian!"

"Back, Nikki, back, now. You're safe, relaxed, back here in my office. You are no longer on Remmel, you are back here and you are safe in Los Angeles. You are fine, you are rested, you are not anxious or afraid, relax, come back, Nikki, when you are ready you will open your eyes ... You will remember everything you've said this evening but you will not be afraid, you will have no anxiety, no more nightmares, you will know you are safe. Come back to me, Nikki, when you are ready." Anne

Lessing could hardly speak. She fought to regain her composure.

L.A. Over. It's really over. I hear Anne calling. Eyes open, jerk in the chair, clutch, then let go, sweat on my upper lip, taste it ... Sweat soaked hair, too, shivering, the leather jacket still damp ... Rain ... rain tonight ... pull it close, tight, everything coming in now, I remember, I was up there ... again.

"Nikki? How are you ..." Anne leans forward, her voice trails off.

I see her fight the urge to touch me ... knows I couldn't handle that ... not yet, not right now.

"Yeah, fine, fine." Wipe my face on the backs of my hands, try to stop trembling.

L.A. L.A. My hair, spiky, punked out, L.A., not Remmel ... but Remmel is here, too, from somewhere far away I have carried back part of the mountain ... Sirens outside ... in the street ... L.A.

Anne's client light blinks maddeningly, someone in the outside office. She punches the tape recorder off ... pauses to activate the intercom ... I want to run ... fight it, fight it hard ... Legs won't listen anyway ... they are through running.

"It's Jayne. Anne, let me in fast. They've followed us, downstairs, we haven't much time." The lawyer's voice is controlled but with a definite edge.

I can't see the office clock. Can't focus clearly ... Realize my glasses are off ... in my hand ... Put

them back ... smeary from being held so long ...
Still lost, still in the forest and these people can't
see, don't know it yet.

Anne Lessing moves quickly, opens the door wide.
Jayne slams in, blonde, California cool, business suit
and pumps, and something more ... behind her ...
in the shadowy hall ...

"Nikki?"

The voice is inside me before I even hear it ... a
dream ... no, no more dreams! Real, real as this
winterbound city of angels — Farquhar! Sweet God,
Farquhar! Rushing past the other women, rushing
straight for me!

"How did she —" Anne pulls Jayne off to one
side, I stop listening to them.

"Nikki!" Farquhar holds me, the smell of the city
rain in her hair, but not masking the forest scent
that is her own ... our bodies calling out their
recognized joy ... "Nikki, I got down, wasn't sure
you made it, not till tonight. They took me to Jayne,
these good women. Oh God, I'm glad to see you!"

"She's got a tape, came in with it today, from
Stone. It exonerates Nikki. We have to make a plan,
how we want to play this." Jayne is talking louder
now. She wants me to hear ... I don't care ...
alive. Farquhar alive, off the mountain, down here
with me ... Darrian knew ... she knew!

Sirens getting closer, splitting the night below us.

"Farquhar was with Stacey at Neda's. They kept
her in Venice until this evening. Stacey was tailed
all the way to my place, but there was no other
way. Whatever you got tonight, piece together a fast
statement for the press. Look at a total transcript

later. But with Darrian's tape we can blow this whole issue sky high!" Jayne's excitement rises, even as her voice rises over the screaming sirens.

"Nikki, we can do this ... we have to do this." Farquhar is tight against me, her dancer's body strong, so much like home.

"I know." Won't cry, not again, not this night, not on Darrian's life.

Anne Lessing is in front of us. Behind her, Jayne is hollering to someone on the phone.

Tall, this woman who reminds me a little of another tall, older woman, tall and chagrined, but honest ... like Stone. She puts a tentative hand on my shoulder, gently squeezing:

"When Dian Fossey was buried, the minister who gave her eulogy said that if we think the distance Christ came to take the likeness of man is not so great as that distance from man to ape, then we don't know men or apes — or God. I give you both my promise, Darrian's death is going to matter, and the work you all did on Remmel — we won't let anyone forget. You aren't alone anymore, Nikki."

Below, the land of Lah, plastic and plaster, twinkly lights and macadam ... The night is opened like a present, tinsel, noise, sparkling glitter ... Cops and TV vans arrive, somewhere, an ambulance ... The rain begins in earnest ... the rain, splattering through the sooty clouds ... But above all of this, the stars are singing, and Darrian is in there, kicking ass, looking down, laughing, laughing at us all ...

A few of the publications of
THE NAIAD PRESS, INC.
P.O. Box 10543 • Tallahassee, Florida 32302
Phone (904) 539-5965
Mail orders welcome. Please include 15% postage.

CALLING RAIN by Karen Marie Christa Minns. 240 pp.
Spellbinding, erotic love story   ISBN 0-941483-87-8 $9.95

BLACK IRIS by Jeane Harris. 192 pp. Caroline's hidden past . . .
                                         ISBN 0-941483-68-1   8.95

TOUCHWOOD by Karin Kallmaker. 240 pp. Loving, May/
December romance.   ISBN 0-941483-76-2   8.95

BAYOU CITY SECRETS by Deborah Powell. 224 pp. A Hollis
Carpenter mystery. First in a series.   ISBN 0-941483-91-6   8.95

COP OUT by Claire McNab. 208 pp. 4th Det. Insp. Carol Ashton
mystery.   ISBN 0-941483-84-3   8.95

LODESTAR by Phyllis Horn. 224 pp. Romantic, fast-moving
adventure.   ISBN 0-941483-83-5   8.95

THE BEVERLY MALIBU by Katherine V. Forrest. 288 pp. A
Kate Delafield Mystery. 3rd in a series. (HC) ISBN 0-941483-47-9   16.95
                        Paperback   ISBN 0-941483-48-7   9.95

THAT OLD STUDEBAKER by Lee Lynch. 272 pp. Andy's affair
with Regina and her attachment to her beloved car.
                                         ISBN 0-941483-82-7   9.95

PASSION'S LEGACY by Lori Paige. 224 pp. Sarah is swept into
the arms of Augusta Pym in this delightful historical romance.
                                         ISBN 0-941483-81-9   8.95

THE PROVIDENCE FILE by Amanda Kyle Williams. 256 pp.
Second espionage thriller featuring lesbian agent Madison McGuire
                                         ISBN 0-941483-92-4   8.95

I LEFT MY HEART by Jaye Maiman. 320 pp. A Robin Miller
Mystery. First in a series.   ISBN 0-941483-72-X   9.95

THE PRICE OF SALT by Patricia Highsmith (writing as Claire
Morgan). 288 pp. Classic lesbian novel, first issued in 1952 . . .
acknowledged by its author under her own, very famous, name.
                                         ISBN 1-56280-003-5   8.95

SIDE BY SIDE by Isabel Miller. 256 pp. From beloved author of
Patience and Sarah.   ISBN 0-941483-77-0   8.95

SOUTHBOUND by Sheila Ortiz Taylor. 240 pp. Hilarious sequel
to *Faultline.*   ISBN 0-941483-78-9   8.95

STAYING POWER: LONG TERM LESBIAN COUPLES
by Susan E. Johnson. 352 pp. Joys of coupledom.
ISBN 0-941-483-75-4   12.95

SLICK by Camarin Grae. 304 pp. Exotic, erotic adventure.
ISBN 0-941483-74-6   9.95

NINTH LIFE by Lauren Wright Douglas. 256 pp. A Caitlin
Reece mystery. 2nd in a series.   ISBN 0-941483-50-9   8.95

PLAYERS by Robbi Sommers. 192 pp. Sizzling, erotic novel.
ISBN 0-941483-73-8   8.95

MURDER AT RED ROOK RANCH by Dorothy Tell. 224 pp.
First Poppy Dillworth adventure.   ISBN 0-941483-80-0   8.95

LESBIAN SURVIVAL MANUAL by Rhonda Dicksion.
112 pp. Cartoons!   ISBN 0-941483-71-1   8.95

A ROOM FULL OF WOMEN by Elisabeth Nonas. 256 pp.
Contemporary Lesbian lives.   ISBN 0-941483-69-X   8.95

MURDER IS RELATIVE by Karen Saum. 256 pp. The first
Brigid Donovan mystery.   ISBN 0-941483-70-3   8.95

PRIORITIES by Lynda Lyons 288 pp. Science fiction with
a twist.   ISBN 0-941483-66-5   8.95

THEME FOR DIVERSE INSTRUMENTS by Jane Rule. 208
pp. Powerful romantic lesbian stories.   ISBN 0-941483-63-0   8.95

LESBIAN QUERIES by Hertz & Ertman. 112 pp. The questions
you were too embarrassed to ask.   ISBN 0-941483-67-3   8.95

CLUB 12 by Amanda Kyle Williams. 288 pp. Espionage thriller
featuring a lesbian agent!   ISBN 0-941483-64-9   8.95

DEATH DOWN UNDER by Claire McNab. 240 pp. 3rd Det.
Insp. Carol Ashton mystery.   ISBN 0-941483-39-8   8.95

MONTANA FEATHERS by Penny Hayes. 256 pp. Vivian and
Elizabeth find love in frontier Montana.   ISBN 0-941483-61-4   8.95

CHESAPEAKE PROJECT by Phyllis Horn. 304 pp. Jessie &
Meredith in perilous adventure.   ISBN 0-941483-58-4   8.95

LIFESTYLES by Jackie Calhoun. 224 pp. Contemporary Lesbian
lives and loves.   ISBN 0-941483-57-6   8.95

VIRAGO by Karen Marie Christa Minns. 208 pp. Darsen has
chosen Ginny.   ISBN 0-941483-56-8   8.95

WILDERNESS TREK by Dorothy Tell. 192 pp. Six women on
vacation learning "new" skills.   ISBN 0-941483-60-6   8.95

MURDER BY THE BOOK by Pat Welch. 256 pp. A Helen
Black Mystery. First in a series.   ISBN 0-941483-59-2   8.95

BERRIGAN by Vicki P. McConnell. 176 pp. Youthful Lesbian —
romantic, idealistic Berrigan.   ISBN 0-941483-55-X   8.95

LESBIANS IN GERMANY by Lillian Faderman & B. Eriksson.
128 pp. Fiction, poetry, essays.   ISBN 0-941483-62-2   8.95

THERE'S SOMETHING I'VE BEEN MEANING TO TELL
YOU Ed. by Loralee MacPike. 288 pp. Gay men and lesbians
coming out to their children.   ISBN 0-941483-44-4   9.95
                                                 ISBN 0-941483-54-1   16.95

LIFTING BELLY by Gertrude Stein. Ed. by Rebecca Mark. 104
pp. Erotic poetry.   ISBN 0-941483-51-7   8.95
                                                 ISBN 0-941483-53-3   14.95

ROSE PENSKI by Roz Perry. 192 pp. Adult lovers in a long-term
relationship.   ISBN 0-941483-37-1   8.95

AFTER THE FIRE by Jane Rule. 256 pp. Warm, human novel
by this incomparable author.   ISBN 0-941483-45-2   8.95

SUE SLATE, PRIVATE EYE by Lee Lynch. 176 pp. The gay
folk of Peacock Alley are *all cats*.   ISBN 0-941483-52-5   8.95

CHRIS by Randy Salem. 224 pp. Golden oldie. Handsome Chris
and her adventures.   ISBN 0-941483-42-8   8.95

THREE WOMEN by March Hastings. 232 pp. Golden oldie. A
triangle among wealthy sophisticates.   ISBN 0-941483-43-6   8.95

RICE AND BEANS by Valeria Taylor. 232 pp. Love and
romance on poverty row.   ISBN 0-941483-41-X   8.95

PLEASURES by Robbi Sommers. 204 pp. Unprecedented
eroticism.   ISBN 0-941483-49-5   8.95

EDGEWISE by Camarin Grae. 372 pp. Spellbinding
adventure.   ISBN 0-941483-19-3   9.95

FATAL REUNION by Claire McNab. 224 pp. 2nd Det. Inspec.
Carol Ashton mystery.   ISBN 0-941483-40-1   8.95

KEEP TO ME STRANGER by Sarah Aldridge. 372 pp. Romance
set in a department store dynasty.   ISBN 0-941483-38-X   9.95

HEARTSCAPE by Sue Gambill. 204 pp. American lesbian in
Portugal.   ISBN 0-941483-33-9   8.95

IN THE BLOOD by Lauren Wright Douglas. 252 pp. Lesbian
science fiction adventure fantasy   ISBN 0-941483-22-3   8.95

THE BEE'S KISS by Shirley Verel. 216 pp. Delicate, delicious
romance.   ISBN 0-941483-36-3   8.95

RAGING MOTHER MOUNTAIN by Pat Emmerson. 264 pp.
Furosa Firechild's adventures in Wonderland.   ISBN 0-941483-35-5   8.95

IN EVERY PORT by Karin Kallmaker. 228 pp. Jessica's sexy,
adventuresome travels.   ISBN 0-941483-37-7   8.95

OF LOVE AND GLORY by Evelyn Kennedy. 192 pp. Exciting
WWII romance.   ISBN 0-941483-32-0   8.95

CLICKING STONES by Nancy Tyler Glenn. 288 pp. Love
transcending time.   ISBN 0-941483-31-2   8.95

SURVIVING SISTERS by Gail Pass. 252 pp. Powerful love
story.   ISBN 0-941483-16-9   8.95

SOUTH OF THE LINE by Catherine Ennis. 216 pp. Civil War
adventure.   ISBN 0-941483-29-0   8.95

WOMAN PLUS WOMAN by Dolores Klaich. 300 pp. Supurb
Lesbian overview.   ISBN 0-941483-28-2   9.95

SLOW DANCING AT MISS POLLY'S by Sheila Ortiz Taylor.
96 pp. Lesbian Poetry   ISBN 0-941483-30-4   7.95

DOUBLE DAUGHTER by Vicki P. McConnell. 216 pp. A Nyla
Wade Mystery, third in the series.   ISBN 0-941483-26-6   8.95

HEAVY GILT by Delores Klaich. 192 pp. Lesbian detective/
disappearing homophobes/upper class gay society.

                                      ISBN 0-941483-25-8   8.95

THE FINER GRAIN by Denise Ohio. 216 pp. Brilliant young
college lesbian novel.   ISBN 0-941483-11-8   8.95

THE AMAZON TRAIL by Lee Lynch. 216 pp. Life, travel & lore
of famous lesbian author.   ISBN 0-941483-27-4   8.95

HIGH CONTRAST by Jessie Lattimore. 264 pp. Women of the
Crystal Palace.   ISBN 0-941483-17-7   8.95

OCTOBER OBSESSION by Meredith More. Josie's rich, secret
Lesbian life.   ISBN 0-941483-18-5   8.95

LESBIAN CROSSROADS by Ruth Baetz. 276 pp. Contemporary
Lesbian lives.   ISBN 0-941483-21-5   9.95

BEFORE STONEWALL: THE MAKING OF A GAY AND
LESBIAN COMMUNITY by Andrea Weiss & Greta Schiller.
96 pp., 25 illus.   ISBN 0-941483-20-7   7.95

WE WALK THE BACK OF THE TIGER by Patricia A. Murphy.
192 pp. Romantic Lesbian novel/beginning women's movement.
                                      ISBN 0-941483-13-4   8.95

SUNDAY'S CHILD by Joyce Bright. 216 pp. Lesbian athletics, at
last the novel about sports.   ISBN 0-941483-12-6   8.95

OSTEN'S BAY by Zenobia N. Vole. 204 pp. Sizzling adventure
romance set on Bonaire.   ISBN 0-941483-15-0   8.95

LESSONS IN MURDER by Claire McNab. 216 pp. 1st Det. Inspec.
Carol Ashton mystery — erotic tension!.   ISBN 0-941483-14-2   8.95

YELLOWTHROAT by Penny Hayes. 240 pp. Margarita, bandit,
kidnaps Julia.   ISBN 0-941483-10-X   8.95

SAPPHISTRY: THE BOOK OF LESBIAN SEXUALITY by
Pat Califia. 3d edition, revised. 208 pp.   ISBN 0-941483-24-X   8.95

CHERISHED LOVE by Evelyn Kennedy. 192 pp. Erotic
Lesbian love story. ISBN 0-941483-08-8 8.95

LAST SEPTEMBER by Helen R. Hull. 208 pp. Six stories & a
glorious novella. ISBN 0-941483-09-6 8.95

THE SECRET IN THE BIRD by Camarin Grae. 312 pp. Striking,
psychological suspense novel. ISBN 0-941483-05-3 8.95

TO THE LIGHTNING by Catherine Ennis. 208 pp. Romantic
Lesbian 'Robinson Crusoe' adventure. ISBN 0-941483-06-1 8.95

THE OTHER SIDE OF VENUS by Shirley Verel. 224 pp.
Luminous, romantic love story. ISBN 0-941483-07-X 8.95

DREAMS AND SWORDS by Katherine V. Forrest. 192 pp.
Romantic, erotic, imaginative stories. ISBN 0-941483-03-7 8.95

MEMORY BOARD by Jane Rule. 336 pp. Memorable novel
about an aging Lesbian couple. ISBN 0-941483-02-9 9.95

THE ALWAYS ANONYMOUS BEAST by Lauren Wright
Douglas. 224 pp. A Caitlin Reece mystery. First in a series.
ISBN 0-941483-04-5 8.95

SEARCHING FOR SPRING by Patricia A. Murphy. 224 pp.
Novel about the recovery of love. ISBN 0-941483-00-2 8.95

DUSTY'S QUEEN OF HEARTS DINER by Lee Lynch. 240 pp.
Romantic blue-collar novel. ISBN 0-941483-01-0 8.95

PARENTS MATTER by Ann Muller. 240 pp. Parents'
relationships with Lesbian daughters and gay sons.
ISBN 0-930044-91-6 9.95

THE PEARLS by Shelley Smith. 176 pp. Passion and fun in
the Caribbean sun. ISBN 0-930044-93-2 7.95

MAGDALENA by Sarah Aldridge. 352 pp. Epic Lesbian novel
set on three continents. ISBN 0-930044-99-1 8.95

THE BLACK AND WHITE OF IT by Ann Allen Shockley.
144 pp. Short stories. ISBN 0-930044-96-7 7.95

SAY JESUS AND COME TO ME by Ann Allen Shockley. 288
pp. Contemporary romance. ISBN 0-930044-98-3 8.95

LOVING HER by Ann Allen Shockley. 192 pp. Romantic love
story. ISBN 0-930044-97-5 7.95

MURDER AT THE NIGHTWOOD BAR by Katherine V.
Forrest. 240 pp. A Kate Delafield mystery. Second in a series.
ISBN 0-930044-92-4 8.95

ZOE'S BOOK by Gail Pass. 224 pp. Passionate, obsessive love
story. ISBN 0-930044-95-9 7.95

WINGED DANCER by Camarin Grae. 228 pp. Erotic Lesbian
adventure story. ISBN 0-930044-88-6 8.95

PAZ by Camarin Grae. 336 pp. Romantic Lesbian adventurer
with the power to change the world.   ISBN 0-930044-89-4   8.95

SOUL SNATCHER by Camarin Grae. 224 pp. A puzzle, an
adventure, a mystery — Lesbian romance.   ISBN 0-930044-90-8   8.95

THE LOVE OF GOOD WOMEN by Isabel Miller. 224 pp.
Long-awaited new novel by the author of the beloved *Patience
and Sarah*.   ISBN 0-930044-81-9   8.95

THE HOUSE AT PELHAM FALLS by Brenda Weathers. 240
pp. Suspenseful Lesbian ghost story.   ISBN 0-930044-79-7   7.95

HOME IN YOUR HANDS by Lee Lynch. 240 pp. More stories
from the author of *Old Dyke Tales*.   ISBN 0-930044-80-0   7.95

EACH HAND A MAP by Anita Skeen. 112 pp. Real-life poems
that touch us all.   ISBN 0-930044-82-7   6.95

SURPLUS by Sylvia Stevenson. 342 pp. A classic early Lesbian
novel.   ISBN 0-930044-78-9   7.95

PEMBROKE PARK by Michelle Martin. 256 pp. Derring-do
and daring romance in Regency England.   ISBN 0-930044-77-0   7.95

THE LONG TRAIL by Penny Hayes. 248 pp. Vivid adventures
of two women in love in the old west.   ISBN 0-930044-76-2   8.95

HORIZON OF THE HEART by Shelley Smith. 192 pp. Hot
romance in summertime New England.   ISBN 0-930044-75-4   7.95

AN EMERGENCE OF GREEN by Katherine V. Forrest. 288
pp. Powerful novel of sexual discovery.   ISBN 0-930044-69-X   8.95

THE LESBIAN PERIODICALS INDEX edited by Claire
Potter. 432 pp. Author & subject index.   ISBN 0-930044-74-6   29.95

DESERT OF THE HEART by Jane Rule. 224 pp. A classic;
basis for the movie *Desert Hearts*.   ISBN 0-930044-73-8   8.95

SPRING FORWARD/FALL BACK by Sheila Ortiz Taylor.
288 pp. Literary novel of timeless love.   ISBN 0-930044-70-3   7.95

FOR KEEPS by Elisabeth Nonas. 144 pp. Contemporary novel
about losing and finding love.   ISBN 0-930044-71-1   7.95

TORCHLIGHT TO VALHALLA by Gale Wilhelm. 128 pp.
Classic novel by a great Lesbian writer.   ISBN 0-930044-68-1   7.95

LESBIAN NUNS: BREAKING SILENCE edited by Rosemary
Curb and Nancy Manahan. 432 pp. Unprecedented autobiographies
of religious life.   ISBN 0-930044-62-2   9.95

THE SWASHBUCKLER by Lee Lynch. 288 pp. Colorful novel
set in Greenwich Village in the sixties.   ISBN 0-930044-66-5   8.95

MISFORTUNE'S FRIEND by Sarah Aldridge. 320 pp. Histori-
cal Lesbian novel set on two continents.   ISBN 0-930044-67-3   7.95

A STUDIO OF ONE'S OWN by Ann Stokes. Edited by
Dolores Klaich. 128 pp. Autobiography.   ISBN 0-930044-64-9   7.95

FAULTLINE by Sheila Ortiz Taylor. 140 pp. Warm, funny,
literate story of a startling family.   ISBN 0-930044-24-X   6.95

THE LESBIAN IN LITERATURE by Barbara Grier. 3d ed.
Foreword by Maida Tilchen. 240 pp. Comprehensive bibliography.
Literary ratings; rare photos.   ISBN 0-930044-23-1   7.95

ANNA'S COUNTRY by Elizabeth Lang. 208 pp. A woman
finds her Lesbian identity.   ISBN 0-930044-19-3   8.95

PRISM by Valerie Taylor. 158 pp. A love affair between two
women in their sixties.   ISBN 0-930044-18-5   6.95

BLACK LESBIANS: AN ANNOTATED BIBLIOGRAPHY
compiled by J. R. Roberts. Foreword by Barbara Smith. 112 pp.
Award-winning bibliography.   ISBN 0-930044-21-5   5.95

THE MARQUISE AND THE NOVICE by Victoria Ramstetter.
108 pp. A Lesbian Gothic novel.   ISBN 0-930044-16-9   6.95

OUTLANDER by Jane Rule. 207 pp. Short stories and essays
by one of our finest writers.   ISBN 0-930044-17-7   8.95

ALL TRUE LOVERS by Sarah Aldridge. 292 pp. Romantic
novel set in the 1930s and 1940s.   ISBN 0-930044-10-X   8.95

A WOMAN APPEARED TO ME by Renee Vivien. 65 pp. A
classic; translated by Jeannette H. Foster.   ISBN 0-930044-06-1   5.00

CYTHEREA'S BREATH by Sarah Aldridge. 240 pp. Romantic
novel about women's entrance into medicine.
                              ISBN 0-930044-02-9   6.95

TOTTIE by Sarah Aldridge. 181 pp. Lesbian romance in the
turmoil of the sixties.   ISBN 0-930044-01-0   6.95

THE LATECOMER by Sarah Aldridge. 107 pp. A delicate love
story.   ISBN 0-930044-00-2   6.95

ODD GIRL OUT by Ann Bannon.   ISBN 0-930044-83-5   5.95
I AM A WOMAN 84-3; WOMEN IN THE SHADOWS 85-1;   each
JOURNEY TO A WOMAN 86-X; BEEBO BRINKER 87-8. Golden
oldies about life in Greenwich Village.

JOURNEY TO FULFILLMENT, A WORLD WITHOUT MEN, and   3.95
RETURN TO LESBOS. All by Valerie Taylor   each

These are just a few of the many Naiad Press titles — we are the oldest and
largest lesbian/feminist publishing company in the world. Please request a
complete catalog. We offer personal service; we encourage and welcome direct
mail orders from individuals who have limited access to bookstores carrying
our publications.

I0659520

VOICE FROM THE DARK

Christopher Duprea

LMH Publishing Limited

Executive Editor: Charles Moore

Editors: Neil Morgan & Charles Moore

Cover Design: Leequee Designs

Book Design & Layout: PAGE Design & Services

Prepared forPublishing by:
LMH Publishing Ltd.
Suite 10, 7 Norman Road
Kingston, C.S.O.
Jamaica, West Indies
Tel: 876-938-0005/0712
Fax: 876-759-8752
Email: lmhbookpublishing@cwjamaica.com
Website: www.lmhpublishingjamaica.com

Printed in the U.S.A.   ISBN   976-8184-93-0

Dedication

To my wife Janet for your love and support.

Acknowledgements

Special thanks to Mrs. Rita Marley and her daughter Stephanie for taking me to numerous countries across the world and opening so many paths of experience.

I want to thank my wife Janet, my daughters Catherine, Christine and Phillippa for being patient with me until I fulfilled my dreams.

Also, thanks to Steven Stedesco for helping me in the United States and also to Merl and Nick.

It is the gift of kindness, the gift of a smile and the gift of love that makes life worthwhile.

Written by: Dr. Pratap C. Singhai, M.D.

Table of Contents

PART I:

'Chant and Confrontation'

"In the end, we will remember not the words of our enemies, but the silence of our friends."

(Martin Luther King Jr)

A Getter

You don't wait on others
To tell you who you are or
Where you should be going;
If you can reach the stars,
There is no limitation to what you can achieve.
Tell yourself that the heart
Sticks to what it believes.

You don't wait on others to respect you
Or your investments in life;
You don't see others as better to yourself;
It avails you to remain on the floor.
Go out and get —
Not regret
What your dreams are for.

What's in store if you fail?

Don't wait on others to realize your dreams;
No one owes you.
Don't be shut out behind the scenes.
You, who work endlessly,
You who put out nothing less than your best

Others will come to honour you;
Others will attest to your success.

Care

Don't go hurting others
Because they might hurt you;
You'd be just as guilty
For better you know to do.
Consider their plight -
What you call wrong they might see right.
Be patient and understanding,
And a genuine friend you'll win.

Don't go hurting others
Wanting to see yourself in them.
You might not see eye to eye
All of us have our problems
Respect the opinions of others,
Meet them half way without ruining your happiness
Allowing hatred to cloud the day

Don't go hurting others
Because their ethic differs from yours:
They might not have been fortunate to be brought up
With the care and love a mummy and daddy ensures.
All your life you've been sheltered
Knowing from where you will get your bread;
Unlike you, others don't have such a privilege.

Don't go hurting others
Lend them a hand to reach their goal
Though they prove themselves ungrateful;
Waste none of your time to contrive their down fall
Pause, first, to remember;
The world is created not for some, but all.
Don't prejudice in your dealings and
Plot your downfall.

Crab Mentality

Shun the cynic around you
If you want to get ahead.
If they cannot succeed on your advancement
They will try to impede on your happiness.

Avoid this crab mentality!
Shake off those who are prophets of doom;
Be firm in whatever you do
Or else you will never get through.

Don't be subdued by negative criticism:
See the sun in through the rain clouds;
An achiever doesn't easily give in -
An achiever goes out there to win.

Be different from others -
Risk the condemnation;
Risk the insurmountable barriers set up to foist you.
Make use of opportunities when they avail themselves.

Be meek when you reach the end of your travels;
Remember, before one walks, one has to creep.
Success will always remain with the humble -
Those who haven't forgotten the pain.

The world is a classroom:
Rise with the current swelling the air
Or retreat with the lapse in tides
Scooping clear water from the heart;
Accomplish your dreams as you stride.

Underestimated

Don't look down on others
Whoever they might be
No matter where you are today
There is a lot more left to see
You might see yourself flying like a kite
Others might be slow in starting
But they too have their heights to soar

Don't look down on others
Because you do not agree
A difference of opinion
Don't make you wrong or right
Many have been to the same class room
Some successful while others failed
All could not be doctors and lawyers
Someone has to deliver the mail...

Do not look down on others
Because you had to part company at the cross road
Try and be more understanding
Everyone knows the weight of their load!
We all might be on the same ship
Sailing on the same sea
But at the end of the journey
It's the same faces you see.

Do not look down on others
Because your pedestal will topple or swing to and fro
Others might be more contented in a hut or under a
tree.
You might be of a different pigmentation
Or segregate yourself in another class
What you should fight to keep is your freedom
Remember others had a to pay a high price as well.

Pawn-Yuh Machete

You don't have to mortify your brother
To reach your destination.
You don't have to sow a negative seed;
It will never be healthy when it germinates.
Your intention doesn't have to be evil
Because you're overshadowed by the lack of gain.
Instead let it be an example, and with hard work
You can attain your aim.

You don't have to covet what others have;
Because your brother labours to get success,
You dig a pit and await his fall.
All was bestowed with talent;
Not all had utilized it right.
Should you in your failure
Pounce on others who were strategic
In winning their fight?

You don't have to be a pawn-yuh-machete:
Prattling to elevate yourself in extremes.
How sordid for a human being to descend
Flippantly,
Plotting schemes until their dying day.
What good will it do you
To see others in pain?
In the latter, it'll return to haunt you
And your actions will be pure shame.

Covet

Why would you covet
What God has blessed others with?
If you work hard and yielded to your synergy
You'd have the same outcome.
Why waste so much energy envying the success of others?

Why covet others for what they have?
How do you think they got it -
Squandering, impatient, living life in one day?
Not making the sacrifice for when they become old and
gray?
Don't eat all your cake believing you still have it;
If you don't invest, you'll not make a profit.
Remember, with the ceasing of the sun,
Comes the cold and the rain
A little insurance must be put aside
Else all will be in vain

With the candles lit at both ends,
You'll always be indebted -
Never in a position to render a helping hand to a friend.
Be cheerful and encouraging when your brothers and
sisters advance;
Neither of you will make it alone
If none is prepared to take the chance.

Never feel that you're too proud if you reach the top;
The same people who cheered you on your way up
Will point at you if you drop.
Try and help someone as you travel on your pathway
Embrace your journey, as rough as it is
Stop not to abuse people
Because they lack opportunity and zeal;
In life success isn't guaranteed.
Would you like to be treated in
That manner should your courage fail you?

Higgler's Business

I walked with bags of gungo peas
To Pedro and Flagaman;
Through woods climbed o'er the fence
Crawling on knees and hands
Harassed by pesky, stinging insects.
I'm in the higgler's business
To get rich or die.

I walk with kegs of corn pork, banana and lemon
From house to house I sell;
To Munro and Devon
My back ached beneath the load,
My feet quivered as I travelled the road.
I'm in the higgler's business
To get rich or die.

I walked with baskets full of avocado and melon
Selling irish potatoes, broccoli and yam;
Through flood and rain, swamps and plane
To Treasure Beach, and Frenchman's Cove.
I'm in the higgler's business
To get rich or die.

Career

Get some security:
Get a trade or career
Before your heart leads you into a situation
For which you are unprepared.

Waste not your young life
Roaming with blind eyes,
Fantasizing relentlessly;
Be focussed and sincere,
Keep your head firmly screwed on,
Trust in your instinct, as it tells you what to do –
You'll be more times right than wrong.

Don't patronize you peers with what you don't
understand,
Don't lash out because you're left behind in places you
don't belong;
It could be time to realize your future direction.

Try to be peaceful, caring and true;
Remember today for me, tomorrow for you.
Be co-operative and patient, don't be easily despaired;
Don't resort to bad habits when others treat you unfair.

Never make a decision that you'll come to regret;
Never make promises that you know you cannot keep;
Don't jump into waters, if you don't how deep;
Don't start anything that you have no intention to
complete.

Police Abuse

Approaching the Ghetto
So you treat it like pig sty.
Intoxicated, you're on a high;
Drink up plenty rum,
Load up with automatic gun,
In the ghetto yard –
Killing who you don't regard!

You've butchered with your licensed firearm
Beating them to your will.
A part of being infamous is having to kill
Your way to the top;
Making havoc shudder through the crowd;
Ghetto children bawling out loud in twisted
admiration.

How can you kick
A pregnant mother?
Shoot an innocent brother?
Lie on another
And then make love to lover?
How would you like your children
So meek, so mild
Coldly shot by a member of your gangrene?

How can you
For a month's pay
Go on in this way?
You don't realize
Old age sneaks your way?
You'll become a languid babe,
You'll need someone, a friend
When you are too old to move around.

I pity you!
Storm in the calm,
Pitiless in duties performed,
Refuse of society
Abusing your authority
Giving in to fun
You can't live without the gun.

Splinter in My Tear

Empty vibrations felt
Are reasons within themselves:
Nothing seems to make sense.
Had to be building a resistance
For existence to flesh itself out...

Have you experienced joy and sorrow?
Are you familiar with failure and error?
Why does the spirit adjust so easily
To the different seasons?
And man to envy, and distrust
Locked away in prison!

Are we here passing time
As entertainment to the bosses of the capitalistic
swarm?
Working daily,
Worrying endlessly,
Carrying their crosses!

Echoes, when I question our poverty,
That we didn't get any of the good things created.
Will we always have to work harder
For a passport?
To cross into the world of living easy?
We're out of breath working relentlessly,
Unable to erase our debts,
Hardly able to provide meals for our plates...
Who's blessed with such faith?
Must we die and be reincarnated before the path
clears?

The Pen

There's not an invention more welcomed
Than the pen.
You can jot your thoughts
Down to remind you where or when.

A thought in mind is special;
A speech is sometimes misquoted.
A scribble of the pen on paper
You can forever retract your note.

The pen will make an impression
To an unborn generation,
Convey a conversation across
The sky and ocean;
The pen can unite a nation.

Struggling Soul

Oh! You bitter,
Wandering soul!
Toiling hard to reach your goal.
Obstacles stretch out hands to hold you in the cold.

Oh! Struggling soul!
Slaving away;
Knowing there will come a day
To lift yourself
From the miry clay!

No one can stop you from reaching your destination -
Nor imprison your inspiration.
You're left in bitterness.

Propose to buy a piece of land
Build a house,
Uplift yourself,
Be a man!
To accomplish the end,
You got to have the means.
Get in the front line.
Obstacles merely threaten you in this time.

Kibba yuh mout'

Where do you find time to
Flush other lives in slime?
Never uttering a word
About what you see,
Always, I heard!
Your life is on the ground,
But you find time taking others to task,
With your squalid remarks.
Everyone yuh label
'Bout yuh hear say
Him eligible or unstable!

Yuh chat 'bout people's shoes' size an'
Who and who economized.
The dread down the road knows better
Because he deals with a different vibration.
You criticize his belief in another master
Want to know how much load in the higgler's basket.
Yuh turn Christian today
Convincing me that riches made you lose your way.
You squandered your life in your hey day.
Now eating out a garbage bin
You never stop bragging
And bragging.
Now yuh have life worse than dog.

Never Say Never

Never shouldn't be a final word;
Never say "I never".
This could be an embarrassing word
To retract a situation
You swore you'd never.
Never seems so appropriate
The moment it's expressed;
But confronted in a dilemma,
You'll do what you said you'd never.

Life is a gamble.
Today you see success,
You think you're so clever.
That's when you're inclined to boast
I "never"!
Never, what's "never"?
When one's out of danger
Don't be hasty to condemn
Others for what you think you'll never;
You might tumble into a troubled era
And call on the escape route "never".
Today you criticize, "never" tomorrow;
"Never" could be you
So when you speak make sure you think before
You use the word.
Don't be a victim
In a situation you swore you would "never".

Dirt under your collar

Get your snout out of the dirty trough!
Why make vanity lure you into filth?
You get your gain from exploiting
The little man sweating in fear,
Swindling his pocket
As he struggles from strain of minimalism.

Sheep sweat hard behind thick wool.
You don't show the dirt under your collar,
Yet what you hide will one day show.
Cologne turns to stench,
Becomes stagnant as breeze start blow
When you start to get that dirt off your shoulder

Pearls dished out to swine;
Hogs can't appreciate good wine!
The blind cyaan lead blind!
It's time to draw the line towards your path.
Stop running away from your aggression,
Have a heart, remember where you coming from.
If you continue to squeeze,
One day the people will squeal.

Pressure

Firmly hold on to the reins,
Blindfold yourself from seeing people's pain;
Everyday you tighten the noose.
Soon, the chicken will have to abandon their roost.
Taxes outweigh their measure,
People forget how to have pleasure.

Cost of living reaches the maximum,
There's no consideration for the suffering in the slum.
So much malnutrition and
Like rain, down comes the taxation.

Who has patience now
To sit around in the air condition' for a few cents per
hour?
Trying to make ends meet from 8 to 5,
Always on their feet,
From hand to mouth
She has become a slave
Taxation pressures mother to an early grave.

Dependency

Rise above your slavish mantle;
Go for the task of self-will.
Free yourself from the pawn of handouts;
Don't be tricked into thinking copper is gold.

Rise and awake your consciousness,
Sanction the willingness to succeed;
Shake off the yoke of dependency,
Demand your little piece of this earth!

Rise from your wayward thinking,
Rise to the task set at hand;
It's not a rule but a challenge,
The need should be endurance.

Rise from your passive upbringing,
Demand self-worth;
Begging, prostituting, cheating, killing -
You're deep in the dirt.

Rise from a low down living,
From dependency, why not convert?
Working is the best take out policy,
Life could be like heaven on earth.

Worthless Man

Young man you are so bitter;
To whom will you turn to complain?
You're a son of the soil,
You're no quitter!
In your anguish, who will you blame?

You're advised to seek redress;
The parson says poor men must to their God bless.
Poverty manifests in all you investments;
How did you get in such a mess?

You don't want to escape your responsibility.
You are not looking hand out.
You don't want any sympathy.

A nuh this yuh bitter 'bout.

You do not want to migrate to the states,
You don't want to be caught in idle debates,
Sufferation has you deeply frustrated;
God gives and takes away faith.

There seems no opportunity on the land,
This is causing a big division.
Although you toil till arthritis numbs your hand,
You appear a worthless man.

Hustling with your load on your head,
And the table still short of bread.
And the worst that you dread
Is to see your child go unfed.
How can you with this minimum wage
Inna dis day and age?

Cost of living reach such a high stage
You rant in rage when you turn
The gleaner page.
You can't afford to get sick,
You'll have a heart attack if you think about it.
When you going to stop pay rent,
And lay a brick,
And be constructive in spending a bit?
So long you don't buy your woman a dress,
Only Lawd knows how we poor and distress'.
If you want good, it is said, you nose have to run
But bitterness overcome all the fun.

PART II:

'My Own 'Personal Gravity'

"Reality is merely an illusion,
albeit a very persistent one."

(Albert Einstein)

Destiny

I believe in destiny,
What is to be must be.
No matter how carefully you ordain
The sun and the rain to remain: they won't.

I believe in the creator
And his omniscience overshadowing everything
Do you doubt him?
Do you really believe he doesn't limit the pain you
feel?

I believe that today in my sorrow
Will not make me fear them tomorrow;
When the critic observing my errors
Usurps the happiness on my page,
It is the type of thing he would repel.

I believe there's nothing you can avoid;
No tide, once insurmountable, can be swayed.
Imprisoning yourself behind the grill
Will not prevent you from being killed.

I believe there's no substitute
For the barren tree which doesn't bear fruit;
I believe that through destiny
It is in man to squander or save their morality.

24

Music

Music
With her silky hands
Caresses the surface of my heart;
Sweetly, seduces my body with traumatic passion
Oh romantic music...

Music
Which echoes
Around the valley
Of my dreams;
Such harmony
Oh! Placid melody
Rocking me to sleep,
Oh Music, don't leave me.

Music
Such a lovely rhythm...

If I Knew

If I knew —
Three words which
Influence our lives so...
Strangle-holding the weaklings
Deserting you when you're in need
Like cowards, they strongly criticize
When you've done the deed

If I knew -
What an illusion!
Always showing up in hindsight
Like a premonition after the damage was done,
Never mind it when you've made a decision.

But when they appear
You can't help but be astonished

How come you never
Possess their precisions?

Loneliness

How I feel lonely in my soul
And far-far away
From the boundaries of my goals.
Loneliness grips me within;
Her slumbering strong clasp
Shunting the fire burning deep in my soul.

Loneliness grips me
Making it hard to see.
I asked God in meditation:
Was this ordained to be?
This pain, this misery,
This torment I feel.
I must squeal
Because at times
It doesn't seem real!

Myself

Who am I?
A philanthropist
An explicit Jamaican
Not what society wants me to be;
I'm floating in a vacuum
Suppressed by your negation, your plans.
I'm a simple farmer
A determined, struggling man.
I will die for my freedom,
But I will not travel in your crowd.
You beat down on my rights
With your bitter lies.
I have no faith in this system
Which is outliving its time

Exile

Loneliness has stayed with me so long
The world of dreams eludes me;
All I see is your pity.
Leaving me with my ego and pain
No serenity engulfs my brain.
God
Will you now stand by me
Through tumult and rain
And spiritually rid me of the turmoil
I feel each day when the sun slips?

I have no use
For your polluted atmosphere
Smeared with hate, envy and fear.
In my hammock with a book, at home
How better 'tis to pass the time
Than in a war, or behind prison bars.

They who never cease
To nurture the growth of gossip
Tread upon the turf of peace;
They merely descend into insanity
Sinisterly giving out their so called pity.
I don't ponder your phenomenon;
Don't ponder mine... we have nothing in common.

At the Cross

I stand steadfast
At the cross
There are no contradictions
At the cross
I rest from effortless toil
At the cross
I am no longer defiled

At the cross
I erase all pretenses
At the cross
I unclothe my remnants
At the cross
I kneel and give thanks
At the cross
I needn't compete to close ranks

At the cross
I'm not a color
At the cross
We don't live like dogs
Biting at each other
At the cross
Freedom has no price
At the cross
Freedom comes
At last...

Death

Grief,
So hard to bear;
A destiny we all must share.
Doesn't matter how well you prepare
Death always catches us unaware.
Oh! Why, why such a time span bestowed on humans?
Living, beautiful creatures created by God's hand
From dust to ash you arrive and return;
It doesn't care how tall you rise.
You fill your mind with wisdom
Your end is due
The pendulum's swing
Is not controlled by you.

Death, I contemplate,
Must be a passionate subject;
I find it hard to debate.
Look at all the inventions of man
Yet, death lies awaiting its hour
To carry you from this land of
All the things you cherish;
A time comes when they too will perish.

Loafter

Up the mountain;
Neither my aim nor my digression
Deters me to win or gain.
I'll endure whatever strain;
The sun sometimes shines a little brighter
No use for me to sit and complain.

Hardships frosted my awakening;
My will to attain isn't shaken.
Tiresome time, whispers lie;
You'll become naught if you comply.
Patient, idle the day
Start don't complete the way -
You have a next day, a next year, or forever
To achieve your endeavour.

Bewitching

Woman of my dreams,
So bewitchingly beautiful-
You delusion of my youthful inclination!
Are you real?
Are you a shadow revealed at last when I awake
Or are you swept away by streams of oblivion?

Woman of my dreams
Your empty presence
I must constantly bear!
With the approach of morning,
Can you ever stop the tides
From washing your image away from my mind?

Say but a word;
Let your presence be felt.
You exist, somewhere out there
I dreamed of us
Strolling amongst the panorama of eroticism

I trembled
Me, a strong man being drained of my potency
Acting stupid, making empty promises
Love, leave me not
To the dungeon of loneliness-
Stay! Stay! My bewitching lover...

Profiteering Vagabonds

Standing at a cross roads
As I carry the heavy load;
God! Guide me to make the choice,
Give me strength to sacrifice
On a journey to Zion Hill
Where sins, and grief, cannot be found
And Satan is hell-bound.

I shut my eyes
In silent prayer
For God to lift me higher!
Guide my path that I'll not falter
Leaving my burden at the altar!
Freedom from oppression,
And poverty's condemnation!
Lead me out of the corrupted hands
Of profiteering vagabonds.

Hear the foreboding voice inside;
By your laws let me abide
Obstacles in this impoverished plane
Tempt me to give in to selfishness-
Help me to carry this cross
With each step... not counting the cost.
Hold my hand, and pull me through-
Oh Lord! I'm depending on you.
When I'm provoked to sin,
With your love, the exploiter can't win!

"You"

by J. Neil - to C.D.

Who are you?
You come into my life so suddenly
Captivating me
Demolishing my laws, and building up yours.
In awe, I watched you rule.
It didn't take long for my activities
To be revolutionized.
Childishly, I complied with your perceptions
You became my world;
My life, my dreams,
My hopes were all centered around you.
This wasn't for long though;
You vanished without muttering a syllable.
Now my world is like a vacuum;
Dark and blank.
I never seem to understand your actions
Puzzling –
Your disappearance startles me as much
As your appearance.

Evading Happiness

Out there along
The plains
My thoughts roam;
Evading happiness.
Such warmth I feel,
Such peace, it's not real.
Melancholy lurks
Sucking away like quick sand
Twirling,
I shout for liberty!

Out there along the rivers and seas
I found happiness, for a moment
My heart was glad;
My mind became sad
With the approaching
Twilight overshadowing
This promising gleam.
I shout for liberty.

Out there amidst the trees,
Birds, singing early.
Free to pollinate the blossoms
No care, no fear
No bondage so free;
While acrid within my breast
Longing, hoping to rid the constant gloom.

Whisper in the Dark

Thoughts revealed
In the dark
Grappling my heart
So much to reminisce
After a long kiss
Could distance separate
The warmth we shared?
We couldn't stay apart at the start

Oh! Love has died unfairly;
I'm broken with despair
All those years waiting,
Preparing for our concurrence
Like the dark, you're cold
Where's the raging fire?
Where are the romantic verses
So boldly you once told?

My advice you once admired
Responding with endless desire;
Sad, was our reunion
Dampening all my feelings with sympathy.
Let's deal with reality:
Love's grown cold.

Sometimes

J. Neil to CD

Sometimes, I love you;
Sometime, I adore you;
Sometimes, you engulf my whole being;
Sometimes, your face haunts me;
Sometimes, I think I cannot exist without you;
Sometime, I hate you so much;
Sometimes, I want to hurt you;
Sometime, I want to destroy you;
Sometimes I wonder what my true feelings
    are towards you;
Sometimes, you make me want to do things
    I wouldn't do;
Sometimes, you bitch, and it really hurts;
Sometimes, I see your face in others;
It disgusts me
Sometimes, I wonder who dares you
To leave me
Alone
And cause me to be so terribly lonely...

Lasting Peace

Silence, Oh silence;
No noise, not a sound.
I probe my thoughts silently
To create a tranquil grounding
Where lasting unity and peace
Resound
And justice without favour
All year around

Silence, Oh Silence!
Neither conflict nor battle
Brothers killing brothers like lamb to the slaughter
Inflicting environmental hazards and famine and
destroying our towns.
Soon there'll be nothing left.

Silence, Oh! Silence,
Let peace be a part
Of the thoughts in your head;
Nuclear weapons —
A dream once that was dreamt
To help one another
Up the rung of the progressive ladder.
Not seeking lasting power
To destroy progress in an hour.

Fragile Affair

So many years have lapsed
So many tears
Our relationship has collapsed;
Nothing
Remains of the love.
Men are sometimes weak,
They fell prey to a woman's stare.

The wives at home have crosses to bear;
Their behaviour is premature.
Flirting with desperate longings far from home shores
God, blessed us with two beautiful children

Yet
You've changed:
The simplest things make you sore with anger
You've become so violent...
All my efforts are in vain
The best years of our lives have been
Flushed down the drain.
I'd gotten used to your desire.
I
Grew old;
You
Found others to admire...

Silent Hill

The hills make
Nostalgia overwhelm my reflections;
The rivers and springs,
The rocks and cliffs-
Grandma's endless cultivation

Donkeys and mules
Resting under the cool trees;
The sugar cane we milled,
The water drums filled,
Carrying bundles of fire wood
On our heads uphill.

Long have I seen
Fruit trees and orchids
Adorning the wild;
Unmanned hills setting up nightly,
Catching birds in their nest
And cook sly meals
As grandma rests…

Take Time

Anonymous

Take time to live; it is the secret of success.
Take time to think; it is the source of power.
Take time to play; it is the secret of youth.
Take time to read; it is the fountain of knowledge.
Take time for friendship; it is the source of happiness.
Take time to dream; hitches the soul to star.
Take time for laugh; it helps to lift life's worries
Take time for God; it is life's only lasting investment.
Take time to meditate; it is the lifting of your heart.
Take time to pray; it is the union of your mind with God.
Take time to love; it is the privilege of good.
Take time to work; it is the price of success.

PART III:

'In The Carnival
Called Life'

*"...the most dangerous creation
of any society is that man who has nothing
to lose."*

(James Baldwin)

Lovers Leap

Lovers Leap
A dramatic scene
Superb look-out
In the south east hills
Where the seas below
Clatter and growl;
Canoes and boats
Fishing in the flawless ocean sun-dried mix.
Waves roll, and rattle
Lyrically against the rocks
Scrubs lush, surpassing the low shore.

Lovers who embrace
In the dim light,
Refreshing their lives,
Renewing vows
Under the beaming beacon.
The night inspires a panoramic view of
Munro, Pedro and Flagaman
Corby, Plowden and Alligator Pond
Lover's Leap where lovers meet.

This boundless beauty,
All this memory
You'll keep forever.

Hustle and Bustle

Time to climb out of the gutter;
Time to acknowledge how your bread gets buttered.
Stop being carefree and
Take hold of your responsibility -
Use the educational key
To enter the gates of prosperity.
Nothing in this life comes easy
The sailor in the boat works hard at sea.

Take your minds off food rations;
Become self-reliant, get off the welfare cushion.
Don't wait until it's too late to be a man
Supporting your family
Instead of being restricted to depravity;
Rise above brawn and muscle
It's all just a hustle and a bustle.

A head isn't made to wear hats solely
Nor bellies made to settle with fat;
You'll never make it to the top of the hill
If you sit still.
Jump and dance, romance and prance
This is as it would; burn out...burn out
Like fire on dry wood.
Secure an old age pension
Don't end up with too many
Unanswered
Questions...

Mother

Mother, there's no other
To take the place of her guidance;
Over the rockiness of hardships
She'll help you through.

So gentle, her arms embrace you;
How safe you'll feel from harm.
Doesn't matter how cold the weather is
Mother will keep you warm...

Her role in life is endless;
Always trying her best
When the journey seems dreary.
Mother never becomes a figure of despair

For nine long months, you were her load;
Fed and clad you with what little she could afford
Through pain and strain, loss and gain
Never counting the cost.

On her advice you depend;
She's a devoted friend.
You can count on a mother
To defend you to the end...

Proud Farmers

Can't wait for the morning to come around again;
The cocks will crow its arrival,
Farmers hasten for the field
Planning the various shrubs that will yield
To rain and the energy unravelling
From wound-up shoulders

Thunder rolls behind dark clouds
Gather all the tools;
We're farmers that are proud.
Labour while it's cool,
Hasten before the day is through,
Plant the seed that we bring,
Hum a lively tune, let's begin.

Plow and sow,
Lift the hoe;
Plants must grow.
Fork the land, plant yam for a rainy day
Slit the cocoa for it will keep my stomach warm;
Plant sweet and irish potato.

Scatter the grains in the row,
The tractor will keep their anarchy in line
Or we weed them out tomorrow
The rain starts to fall -

A productive day's dream has come true.

Age

Age, creeps up on you
Through the door of time -
Sucking away your youthful designs;
Deranging your memory;
Slowly depriving you of your energy:
What games betwixt, you, young and old?
You were a tower of strength
Now it serves me feeble and cold...

Oh! Youth, glimmering in the spring
Of ever green, roaming about
Idly gloating, discovering hidden scenes;
Strength never failing,
Endlessly daydreaming:
Now, I remember such enchanting feelings.
Age moved in with no intentions of co-existing
Elbowing out the young
Overthrowing, capturing, dictating...

Age, with authority, prunes away
Every fibre of youth's remains;
Hair which was black as night
Are replaced with silvers and grays.
Slowing your agility,
You perish with humility...
Age affecting you in every way;
Age is here to stay.

Work

Man, till the soil;
Man, must go the extra mile;
Man, must have a purpose;
Man, stop and think a while.

Man should live a life
In its truest sense:
Eating, drinking, praising God.
The dead don't need this living
Man,
Work incessantly!
Don't be content with merely existing.

So do not live as though you're dead
Roaming in your sleep full of misgivings;
A hard day's work procures
A night's rest, sweetly dreaming.

Aim your ideals at the top
Suffice not with today's accomplishment
The minute's elapsed
You're getting old
Your energy dwindles

Is there a earthen bound section
To enjoy this place called heaven?
What a trick when the trumpet sounds!

Bucky Master

How many times we sigh, and cry?
How long must we suffer
Under this ya situation?
Isn't there a solution?
Help us the small nation;
We must live...we can't afford to die...

How long must a nation be subdued
By your promises?
Your lies?
You make rules to further your causes
While disregarding a nation with handouts.
The poor can take no more;
People have been milked to the core.

How many times
Must they pay
With their blood, sweat and tears?
When will they have their say?
Under your administration
Come no plans to unite a nation...
You oppress children from their food
To feed
Your greed...

People of the Night

Lying on the city pavement,
They are
Outstretched like the dead.
No one cares!
Broken bare and battered feet,
Defecating on the streets.

Lying on the pavement,
A pregnant mother weeps herself to sleep:
She is a victim of the system,
Thwarted by oppression.
Her children roam the streets
Hunting food out of the garbage heaps.
Around the corner, prostitutes willingly sell themselves
To men who could inject unmentioned disease

Lying on the pavement,
Lovers, deep in a meeting, feel no love;
Money becomes the medium of their heart's exchange.
Thieves and rogues are close at hand
The scarcer the goods are
The harder to pay the cost.
Man standing at a loss
Where is the human right?
We count the stars
While being trampled by another man's might...

Hunger

Hunger prowls inside,
The stomach rolling for a bite
Nothing to eat: hunger hurts.
The cost of living and income don't relate;
Prior to being paid,
Thieves raid.

Concocted evasive rationing,
Persistent hunger creeps in;
If you are the tower of strength
To climb on to the top,
Who invites you ever to be bold?
Wishing to enter society's fold
You resist and fight…
Just maybe, you'll reach your goal…

Burn the Coke

Extradition, sedation, execution
Hell-bound in our situation -
Contaminating, penetrating
The new born generation;
Poisoning their consciousness with cocaine
Soliloquizing, fantasizing, dehumanizing…
What's your aim?
Stooping so low,
Destroying humanity
To achieve vanity -
What a blow!

Freaks in white collars
Can't see anything, but the almighty dollar;
Coke messing up the youth's brain.
Refrain from this gesture
Flushing lives down the drain! Shame!
You're creating a Frankenstein
Cocaine barons must sequester
If it's even with the gallows
Stop this lunatic fellow:
Grab him, drag him and flog him;
Get rid of the dope, sniffing coke
There's no hope.

Scars

Do you know the grief that women have borne?
Do you understand why they weep and mourn?
Only God knows the pain they endure
When men wreck their lives and dump them on their
own

Do you know the distress?
The scars which have regressed
Giving up all they had stood for.
Now you place them aside,
Finding others to take as brides,
Treating women like you treat your shoes.

How easy for men
To walk out and start again;
No marks on their bodies to show
Men, proud men
Every woman as prey

Do you know the heartache and sorrow
Of seeing men living carelessly?
As the sparrows, fluttering their feathers,
Treating women as their handmaids.
Men, they think women are fiddles
And each week
Their fingers pick a new tune.

Do you know blood flows through their veins?

Dutty Bundlers

Chilled to the bones
Observing the coiling ferns;
Not accustomed to this weather.
Feeling like captured birds.
Never could I turn to the United Nations
To deviate from the heat.
So inconsistent with who they discredit
Swift to others to hand out merit.

The insignificance with paper sword,
You're expedient in making inroads;
South African violations by the trailer load
United Nations ineffective sanctions gone o'erboard
And different for Iraq, Columbia and Bosnia
Wha' a gwaan yah?
South Africa has the desecrated book
Determine to cloak dem dutty bundle, o'er looked

United Nations ease sanctions without reforms....
Oh Lord! What wickedness
In Cape Town...
They performed...
Apartheid fixed embalmed...
We have to call on God.

Enmity in the City

Why so much murder in the city
Enkindled with enmity?
Is the city becoming a forest
And the people its birds?
Dear Lord, these couldn't be lives
The murders are exterminating;
Using guns and knives.
What a picture they are painting!

Do they have blood in their veins?
Or feeling to feel pain?
Pumping bullets in people's flesh;
Will you require sympathy when you get caught?
You appeal for human rights
When you are condemned to die.
But do you apply these rights when your
Victims appeal to you?
Cry!

Raciality

Is this a ploy
You've employed?
Debasing a whole human race?
Keeping them dedicated to the task
Of remaining uneducated?
You smear a little grease
On their ignorant lips
To keep them in subjection,
And you use you slavish whip
To enact your racist intent.

You take your wealth;
And spread your terror.
Employing goons, a ploy for immune retaliation!
When the people get out of place,
You massacre a large amount of their race.
Resorting to dirty tricks
Carrying out wicked tactics!
How far must you go
To keep the races from mixing?
You playing yo-yo?
Time for your system to go!

Prostitution

Prostitution is a sin
Why do you take this route for a living?
AIDS is a big risk, such scars
Have you ever contemplated tomorrow
When your joy turns to sorrow?
With all your material gains
Your soul will be tormented.
Don't take it for granted;
Your ambition has left its stain.

Some convert to Christian;
Some will turn to beer at 2 am in the morning.;
Some will be mad;
Some will be soothed by ballads;
The consequences will scar your conscience.
Your life is a pretense.

What a situation you're copying!
Throwing yourself to the wind
Don't care how grim things are,
Don't turn to negative obsession;
The possession at time craves
Hastens you to the grave.

Inflation

Inflation on the land,
Who is it polluting
But the poor suffering man?
He works hard
To facilitate
His poor polluted state:
Underpaid,
Overworked,
Through rain and sun;
He has no fun.
Poor suffering man
He owes a lot of debts
Food price gone high.
Pay, when insurance 'draw out'
And tax, can only buy knick knacks;
Wife and pickney empty belly bawl
The rent man a call;
Suffering man look to the sky to ask,
Why?

Grease the Palm

When did mortality lose its accord?
Revulsion scatters without regard
All evil-doers have their reward
Repent, seek a blessing -
Seek the Lord!

When did our nation trade their righteous path?
It once was unselfish,
Moving steadfast.
This generation seems bent on one aim:
Obliterating the love for which Jesus came.

No more Samaritan without greasing the palm;
Hands too immaculate to work on the farm.
Brethren won't hesitate to bring you harm.

People use people without conscience:
Your life...is it worth anything?
Turn a blind eye,
lead your mind away
No one will help;
They would only be willing to push you over the
bridge.
Iniquity and hatred, violence and bad mind
Only God can save
This generation from its subliminal enmity.

Question

Too many sleeping dogs left to lie.
Not everything eaten should be digested:
You extract the best and dump
What's left behind.

Everything which done has a reason;
Each man has a price;
Everything comes in season;
If it's not power they have as an aim,
What they don't own, they want to claim.

It can be reasoned
That all men have some good in them.
Never be hypnotized;
There's always at least one bad morsel hidden
Quietly, from the fruit trees.
There's no perfection;
Believe half of what you see
And nothing, if you don't have concrete justification.

Cease to condemn others based on what you hear;
Be weary of chit-chat:
Question thoroughly in your mind
Why and where's that…
Never swallow a pill
Knowing not, of what good it wills;
Question before you accept a belly full…

Humble

Rumble, grumble,
Voices mumble.
Who has ears let them hear:
From a whisper to a flare up,
Anger echoes loud and clear.
From complaining to law-breaking
Working but can't reach anywhere.
From a mumble to a rumble
This cross is too hard to bear.

Rumble, rumble,
Disgruntled, restricted:
Harden hearts to the wailing cries.
Power is in your hands;
People aren't birds caught in your hands
Peaceful demonstrations yet
Responses come tightly armoured;
Steam will burn as heat gets hotter;
Chaos results from suffocation
The earth will shatter
Volcanic silences
Will soon erupt

Mumble, grumble turn a rumble,
Don't let a spark catch the bramble
Or your power will get burn to shambles:
Too late for you to start act humble.

The Ant

Observe the ants
In their abundance:
Tiresome creatures, yet they labour
Gathering when it's dry.

A thousand times they fail
Persistently retracting their trail.
They will never give up
Until everything's firm in their dens.

Take a leaf from their book;
Adopt their outlook;
Don't be tricked into yielding.
Try and try…one day you'll win.

Unite just like the ant
Pulling hand in hand
Accomplishing when they take a stand
Defending their independence

Ants are well-disciplined
In their doctrine:
They seem to work without lament
Always have their backs bent

Observe their self-will:
Always, they build,
They don't eat all,
They save for the rain.

If you live like the ants,
You'd be better advanced
You don't have to come out the best
At least you've stood to the test

They care about each other
And help one another;
Not complaining who'd work the least
They move jolly and live in peace.

Victory

March on
Oh weary soldier!
The battle must be won;
Bridge the gap betwixt
Ignorance and knowledge.

March on, its time to speak
Nothing is gained succumbing to the strong
It's a fallacy to be poor
So much condemnation to endure

March on we can't retreat:
Victory we must complete.

March on to yonder street:
Barbarism we must defeat.
Demonstrate to the highest seat -
We're tired to be coerced under the emperor's feet

March on,
Tis life or death!
Chained to this situation and full of regret,
Nothing to lose;
Only negation makes the news.

Drought

O'er the oceans climbing the hills
Come the zephyrs;
Blustering wind
Wheeling, whisking, whispering threats
Destroying whatever they can.

Down through the valleys and across the plains
The earth is so in need of rain;
Cattle grazed brown grass
Farmer's spirits are down cast as their crops die;
Hopes
Disappear...

Down goes the weakling as the wind passes,
Weeping willow sways to and fro
Dust blows, casting a shadow
Oh! How the farmers wished rain
Would come at last.

Summer so dry,
Feeling baked in the heat
Surrounding lands hot under your feet
Lignum Vitae and Poinsettia
Blue and red bloom
The dew falls and
The wind swiftly consumes.

Terrorist

Living like dogs
Barking at each other
Hiding in the dark
Unleashing your spree of killings
Fabricating strife, terminating lives
Destruction is all you lend;
How long can you win?

Change your outlawed thinking;
End your repellent barbarism!
Don't you believe in God?
Don't you fear the wrath he'll bring?
As tides runs into rivers,
And streams flow into streams,
If you continue your lives this way
You'll die a refugee…

Everything with life has its end,
What strength is there that cannot be broken or bent?

Plotting, planning, conning your way
When the prison gate shut, you'll pray to see the day

Mother who Fathered

You left me pregnant and went abroad
So, I hardened my mind against you;
There was always the rent to pay.
All the promises, you never meant,
Everything from God and own my strength -
I don't want to hear any arguments...
Nor empty commitments.

Past the worst now,
I stood the test of time -
Children at University
Don't need your pity.
What breeze blew you back here?
You spread your bed, in America
Now you come here telling me you care
Touching, and calling me your dear.

Have properties and a car
Made you reach this far?
It makes you walk like a landlord in the streets
Unfurling your concord ambitions -
You tek mi for prostitute?
I grow the tree,
You come pick the fruit?
Get out you brute!

Poorest Turn Touris'

Pretend you don't know the score
Visiting from foreign shores;
Hand out a couple dollars like you are doing favours
for us
To demonstrate good behaviour.

Life perplexes, I'm vexed.
You migrate from distress
Looking down on
Who remain
Who couldn't obtain a visa
Nor foreign dollars to impress…
You were fortunate to enter greener pastures
While others await your return from graduation…

Can't cope with competition, others have ambition
Though they've never travelled…
Lagging people left behind
Come see them in big mansions
You don't like the expansion

You like to send out barrels
With old stock and at Christmas
Yuh come drink sorrel…

What's going on with God's creation?

PART IV

The Promises of a New Day'

"Sometimes a scream is better than a thesis."
(Ralph Waldo Emerson)

Stress

You are the centre of your life;
Don't let stress overcome you.
No one is worthy of your anger,
Flush negativity from your thoughts;
Open your arms to welcome the Son.
Live not your lives to impress others -
Live for yourself and others will come to appreciate
you.

Live each day in God's presence;
Start today with a positive mind,
Expect that there will always be problems.
There is no solution if you just sit and pine away:
Be loving,
Be kind.
Think of laughter;
Think of the beautiful things in your life;
Think how lucky you are to be alive;
Don't waste your lives on the strife of others.

Don't sleep with hate for another person
Eating away at your health;
Don't allow anyone to trespass on the peace within
you;
Leave the mess outside -
Don't take it indoors.
Don't be like the dog, biting back at who has helped
you;
Confront the darkness as it once was light:
That's the only way you're going to go through.

Going through the Change

It is not every time you can be humble
There comes a time when you have to grumble:
Humble calf suck de mos' milk...
Sometimes humble calf get lef' without milk

A time will come when you must be meek,
This might make you seem weak.
A time will come when you keep to yourself in the
dark;
A time will come when you stand and make your mark.

A time will come when some things cannot be
avoided;
Some might see this as encouragement to take you for
a ride;
Sometimes you have to fight for your right;
Sometimes you have to put aside your pride...

A time will come when you undermine your feelings:
But how long can this be allowed?
Sometimes you must pretend that some things pass you
by unnoticed;
Sometimes you have to pretend you care...

A time will come when you are helpless;
Sometimes you won't have much, but you must share;
Sometimes you rebel because there is so much to
bear...

A time will come when you shed the tears;
A time will come when you put aside your fears;
When you think you cannot take any more,
Turn to the master; he is right by your door.

Success

Yesterday is today's history,
Tomorrow is a dream;
The present is so final,
So unredeemable...

Dreams seem easily accomplished;
Yet, they lay idle, never seeming to come through.
You'll be wretched when old
Regretting another chance wasn't there for you...

The road to success is precipitous;
You decide when it's time to sweat.
Doesn't matter how difficult it gets,
Aim with determination to reach the Zenith

Surmount the barriers that you pass -
Use these experiences to strengthen you everyday.
Confront the future with what you learned from present
and past;
Fulfill what is asked of you.

Be not an addict, repeating mistakes;
Time evaporated cannot be regained.
As minutes tick by, the days and weeks fly,
Seemingly remote years
Creep
Up on you.

Relaxation

When you are downhearted,
Cast yourself into the light;
When there seems no end to the tunnel,
And you're dashing head-first into doom
Your situation isn't unique: press on!
Think about the condemned,
And you'll be strong...

There's so much you can do
When you're overwhelmed with agitation;
Do something active to divert your mind,
Release your pent-up tension,
Talk a walk, window shop, or sight-see;
Read a book or keep yourself active and clean.
Be considerate and volunteer to help,
It will help to blot out negation.

When you become despondent and forlorn,
Impatient with distemper,
Remember the sick and those crippled:
You'll see that you're blessed.
Consider the incarcerated, having lost their rights,
The one's stuffed up with hatred
Tormented because of pride;
Consider being killed in a fracas which you didn't ignite,
And living one mouth full from death
Not knowing from where you get the next bite.

You'll have a problem
Which you can't deal with;
Don't become impotent and deceived
Consuming drugs and becoming alcoholic
Believing you'll get rid of it.
It seems but
Remember it could be worse...
Be confident in someone;
Your freedom, your happiness, don't compromise
It comes first...

Can't

Why are you so weak
When so many opportunities
Lie at your feet?
Everything you want -
Will you die for all your wants?
Do you like being foolishly pushed around?
No one ever reaches the top
If he believes he cannot get there...

When you're constantly let down,
It's easy to stay on the ground -
Nothing gained, like a tortured beacon.
Don't believe you can't;
Summon the strength,
Use your brain.

You,
Who have gained an education,
Apply your dedication to achieve
Success
In your estimation,
Is a matter of who can and cannot -
Where's your ambition?
Why do you adopt this impression -
Thinking you can't
Subjecting yourself to those
Who are glad to degrade you?

Autumn Rain

Rain starts to fall
When autumn calls.
Tributaries overflow onto the seashore,
Farmers become glad -
The long drought ends.

Rain starts to fall;
Labourers earnestly toil
The soil
Coming alive
With seeds germinating.
The birds sweetly sing,
They spread out their wings;
The zephyr brings a sigh of optimism…

Rain starts to fall;
Reservoirs that were low rumble
Expectantly.
Heather and Dahlias
Radiate in their bloom,
Cattle graze grass
Verdantly at noon.

Rain starts to fall;
Autumn calls.
Thunder and lightening
Rolls and flashes,
Pellets of hail shatter window panes;
As a glittering rainbow glows in the rain.

Wait

Wait is an indefinitely closed gate;
Only patience has access.
Its sequel is an open door to progress.
Waiting is a virtue
Only faith can pursue:
Entering a minute late
Could mean disappointment for you.

Wait, it has dual personalities;
You've got to deal with reality.
It could have you up, and down
Pushing you around.
Waiting sometimes abuses your expectations
When you're not conclusive
Waiting can disappoint you

Wait, when procrastinated for long,
You think you can't prolong...
This is when the strength moved you on.
Sometimes you must learn to wait
There will be a time when you desist from waiting.
Wait, when you have it to do,
Can open the new day that'll see you through.

Daily Bread

God is great
In him have faith
Your troubles he'll alleviate
In his hand unfurl from sin
Out of the cold he'll take you in

God isn't dead!
Where would you find your daily bread?
Don't undermine his power
You should glorify him each passing hour;
Why don't you cling to the
Serenity and love He brings?

God is great:
Let's congregate.
Unto him, let's blend
Our voices and sing…
In silent meditation
Declare the wondrous creation
Of which you partake.
God is divine:
His presence manifests in
You at all time.
His love knows no bound.
He won't frustrate
You with frowns;
Just a thought of him
Will make your spirit soar.
You'll never regret it
Your problems you will surmount.

Work A Genesis

Work hard to be a man -
You're man enough to work hard;
Earn and save all you can
Work, so you'll get your reward.

Work, it doesn't kill anyone -
It's a genesis ordained on everyone.
Idle not away precious time,
Stand today and be proud;
To earn your dime.

Work hard for your pay,
Linger not by the clock
To elapse the day.
Shun this phlegmatic outlook
Laziness recompenses a thorn in your side.

Prayer is to assist
Luck's gain from taking risks.
If you don't toil behind
Your dreams,
Luck and prayer will show the way -
It will not provide the means.

Reminisce

No greater persecution
Than the memory of the past;
An intruder you must learn to live with -
They guide you at your future tasks.

Afraid of the shadow you come across?
So many skeletons hidden in the closet?
So many events you wish to erase?
But the past is so common place
It blurts right out in your face.

How strange is your behaviour!
Some say that you are mad
But with a past of so many dazzling tricks,
You've been hesitant about the company
In which you mix.

Yesterday,
So immature
So innocent,
So unsure.
Things we indulged
For folly
Are past you wish
You could ignore.

ABOUT THE AUTHOR

Christopher Duprea

Christopher Duprea has travelled the world over with popular performing artistes and other celebrities. Unable to complete his high school education, Duprea was determined to make a success of his life. This work does not simply recommend lessons for life, but records the lessons that this poet has learnt throughout his life and journeys. He is married with two daughters and continues in his journeys around the world to apply and share his life's lessons.